MY LIFE AS AN ICE CREAM SANDWICH

IBI ZOBOI

Dutton Children's Books

Dutton Children's Books
An imprint of Penguin Random House LLC, New York

Copyright © 2019 by Ibi Zoboi
Illustrations copyright © 2019 by Anthony Piper

Visit us online at penguinrandomhouse.com

CIP Data is available.

Printed in the United States of America
ISBN 9780399187353

1 3 5 7 9 10 8 6 4 2

Design by Kristin Boyle
Text set in Bookman

For Pascale, my inner space cadet,
and the others out there, with our heads in the clouds
and our eyes on the stars—boundless imagination

CHAPTER
1

These clouds are a concrete wall! The airplane won't push past the gray and blue to reach the endless black called outer space. So I have to take control.

I press my back against the seat, push up my glasses, close my eyes, and pretend the plane is aiming for the stars and planets and the very edge of our galaxy. The seatback in front of me is the control board, and I press button after button as the plane blasts through the concrete sky and becomes the Mothership *Uhura*. It's star date 06.23.1984 and I'm now E-Grace Starfleet, space cadet, on a mission to rescue the great and wise Captain Fleet!

"I'm coming for you, Captain Fleet!" I whisper to myself.

The clouds part as the *Uhura* achieves Earth's orbit. Then, in just a few milliseconds, I calculate the hyperspace jump all the way out to Andromeda. This part sometimes makes me queasy because warp speed forces time and space to squeeze my whole body—along with this morning's breakfast rolling around in my belly—into an opening smaller than the eye of a needle. I've never thrown up while on the Mothership *Uhura*. Until now.

Someone touches my shoulder, and I blink right back into the present, back onto this American Airlines Boeing 727, headed for New York City.

"Are you all right, honey?" the stewardess asks. "You look a little sick."

I shake my head because my stomach is a whirling black hole ready to spew out long lost spacecraft and missing astronauts. The stewardess hands me a bag just in time and up come Momma's grits and cheese and ham and eggs.

There's nothing more human than throwing up.

Suddenly, I don't feel like Space Cadet E-Grace Starfleet anymore. Even in this airplane that's supposed to be "something special in the air," I'm just regular ol' Ebony-Grace Norfleet Freeman, rising seventh-grader from Huntsville, Alabama. There's nothing out-of-this-world about a too-stiff white shirt, ugly pleated skirt, lace-trimmed socks, a greasy press 'n' curl, big ol' glasses, and a tummy that feels like volcanic explosions on the surface of Mars.

I lean against the window to look out at the concrete sky, so incredibly close to outer space. The white lady across the aisle thinks I don't notice her watching me out of the corner of her eye as she lights a cigarette. Maybe she thinks it will settle my stomach. I take off my glasses, place them on my lap, and close my eyes again.

When has the brave and powerful Captain Fleet ever needed saving? Never ever. Not when the Sonic King threatened to destroy the *Uhura* with a single meteor. Not when his evil little minions, the Funkazoids, led Captain Fleet on a wild-goose chase all over Planet Boom Box. And not even when Momma made Granddaddy promise to "stop filling her head with crazy stories since she'll be in junior high school soon!"

But now I am the farthest I've ever been from Captain Fleet in my whole entire life. He has no one to help him when he faces the evil Sonic King. He is all alone as I make my way to New York City.

"Of course the Sonic King took the opportunity to capture the great and wise Captain Fleet once and for all," I whisper to myself.

This is where Granddaddy's stories ended before I left for a whole week in New York City. And maybe this is where they'll end forever since I am becoming a young lady and it is "time to do away with comic books and childish stories," as Momma said before I left.

But Granddaddy doesn't always keep his promises to Momma.

"Promise me I won't be gone for too long, Granddaddy," I had told him before I left.

"And promise me E-Grace Starfleet will rescue that old Captain Fleet from the hands of the evil Sonic King," he'd replied.

Granddaddy may not always keep his promises to Momma, but we always keep our promises to each other.

"I'm coming for you, Captain Fleet," I say aloud. I don't even care if the white lady across the aisle looks at me sideways.

Slowly, the clouds begin to part and reveal New York City's skyscrapers—the Twin Towers, the Empire State Building, and the Chrysler Building. Somewhere on those streets, John Lennon got shot. A lot of people get shot in New York City. Back in Huntsville, I would always run to the TV whenever I heard Pam Carleton and Robert Lane start their Nightcast Weekend News report on Channel 48 with all the very bad, terrible, and awful things happening in New York City. And I'd think of Daddy. But Momma always sent me out of the room before the news report finished. She does that almost every time the news talks about New York City.

"I don't want you hearing about all that sinning going on

up there in that town. You can come back down when Reverend Swaggart is on," she'd say with her hard-candy voice.

"No, thank you, Momma," I'd say as I stomped back up to my room. Hearing about sin in New York City was way more fun than listening to Jimmy Swaggart sing sad songs about Baby Jesus.

I put my glasses back on, tighten my seat belt, and search all around my mind—my "imagination location," as Granddaddy calls it—for a new name for this planet, a funky one with lots of soul, as Granddaddy would insist. Planet No Joke City echoes in my mind as if it was coming straight from Granddaddy himself. Ain't nothing funny about No Joke City!

I let out a deep, ringing laugh just like my granddaddy's.

It's not until the stewardess comes over to tell me that we'll be landing in twenty minutes that I start thinking about Daddy and his junkyard in Harlem, and my New York City best friend, Bianca Perez.

Last Tuesday when he called, Daddy sounded happy to have me for a whole week, even though he promised Momma that this time he'd sign me up for a day camp with ballet classes, piano lessons, and math enrichment, as well as making sure that I get to a good church on Sunday. But he'd also secretly promised me that he'd let me play in the junkyard, even if it meant getting in trouble with Momma.

Momma had been eavesdropping on the other phone line. "Julius, you better keep Ebony-Grace away from all those greasy men and little street urchins!"

If Daddy keeps his promise to Momma and signs me up for day camp, I won't see Bianca the whole time I'm there. She'll be stuck in her tiny apartment with no TV helping her grandmother sew dresses for rich ladies. Bianca's definitely gonna need my help, too.

"I'm coming for you, Bianca Pluto!" I say under my breath. Surely, I can use a bigger crew to help on the *Uhura*, and Bianca Pluto has already proven herself to be a worthy first officer.

When the airplane finally touches down, I squeeze my eyes shut and I'm on the *Uhura* orbiting Planet No Joke City. I promise myself not to laugh after I beam down or else the aliens will recognize E-Grace Starfleet and take her prisoner. So before the airlock opens, I let out a giggle that becomes a chuckle that turns into an avalanche of big, bright joy. I laugh until I am a bubble floating up into zero gravity.

"Ebony-Grace. We have to exit the plane now. Do you need help with your things?" The stewardess's voice pulls me back down to Earth.

She is not smiling, so I quickly stop laughing.

When I step off the plane and walk through a long, narrow, dimly lit hallway, no one welcomes me, there's no parade for E-Grace Starfleet, the granddaughter of the brave and powerful space hero, Captain Fleet. No cheers, no laughter, no joy.

Ain't nothing funny in No Joke City, all right.

CHAPTER
2

I keep my eyes on a lonely blue suitcase as it rides the baggage carousel around and around, through the black curtain leading to the portal and back toward all the people walking away with their own suitcases. The bag is waiting to be claimed, just like I am. Soon, someone will come sweep it away, and then maybe, that spinning carousel will be all mine.

"Is that blue one yours, too, honey?" a new stewardess asks. She'd been nice enough to pull my two suitcases off the carousel while I just stood there and stared.

I shake my head no.

"Well, you've got two here so far, uh . . . " She leans over to get another look at my name tag—Ebony-Grace Norfleet Freeman scribbled on masking tape with black Magic Marker. "Well, do I call you both names? Ebony-Grace, or just Ebony, or do you prefer Grace?"

"Cadet E-Grace Starfleet," I say, placing both my feet together and giving her a sharp salute.

She cocks her head to one side and only says, "Okay. If that's all, then maybe we should wait by the main doors now?"

I salute her again. But she turns away.

E-Grace Starfleet sees her chance! I stretch one skinny leg over the edge of the carousel and try to get my footing. I

6

have to catch my balance really fast because, before I know it, I'm moving away from the stewardess. I crouch down and hug my legs before I reach the black curtains that lead into the portal.

I'm coming for you, Captain Fleet!

I squeeze my eyes shut really tight and brace myself.

"Hey, hey, hey!" I hear in the distance. But the portal is just a few seconds away . . . 5, 4, 3 . . .

It's not sudden zero-gravity weightlessness that makes my arms and legs flail like a headless chicken. A man pulls me off the carousel and back onto the cold, grimy airport floor.

"Young lady! You could've gotten hurt," the man says. He's so close to my face that I can smell his cigarette breath. My glasses even fog up a little. He keeps a tight grip on my arm as the stewardess rushes over to us with her eyes wide and her face tight, making her glasses look bigger than they already are.

"Is that how you want your father to greet you?" she says. "Escorted out by security guards?"

I smile and nod. That would be outta sight! I think to myself.

But the officer man lets go of my arm, and the stewardess looks down at my clothes while shaking her head. My skirt is all twisted and bunched up. Stupid skirt. I'd spent the whole airplane ride trying to cover up my knobby knees. Momma made me wear it even after I had begged her to let me put on some blue jeans just in case I had to parachute out of that airplane. Now the whole world has seen my underwear as I got onto that carousel.

I look back toward the black curtains—Mission Portal →Home→Granddaddy aborted.

The stewardess grabs my arm. "Don't even think about it," she says through clenched teeth. Her narrowed eyes are hazel, almost the same color as her hair, which is the same color as sand, or as a dry, humanless planet. She's an alien, of course, set out to deliver me to the ruler of this new world, master of no-laughter, leader of Planet No Joke City, the imperious King Sirius Julius: my daddy.

He's like the star Sirius, all right—the brightest in the night sky. Granddaddy says that Sirius is also called the Dog Star. And since Momma sometimes mutters to herself that my daddy is nothing but a low-down, dirty dog, the name King Sirius Julius fits him like a crown.

Even after three years of not seeing him, I can still spot Daddy's thick mustache. I can hardly tell whether he's happy to see me or not since I can't see where his lips are moving, his mustache is so doggone thick. So of course, he looks serious.

It takes him a long minute to spot me. And the stewardess isn't even looking Daddy's way. She would never think that the man in the blue coveralls with grease stains at the knees and the sweat ring around the collar was actually once married to my fancy momma. Daddy's coveralls looks like Granddaddy's NASA space-flight suit, except way dirtier.

Back at the airport in Huntsville, Momma had used her syrupy-sweet voice to ask all kinds of favors from the stewardess. She made sure that I'd have a full lunch and a nutritious snack, that I'd wash my hands each time I used the bathroom, and that I'd read *Little Women* instead of one of Granddaddy's comic books I snuck into my bag. Momma smiled big and bright, showing her Vaseline-covered white teeth, and batted her blue-shadowed and mascaraed eyes before slipping a twenty-dollar bill to the lady. I pretended not to see. I'm very good at pretending not to see.

So when Daddy finally spots me and spreads his arms big and wide, the stewardess holds me back. "Who is that man?" she asks.

"That's my daddy," I say, and push her out of my way.

But she grabs my arm. "Are you sure?" she whispers, looking at my daddy sideways as if he were a kidnapper.

I pop my eyes out at her, something Momma would twist my ear for doing. It feels good to be a little insolent, as Momma calls it. She isn't going to be around for a long while, and I can be as insolent as I want to be. I roll my eyes at the stewardess and pull away from her so I can run to my daddy.

His long, strong arms wrap around me almost twice, and I press the side of my face against his chest and smelly jump-suit, and sniff and sniff.

"Baby girl!" Daddy says. He gently pushes me away from him. "Lemme take a look at you. Still my little broomstick. Taller, but not much wider." His voice smiles, but not his face, of course.

The officer man who had pulled me off the baggage carousel comes over and pushes the luggage cart toward Daddy. "Is that your daughter?" he asks. "She almost got us all in trouble climbing onto that carousel like that."

But before Daddy can ask me anything, the stewardess comes over and clears her throat. "I hope you enjoyed your flight with American Airlines," she says to Daddy and not me. Then she turns around and starts to fidget with my white shirt. I quickly pull away from her again. "Don't you want a pin?" she asks.

She shows me a brass pin with wings and the blue-and-red double-A logo for American Airlines. I grab it from her and pin it on myself. She just stands there in front of us when I'm done, and clears her throat again.

"Oh, uh, Ebony-Grace, aren't you going to thank the lovely lady?" Daddy says.

Momma isn't here, so I barely whisper a thank-you while rolling my eyes again. Daddy is too busy pulling the luggage cart toward the exit doors to notice my insolence.

CHAPTER
3

Daddy's Buick is dirt brown and has dents, scratches, and duct tape all over it.

"Did you build this car yourself, Daddy? Did you make any special modifications?" I ask.

"No, Broomstick, it's just a little beat up, that's all," he says, as he slips the last suitcase into the back seat. He has to push the front seat forward 'cause there are only two doors on his car—unlike Granddaddy's new Cadillac with its four doors and leather seats.

I ask Daddy if I can sit in the back seat to stretch out my legs. I lie down on the rough and torn seats, rest my feet on my suitcase, take off my glasses, cross my hands over my belly, tilt my head back, and look out of the car window. After a few minutes of seeing only wide, blue, open sky, the tall buildings in No Joke City appear from out of nowhere. I sit up in my seat as we cross a bridge over a green-brown river. In the distance, I see short-and-wide buildings and tall-and-skinny buildings. The whole city looks like it was built by robots and machines.

"Welcome back to Manhattan, baby girl. The Big Apple. New York City! And soon, we'll be in Harlem—the heart of it all—where the beat is, the bass, the drum. Ain't that right, baby girl?" Daddy says from the driver's seat.

"It's No Joke City, Daddy," I say, easing toward a window.

"'Cause this place is serious with them tall buildings."

"You got that right," is all my daddy says.

We drive down a winding highway that runs along the green-brown river and on the other side is a sea of shorter-and-wider buildings that Daddy says is Brooklyn. Soon, we turn down Park Avenue where above us a long and wide bridge seems to extend just as far as the whole city. I roll down the window and stick out my head to look up at the giant structure. I remember what it's up there for from the last time I visited Harlem. It's an aboveground train track.

"Daddy, ain't that the Soul Train?" I ask.

He laughs a little. "Could call it that. It is the Harlem Line, after all. The Metro-North. Goes up to somewhere fancy called Connecticut."

"Can we get on the Soul Train to meet Don Cornelius?" I ask him. Momma never lets me watch Soul Train, and Granddaddy says it's changed so much from when it first started with all that glitter and dirty dancing.

Daddy laughs even harder. "I don't see why not. But you gotta dance up there on the Soul Train, baby girl. Whatcha gonna dance to?"

"No, sir. I'm not dancing. Ain't gonna laugh either. 'Cause ain't nothing funny about No Joke City!"

"I see you're not gonna let that one go," Daddy says. "Don't worry. Harlem'll set you straight."

I shake my head to disagree with Daddy, but he can't see me from the driver's seat. Soon, we're making a left onto 126th Street, Daddy's block.

This street is full of fast-walking people packed onto the sidewalk like Granddaddy's sardines, sitting around on stoops, and everything in between. I know better than to trust any of them. The white-teeth smiles or the slap-knee laughter in Daddy's Harlem—they're just traps and they don't fool me. The world here is square and rectangular with its high walls and sharp corners made to keep everything round and bubbly and soft—everything happy—in a cold, hard box.

Except it looks like the box has sprung a leak. Water sprays out of the mouth of a small robot at the edge of a wide sidewalk and it's free like air, like starlight, like rockets.

"I gotta roll up the windows, Broomstick," Daddy says. The window squeaks as it slides up and there are tiny cracks in the middle of the glass.

"What's happening?" I ask, sitting up to watch big-headed and knobby-kneed Harlem kids run through the spray. An iridescent rainbow forms on the ground and no one seems to care because they run all over it with their bare feet.

"Just the neighborhood kids having a good time. But it ain't hot enough out here for all this mess," Daddy says. "School ain't even let out yet for the summer. But what the heck . . . Could use a good car wash!"

Daddy slowly drives the car through the water as the kids make way for him. A boy with a pigeon chest wearing only a pair of red shorts goes over to the small robot and puts his hand in front of the water as it flies even higher. I press my face against the window and the water pounds Daddy's Buick as if it were the torrential rains of the Second Coming, as Momma would say.

"Wow!" I whisper.

"Could come out here later, if you want," Daddy says.

The water splashes my window, I squeeze my eyes shut and press my forehead against the coolness. Soon, we're out of the spray and the kids run back in. I watch everything from the rear window, through the sliding droplets that make everything look bigger and stranger, like a house of mirrors at a carnival.

Still, I don't trust all that laughing and fun because ain't nothing funny about No Joke City! "It's a trap," I whisper to myself.

"Broomstick!" Daddy says. I jump in my seat. "As long as you change out of those nice clothes, you could run back out there before they turn off the fire hydrant."

"Fire hydrant?" I ask, wishing that the little robot had more of a funky name.

Fire Crusher pops up in my imagination location. Fire . . . Destroyer!

Before I can think of what a Fire Destroyer might do, I'm out of the car and setting foot on the surface of Planet No Joke City. "Welcome home," King Sirius Julius says as he pulls my bags out of the back seat. I run to him to help. But a short man wearing a long, dirty coat beats me to it.

"This here your daughter, Julius?" he asks with a scraggly voice. "Looks just like you. You spit that baby girl out!" He tries to grab one of my bags, but Daddy shoos him away. "Lemme help you with those, man."

"Get back, Lester. I don't need any help," he says.

I try to take one of my bags from Daddy again, but before I can even open my mouth to tell him I can carry my own bags he looks down at me with needle eyes. "Broomstick, you go on over there and stand by the steps until I open the door. You hear?" His voice is harder than before—more like the King Sirius Julius he's supposed to be.

I do as he says and watch as my daddy and this Lester fight over my bags. Lester doesn't budge. He tries to grab my green backpack, my brown satchel that used to belong to Nana, and Momma's old makeup case. She had filled that case with all the dolls I never played with. But before we left for the airport, I took out those ugly dolls and replaced them with things more useful and more fun.

"Lester, I'ma have something for you to do in just a minute, if you just let go of these bags and let me take care of my baby girl," Daddy says, softer now.

Lester steps back and bows as if Daddy really were the king of this place. I get a glimpse of Lester's sneakers—no laces and one of his big toes sticks out of a hole. He scratches his head and neck and keeps his eyes on my bags as if there were nothing more he wanted to do in the world than to carry one of them up the steps to Daddy's brownstone.

I'm so focused on Lester and his scratching that I don't notice the small crowd of kids walking up toward us—even the skinny boy with the pigeon chest and red shorts. I turn the other way. More kids. They're coming from every corner of this block.

There's nowhere else to look but down at the brown and gray concrete. Blades of grass stick through the cracks as if there were a secret tiny forest underneath the sidewalk, with teeny-tiny aliens who do nothing but laugh all day. This itsy-bitsy forest beneath the concrete is their prison and punishment for being so happy.

"That's your daughter, Mr. J?" someone asks. It's a boy's voice and I refuse to look up. I imagine one of those tiny laughing aliens climbing over my shiny black Mary Jane shoes, swinging across the lace trimmings of my socks, and scurrying its way up my skinny, Vaseline-covered legs. I let out a snort and quickly cover my mouth before a forbidden laugh bursts out.

I look up to see all the kids' eyes on me. Then, Daddy yells out my name: "Ebony-Grace! Don't be rude."

Get ahold of yourself, E-Grace. Not one snort. Not one giggle. Wipe that smile off your face! I tell myself. I furrow my brows and purse my lips so tight they almost go numb.

"What's wrong with her, Mr. J?" Pigeon-Chest Boy asks.

There are almost a dozen of them—all different shapes and sizes. They talk at the same time—No Joke City gibber-ish. But luckily, my super-duper bionic ears can decipher it all. The words and questions spill out of their mouths as fast as shooting stars.

"Why her face like that?"

"Why she just standing there?"

"What's your name, girl?"

"Can you see through walls with them Coke-bottle glasses?"

"She looks like she been sitting out in the sun her whole life!"

"You know my people down in 'Bama?"

"Is that a perm or a press 'n' curl?"

"Subspace frequencies jammed, sir. Wormhole effect!" I say and cover my ears and shut my eyes because it's sensory overload. I need my helmet. I need to go back home. "Beam me up, Granddaddy!"

But still, they poke and prod and ask more questions. They move in closer and they smell like hot sun, salty sweat, city streets, and car exhaust. I brace myself to be beamed back up onto the *Uhura*. I wait for the atmospheric pressure to squeeze my whole body into a teeny-tiny wormhole in the universe, and I'd zoom up through an invisible portal, cat-apult into space, and stumble onto the cold, logical metal floors of the Starship *Uhura*.

"Beam me up, Captain Fleet!" I yell out loud. "Beam me up, please!"

CHAPTER
4

"Hey, hey, hey!" Daddy's voice booms through all the gibberish. "Y'all step away from her. She's fresh from Alabama. She's gonna need her space."

It's only when Daddy pulls my hands away from my ears that I open one eye to recognize Bianca Perez making her way through the crowd. She grabs my other hand, stretches her arm out in front of Pigeon-Chest Boy and all the other kids standing around, and pulls me toward the steps of Daddy's brownstone.

"To the rescue!" I say.

Still, those nefarious minions stand right outside the rusted iron gate, shouting their comments and questions. They're nefarious because they're so rude and mean. Who yells at a stranger like that, as if they'd have no home training, as Momma would say? And they're minions because they're all working under the orders of King Sirius Julius, who wants them to be friends with me. But they have no manners!

"Hey, girl! You wanna go in the fire hydrant?"

"You know how to jump double-Dutch?"

"I bet you she's double-handed. They don't jump double-Dutch Down South."

"She look country. Look at her knees!"

They all laugh and point and I know it's a trick to get me

to laugh, too. Then, King Sirius Julius will take me prisoner in Planet No Joke City forever! I can just hear him now, calling my momma and granddaddy to say, "I told you she'd be happy here. Now let her stay with me."

I look around for King Sirius Julius, who's already disappeared up the steps and into the brownstone, leaving me and Bianca Pluto to fend off his nefarious minions. They keep laughing and pointing, but I won't be fooled. No Joke City jokes aren't funny.

Bianca doesn't laugh, either, thank goodness. "¡Déjala sola!" she yells at the nefarious minions. "Why don't you go wash off your funky butts in the fire hydrant?"

More shouting, more questions, and more gibberish. I cover my ears and shut my eyes again, until a deep thumping sound comes from somewhere down the block and reaches my bones. It forces me to stare up at the gray-blue sky and hazy yellow sun. Music. Heavy bass music like the Sonic Boom from Planet Boom Box. I can see the sound waves vibrating across the roofs of the brownstones forming a force-field around all of Harlem. I stand on the steps and point.

"Look!" I whisper.

Bianca stands next to me and looks up, too. "I don't see nothing," she says.

"The Sonic Boom," I say, really slowly so as not to alarm anything that might be inching closer to where Bianca and I are standing.

"The what boom?" she asks.

"The Sonic Boom, sent by the Sonic King and the Funkazoids from Planet Boom Box!"

Bianca rolls her eyes and sighs. "Calvin has a new boom box. You wanna go watch him break-dance?"

I look at her all crazy because now she's talking nonsense.

"Who wants to watch anybody dance when an evil king is sending mind-controlling sound waves over your city?"

"Broomstick!" Daddy shouts from inside the brownstone, and in an instant, the waves disappear. "Ebony-Grace! Come on in here and wash up. We gotta call your mother, and then I got some lunch for you. You can join us, too, Bianca, if your grandmother says it's all right."

Daddy's telephone is at the very edge of the kitchen wall, just like Momma's phone down in Huntsville. Bianca runs to wash her hands in the bathroom as Daddy picks up the receiver to call Momma in Alabama. The long spiraling cord hangs across the black and white kitchen tiles. I watch him turn the phone dial with each number—all eleven of them, starting with 1, then 256. Of course, he knows my Huntsville number by heart because he calls every Saturday morning. Our short conversations have never changed.

> DADDY: "How's my baby girl?"
> ME: "Good."
> DADDY: "You're getting high marks in school?"
> ME: "Yes."
> DADDY: "How 'bout you come up to the Big Apple and stay with your daddy for a while?"
> ME: "No."

And even now that I'm with him (not for a while, just a week), he still doesn't have much to say, unlike Granddaddy, who can step in and out of his own imagination location with no problem.

> CAPTAIN FLEET: "What have you to report from your mission, Cadet E-Grace?"

E-GRACE: "The Funkazoids have dispersed all through-
out the galaxy to retrieve the golden Dog Star . . ."
CAPTAIN FLEET: "Retrieve the golden Dog Star, huh?
Is that right?"
E-GRACE: "Affirmative, Captain."
CAPTAIN FLEET (AS REGULAR OL' GRANDDADDY):
"Ebony-Grace, are you trying to tell me you want a
golden retriever for your birthday?"
E-GRACE: "Affirmative, Granddaddy."

And I was supposed to get that golden retriever this
summer, right before signing up for that new space camp.
No matter, because I won't be staying in Harlem. E-Grace
Starfleet won't be Planet No Joke City's prisoner forever. I'll
make it back to Huntsville in time for my new puppy and for
space camp.

So I try very hard not to smile big and bright as Daddy
dials and my heart is beating fast waiting to hear Granddaddy's version of what's really happening here in No Joke
City.

Daddy has to wait a few seconds for Momma to accept
the collect call from New York. Daddy always calls collect
because Granddaddy is rich. Still, I've heard Momma say
Daddy could spare a few dollars just to hear his daughter's
voice. And I've heard Daddy say that he'd rather spend
those few dollars on me when I get here to live with him
for good. With my bionic ears, I hear all sorts of things I'm
probably not supposed to.

Bianca is back from the bathroom when Daddy's thun-
derous voice seems to make the whole kitchen shake. Bianca
jumps, and I cover my mouth to hold in a laugh.

"Gloria! How you feelin'? All right? That's great . . . Well,
she's here. Safe and sound. And happy, too," Daddy says,

without even smiling or winking or nodding at me to make sure that he's right about my being happy.

So I rush over to him and try to grab the phone. King Sirius Julius can fool Momma, but he can't fool me. "Let me speak to her, Daddy!"

"Hold on, Broomstick. That's rude. Lemme finish talking to your momma."

I step back with my face twisted into a tight knot, my arms crossed, and I tap my toe on his dirty kitchen floor and listen to him lie to Momma.

"Her flight was fine . . . Yes, she was behaving . . . She was reading her books . . . I'll sign her up at the Y first thing Monday morning . . . I know a dance school over on 145th . . . I already asked Diane to watch her while I'm at the shop . . . Gonna pay her, too . . . No, I don't need your money or your daddy's . . . Street urchins? Gloria, those are good neighborhood kids . . . She's gonna be just fine and happy . . . "

When he finally hands me the phone, I step away from him as far as the cord will take me—which is all the way through the narrow hall leading to the foyer. I pull the long white cord as it spirals along the wall like a vortex. This is like the portal the *Uhura* has to go through when it leaves Andromeda for a whole other galaxy!

Finally, I bring the phone up to my ear and I don't even wait to hear Momma's voice before I say, "Where's Granddaddy?"

"Now, you know better than that, Ebony-Grace!" Momma says. She has a way of yelling without yelling. Her voice is sweet, but her words shout—like cough syrup that's candy on my tongue, but hot peppers on my sore throat. "Say you'll stay away from that dirty shop."

I lick my lips and swallow hard, getting ready to give Momma my very best Funkazoid robot impression: "You. Will. Stay. Away. From. That. Dirty. Shop."

Bianca, who has followed me into the foyer, lets out a laugh. I move my arm about like Michael Jackson in that old "Dancing Machine" video.

Momma keeps sweet-yelling over the phone, telling me what I should and shouldn't be doing at Daddy's house, in his shop, and on "those crazy Harlem streets with those little street urchins."

Until I yell out again, "Where's Granddaddy?"

Then, it's as quiet as outer space. I know better than to yell at Momma. But she's all the way down in Huntsville and fortunately she knows nothing about teleporting through spiraling portals.

"Little girl," she says. Now, her voice is like a big round jawbreaker—still sweet, but can make you lose a tooth if you're not careful. "If I could reach into that phone line and twist your little ear, I would. Now, listen to me, and you listen to me good . . . "

I don't listen to her. Her words are just like the No Joke City gibberish. Except it's more like having a dozen pieces of butterscotch or peppermint candy in my mouth during church and trying to sing "Amazing Grace" with all the other church folks, but it comes out sounding like gobble-gobble. Momma's words are hard-candy gobble-gobble.

When she's done and it's quiet again, I ask, "Can I speak to Granddaddy now?"

"Put your father on the phone, Ebony-Grace," is all I hear and all I understand.

CHAPTER
5

After such a long trip, I'm expecting a tall pitcher of sweet tea, fried catfish, maybe some grits or black-eyed peas, and a bowl of peach cobbler with vanilla ice cream. That's how Momma does it after Granddaddy comes back from an engineering conference. But Daddy's kitchen is dark, hot, and musty, unlike my house down in Huntsville with its brand-new General Electric air conditioner. I can barely make out two plastic plates holding a set of beige squares—Wonder Bread, slices of ham and cheese, and Hellmann's Mayonnaise. Daddy sets a gallon of milk and two plastic cups in front of us and walks out of the kitchen.

I'm not even on my third bite before Bianca finishes all of her sandwich and pours us both some milk. Even if I did finish my sandwich, I'd still be hungry. Already, I miss Momma's cooking and Granddaddy's voice and stories.

But Bianca is almost something like home. The way she just sits here with me as if I'd never left, as if we're both still nine, pretending to be astronauts. That was when I first gave her the name Bianca Pluto, first officer on the Uhura. We'd been friends ever since we first met when I was five, when Momma and Daddy were trying to make things right again.

After Momma and Daddy got divorced, Daddy moved

back to Harlem from Huntsville to start his own business—the auto repair shop and junkyard at the corner. I was only four. A year later, Momma and I visited Daddy for the first time, and for that whole summer, we were like a family again. Until we had to leave because Momma said the schools and streets weren't very good in Harlem.

When I first met Bianca, Momma had been in this same kitchen—making something really good, I'm sure—when a lady holding a little girl's hand rang our doorbell. Daddy was standing in the middle of the living room shaking his head at me when he saw what I had done to the telephone. (He once told me it was the fourth phone he'd rented from Ma Bell since I figured out how to unplug a phone cord and turn a screwdriver.) And that's exactly how Bianca first saw me that day: Phillips screwdriver in my hand, and my legs wrapped in the cord. She pulled away from her abuela to help untangle me.

She stayed for a long while after that and came back the next day. When she brought her baby doll to share, she didn't mind that I took the little eyes out just to see what made them open and close. Soon, Bianca was breaking things and putting them back together again with me, too.

I'm pulling out the ham and cheese to just eat the Wonder Bread when Bianca starts laughing. "Why are you doing that? Abuela would beat your butt for wasting food," she says.

"Are you trying to trick me with all that laughing?"

"Huh?"

"The Funkazoids chased E-Grace Starfleet all the way to Planet No Joke City! Did you see the signal the Sonic King sent us?" I say, pulling off the crusts from the bread.

"What signal?"

"The sound waves! The Sonic Boom!"

I watch her face—the brown eyes, the curly jet-black hair, the milk mustache. Her shirt is too tight because she's blossoming, as Momma would say, and I don't like all the striped colors on it—the pinks, blues, and purples. I'll make sure to lend her some of my clothes that I sneaked into my suitcase—my NASA, Superman, and Empire Strikes Back T-shirts. Even the new E.T. one that I got from a boy at my old school. I'd traded it for a Transformers T-shirt. I have to hide all these shirts from Momma, who thinks little ladies ought to dress accordingly.

Bianca just shakes her head as if she doesn't know what I'm talking about.

So I try again. "We're gonna have to stop King Sirius Julius from keeping me as prisoner. You have to help me find the *Uhura* so we can save Captain Fleet."

She shrugs. "You wanna go in the fire hydrant instead? Then we can go dry our clothes in the park. Or maybe we could jump some double-Dutch. When my sneakers are wet and I'm jumping rope, they make a squishy sound and it's like music when we sing 'Jack be nimble, Jack be quick . . .'"

"No, let's go check out the junkyard instead. Is my old rocket ship still there? The one that made it to the moon? Maybe we can use that to get to the *Uhura*?"

My very first summer in Harlem without Momma was when I was nine. Bianca and I spent almost every single day in the junkyard behind Daddy's shop. I wasn't allowed to go anywhere out of Daddy's sight. But Daddy's sight was always under the hood of a car or on some rusty car parts.

On one of those days, I sat by the window of Daddy's brownstone all morning waiting for a giant storm cloud to ease up from New Jersey and Central Park and sit its wide, cloudy butt right over Harlem. When it finally crossed 125th

Street, the hot August sun had nothing else to do but back off and mind his own beeswax.

I pulled away from the window and hurried down three long flights of creaky stairs to the ground-floor apartment. I knocked really hard, three times. Bianca opened the door holding her toolbox and wearing a smile as bright as Venus.

"It's time," I whispered. "Come on, we gotta hurry!"

We ran next door to the shop where cars were lined up with hoods open in the front yard. Past the broken cars was the glass door to the shop, left wide-open to let out the heat and all the car grease smells. Daddy was in front of the counter talking to one of the mechanics.

I grabbed Bianca's hand and raced to the back of the shop where the huge rolling gate was halfway up so we could just run straight into the junkyard.

We'd already set up a blue tarp in the middle of the yard where scrap metal, car parts, broken appliances, and even pieces of a staircase from someone's building were stacked up along the gate. To the far right of the yard was an old supermarket refrigerator where Bianca and I kept our supplies.

Albert, the shop's guard dog, was at my legs, wagging his tail, when I opened the refrigerator door and reached down for my toolbox. I petted the old Lab just as thunder ripped through the sky. Albert whined and headed for cover beneath a car door. Bianca and I started setting up on top of the old blue tarp. She pulled out two empty soda bottles, a broken toilet plunger, a wrench, a pair of scissors, goggles, and a whistle.

"What's the whistle for?" I asked.

"For when our rocket ship breaks the sound barrier," Bianca said. "But wait. Did you bring earmuffs?"

"It's not gonna even reach Mach one, Bianca. We gotta get it out of the junkyard, and then out of Harlem first," I said, shaking my head. I pulled out my supplies—aluminum foil, duct tape, three PVC pipes, and a pack of Granddaddy's seltzer tablets all the way from Huntsville.

I hummed the theme music from *Star Trek*. "Space, the final frontier," I said, deepening my voice as I gathered all my materials in front of me.

"To boldly go where no muchacha has gone before," Bianca added. "You think it'll get to the Bronx? Maybe land on the Grand Concourse? I can call my Tío Jorge to catch it for us." Bianca held a pipe to her eye and looked up toward the sky.

"Who cares about the Bronx when you can get to Jupiter and Saturn and beyond?" I said.

I placed the toolbox next to Bianca and looked around the junkyard for any nosy bystanders, like the boys from down the block who used the junkyard for kickball games. But thank goodness the storm had chased them all into their apartments. They're not into rockets, anyway.

I glanced up at the dark gray sky—perfect for launching so we wouldn't go blind from staring at the sun. Plus, when the storm clouds hung so low, it looked as if outer space were close enough for us to just tiptoe and touch. Harlem only got quiet during thunderstorms—no one would be outside getting their hot-combed dos, Jheri curls, and white Adidas all messed up. So it sounded as if the whole universe could hear our countdown.

Another roar of thunder made all of Harlem tremble and a single raindrop landed on my nose. "Let's hurry!" I yelled to Bianca.

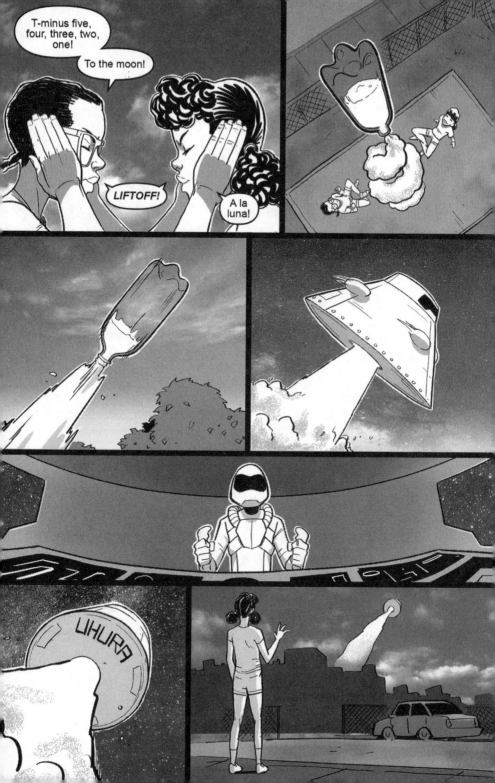

CHAPTER
6

When we're done with our lunches, Bianca and I head out to Daddy's shop. I look up at a faded red-and-blue sign that used to say FREEMAN'S AUTO REPAIR. Now it just reads MAN'S AU PAIR. The shadows of the missing letters are like ghosts, and maybe we need to call the Ghost Busters to get those missing letters back! The red is now a dull pink and the blue is more gray, as if it'd been way more than three years since I last saw that sign.

A rolling thunderclap makes my insides drop and I quickly look toward the aboveground train tracks at the end of the block. But there's no train.

I look all up and down the street. The brownstones are lined up next to one another like soldiers—broken, raggedy soldiers. Some are now boarded up with padlocked chains hanging in front of wooden slats instead of doors. A few brownstones have missing windowpanes and even steps. A giant cardboard box surrounded by shopping carts sits in front of one of the buildings.

Suddenly, the Soul Train comes speeding down the aboveground tracks at the end of the block—with a roll and a thunder, and a thunder and a roll. My eyes almost pop right out of my head and I take a gulp of that No Joke City air. "The SOOOOUUUUL train!" I sing.

Then I quickly cover my mouth because a smile, then a laugh, and then a boogie-down dance is starting to take over my whole body, my whole soul—almost like the ladies who catch the Holy Ghost in Momma's church.

"That's not the Soul Train," Bianca says. "That's the Harlem Line!"

"Well, my daddy says it's the same thing," I say, uncovering my mouth and watching the very last car of the train speed past our block.

"Nuh-uh," Bianca says, rolling her neck.

"Uh-huh," I say.

She shakes her head. Then I whisper, "Well, it's the Sonic Boom! The Sonic Boom is destroying everything!"

Down the block is an empty lot where some of the kids who'd been in the fire hydrant are playing. I can't tell from where I'm standing, but they're jumping on something wide, square, and springy—a mattress maybe. Who would bring a mattress out into an open lot?

"Let's go over there," Bianca says, grabbing my hand.

I quickly let go. "The junkyard is better!"

"I'm not going to that junkyard. It's dirty and junky. Calvin and them are in the lot."

"You mean to tell me that that's not dirty and junky, too?" I say, pointing to the lot with big, metal trash bins that Daddy said were oil drums, old tires, and torn mattress. And, of course, the nefarious minions. I've never seen this much trash in Huntsville. The garbageman comes down Olde Stone Road twice a week, and it's Granddaddy's job to put our metal bin out on the sidewalk. But no one ever, ever puts trash on the street. And surely, there's nothing funny about that. No Joke City, all right!

Someone shouts Bianca's name and we both turn to see

another group of nefarious minions—all girls wearing short-shorts, too small and too colorful T-shirts, and each one holding onto a long white telephone cord. They walk across the street to where Bianca and I are standing.

I can tell right away there's a leader—a girl with two long, swinging ponytails wearing a Rainbow Brite T-shirt. "Is this your friend from Alabama that you were talking about?" Rainbow Dull starts to say even before she reaches the sidewalk. She and her minionettes keep their eyes on me, and my pleated skirt, lace socks, Mary Jane shoes, and stupid curls. I wish I had changed into an appropriate E-Grace Starfleet uniform before braving the streets of No Joke City.

Bianca nods. "This is Ebony."

"So you two are Ebony and Ivory singing together in perfect harmony?" Rainbow Dull asks. "What happened to PJ, Bianca?"

What a stupid thing to say, even though I know it's from that Stevie Wonder and Paul McCartney song that Momma likes. So I ask, "Who's PJ?"

"Her boyfriend!"

"No, he's not!" Bianca shouts.

The nefarious minionettes giggle. Another ploy, as Captain Fleet would say, to get me to smile, giggle, or laugh, too. I furrow my brows even deeper this time, and stare at each one of them, narrowing my eyes, tightening my jaw, and clenching my fists.

"You look like you wanna punch somebody!" Rainbow Dull says, and an avalanche of No Joke City gibberish pours out of everyone's mouth like shooting lasers from a spaceship.

"You wanna fight?"

"Why is she so weird?"

"Why does she have on church clothes?"

"Lemme hear you talk country."

"They don't know how to fight Down South."

I block their laser-beam gibberish by throwing up my arms like Wonder Woman with her Bracelets of Submission. "Pew! Pew!" I say with each swing of my arms.

"What is wrong with your friend?" one of the minionettes asks.

"Ebony, stop acting weird!" Bianca says.

But her words are laser shots and I block them, too. "Pew! Pew!"

"Stop it!" Bianca yells through clenched teeth.

But I have to protect myself. And her. "They've got you, too, Bianca Pluto! Save yourself! Block the gibberish laser beams with your Bracelets of Submission!"

She grabs both my arms to stop me, but I pull them away.

"I'm not gonna let you take me prisoner!" I yell over the laughing minionettes.

"What are you talking about?" Bianca yells back. "You know what . . . Never mind."

She reaches into a tiny pocket in front of her striped shirt and pulls out a small folded green paper that opens up into a clean, crisp five-dollar bill, and she smacks it over the bony part of my chest. "Your daddy gave me five bucks to be your friend."

I grab the five before it falls to ground and look at it. "Five bucks? To be my friend?" I say, almost whispering.

"I'm gonna need at least twenty bucks just to put up with all this loca!" Bianca says.

The minionettes laugh even louder and harder. One of them takes her index finger and swirls it around near her temple. A mind-controlling trick! So I shut my eyes and cover my ears. I should've known that Bianca Pluto had already been taken prisoner. I have to save myself first, then I can save her.

E-Grace Starfleet will not fall under the hypnotic spell of the Sonic Boom!

I let the minionettes walk away with Bianca Pluto.

"If you can hear me, Bianca Pluto, make sure to use your secret spying senses to get all the information you need from the nefarious minions to defeat the evil Sonic King, the Funkazoids, and the Sonic Boom!" I shout into the steamy No Joke City air and hope that it reaches Bianca Pluto's bionic ears in time.

But she only looks back from the crowd of nefarious minionettes, shaking her head and rolling her eyes.

I throw up my left arm with the invisible Bracelet of Submission one more time just in case the minionettes have secretly sent a gibberish laser beam my way. "Pew!"

I've crushed them!

CHAPTER
7

Daddy's brownstone—66 East 126th Street between Madison and Park Avenues—has four whole floors. Well, half-floors compared to my big house down in Huntsville with its wraparound porch, giant rooms, chandeliers, and backyard wider than Daddy's shop and the nefarious minions' lot put together.

Bianca and her grandmother live on the ground floor, where there's a door leading to the tiny backyard that's not even big enough for me to stretch my arms and spin around like an asteroid.

On the first floor is the kitchen at the end of a long, narrow hallway. There's a small dining room whose walls are lined with books and records. One of those records is faced out on its shelf. On the cover, three people wearing strange clothes are crouched down, posing. I quickly grab the album and stare at the picture because of their outfits. They're all wearing white space suits! There's a lady in the middle with white high-heel boots aiming a phaser straight at me. The two men on each side of her are either wearing their space glasses over their eyes or on top of their heads. One of them looks like Daddy himself! I've never seen them before in any of the *Star Trek* shows or even in *Star Wars*, but from the looks of it, they're definitely space heroes.

I read the words on the album's cover out loud. "Warp Nine. Light-Years Away."

A chill travels up my spine and my skin crawls. Warp 9, as in the absolute fastest the USS *Enterprise* can travel. And light-years, as in beyond the galaxy, beyond Andromeda, where Planet Boom Box exists at the edge of our entire existence. And this must be where these people are from. Surely, King Sirius Julius has had contact with the Sonic King. They're in *cahoots*!

I quickly start to look for other clues that King Sirius Julius has allies out there in the universe. I pull out another album to see a bunch of guys around Daddy's age posing in weird clothes. They call themselves the Sugarhill Gang and they're supposed to be the 8th Wonder.

I hold both albums beneath my arms and search around the house for more signs.

In Daddy's living room is a large green velvet couch. A big, old TV set with dusty wooden side panels is pushed up against the corner. Another smaller TV sits on top of it. It has a wire hanger that sticks out behind it like bunny rabbit ears. Back home, once the antenna on our TV didn't work and the shows became fuzzy and staticky, Granddaddy just bought a new TV. I like Daddy's TV set better, though. It looks like an alien robot. Almost like R2-D2, but square and less funny. That gives me an idea. I tuck the two braids sticking out on each side of my head into their bobos so they look like Princess Leia's round buns.

"R2-D2, where are you?" I hear someone say with a robotic voice in my imagination location.

So I quickly look for an opening on R2-D2, just like when Princess Leia recorded her hologram message to Obi Wan Kenobi. What if I could record a message asking for help for my own granddaddy?

"You must see that this message is delivered safely to my grandfather, who is held prisoner on Planet Boom Box," I say. "This is our most desperate hour."

But there isn't an opening for me to slide in a VHS tape.

I look around the R2-D2 TV set—on top of the smaller TV, and on the floor around the bigger TV. Nothing. If Daddy doesn't have a VCR, then what was the point in packing all those videotapes into Momma's old makeup case? I might as well have left the dolls she packed.

I fidget with the knobs on the small TV trying to turn it on and find my favorite show when Uncle Richard walks in.

"Ha! My main gal, EG! Come and give your uncle a high five!"

I do as he says, slapping his hand so hard that my own hand stings.

Then he turns around and sticks his hand out behind him. "All right now, from the back."

I slap his hand again.

"To the side." He bends his knees and sticks out his hand from his hip.

I slap it again and cover my mouth to hide my smile.

Uncle Richard looks like a skinnier version of Daddy with a scraggly beard and a gold tooth. He wears a black leather jacket even though it's as hot as Venus outside, and he smells like a mix of sweat, wet leaves, car grease, and too-strong cologne.

"What you doing inside, baby girl? It's a Saturday evening in June. Everybody's out on the streets. You ain't seen all them kids?"

I glance out of the tall and wide windows. Bianca Pluto is on the sidewalk jumping over that long, white telephone cord as it swings around her like the rings of Saturn. Two of the minionettes are at each end turning the rope and keeping their prisoner in check. When they say jump, Bianca Pluto jumps high.

I shake my head. Poor Bianca Pluto. E-Grace Starfleet will rescue her when she's good and ready.

Uncle Richard is not one of the nefarious minions, of

course. He's almost like Granddaddy because he can go into his imagination location with no problem. He's all right by me. The only thing is, he never sticks around to hear about the *Uhura* and Captain Fleet and the evil Sonic King.

"Those kids are all strange, Uncle Richard," I say.

He laughs. "Oh, you're just a little bit country—and a whole lot of strange, too—EG," he says. "And call me Uncle Rich, you hear? Emphasis on the *Rich*. Words have power coming out of the mouths of children, ain't that right? They have the ability to *manifest*." He spreads his hands out across the front of his face as if he were making the word *manifest* magically appear out of nowhere.

And I see it, too. *Manifest*. It glitters and chimes like it's written with gold and silver and a million tiny bells.

"Manifest," I whisper.

"That's right," Uncle Rich says as he strides over to the TV set and turns it on. "What you wanna watch?"

"*Star Trek*!" I shout. "You got a VCR, Uncle Rich?"

"*Star Trek*?" He turns back to me and looks at me all funny. "Oh, I forgot. You're extra-galactic. I think we just missed *Kung Fu* on Channel 5. You ever seen *Five Deadly Venoms*?" Uncle Rich stands back and poses like Bruce Lee and says, "Ha-Ya!"

"I don't like *Kung Fu*, Uncle Rich. It's too violent!" I say.

"And *Star Trek* ain't? With all those laser guns going off?"

"Phasers!" I make my hand like a phaser and point it at the top TV, hoping to vaporize it and in its place will be a new VCR. "Pew! Pew!"

Uncle Richard laughs. "You need to stop watching so much TV, little girl. Ain't no VCR in this house. But if you really want one, you could ask your daddy. And he could ask Lester to do him a solid. He's gonna need some cold hard cash for a hot VCR, but if he loves you and wants to keep you here with him . . . "

"Keep me here with him?" I ask, looking at him sideways. He walks up the stairs without answering me.

I can't watch the *Star Trek: The Motion Picture—Special Longer Version* videotape that's in the makeup case, so I sink into the couch and tolerate the news, which Momma doesn't let me watch back home. After a few minutes of an anchorwoman named Sue Simmons (who looks very much like Momma) reporting on all the very bad, terrible, and awful things happening to the good people of No Joke City, Granddaddy's job's logo comes up in a little square next to Sue Simmons's head.

"NASA!" I whisper-yell. I move closer to the TV—almost kissing the screen, as Momma would say—and listen very carefully to Sue Simmons talk about Granddaddy's job.

> *The National Aeronautics and Space Administration announces some of its mission specialists for both the 1985 and 1986 space shuttle crews. The flights are mission 51-D scheduled for launch in February 1985 and 61-D, forecasted for January 1986.*

Images of the space center pop up on the screen and I step back to get a good look at Granddaddy whenever he shows up. But that news is not coming out of the Marshall Space Flight Center in Huntsville. The astronauts and rocket-ship people on the screen are all from the John F. Kennedy Space Center in Florida. The *other* space center, as Granddaddy would say, while rolling his eyes.

> *Mission 51-D is to be the twenty-first space shuttle operation on the ninth flight of the orbiter Challenger. While mission 61-D will be the fourth Spacelab flight and will focus on*

experiments in the field for its seven days in space. It will be the ninth flight of the orbiter Columbia.

I inhale deep and shake my head. "But, Mrs. Sue Simmons," I say to the TV screen, "the *Uhura* has already made it way past Mars and Jupiter and Pluto and out of the whole galaxy. I know it's a top secret space mission and all, but you got these people thinking that the moon is as far as we got."

Sue Simmons can't hear me, so I start to fidget with the wire hanger above the TV so that it can get a good signal from my imagination location. The images on the screen wave, morph, and fizzle like soda pop. And soon, a wide shot of the great and wonderful expanse of outer space shows up on the screen.

CHAPTER
8

I use a Jedi mind trick to sneak past the Funkazoids standing guard and make my way into the empty kitchen where our lunch plates are still on the table. Momma won't be able to see how I didn't clean up after myself, and Daddy doesn't seem to care.

I grab the telephone and dial home while whispering every single number like it's a countdown . . . 2 . . . 5 . . . 6 . . . The operator quickly comes on because Daddy can't make long-distance calls. So I ask for a collect call to Mr. Jeremiah Granville Norfleet. When the operator says, "Hold please," after I repeat several times that this call is from E-Grace Starfleet, lieutenant on the Mothership *Uhura*, I pull the receiver all the way into an empty nook between the refrigerator and the sink.

But Momma picks up the phone, and before the operator asks if she will accept a collect call from E-Grace Starfleet in New York City, I gasp, rush to the phone on the wall while almost tripping on the cord, and quickly hang up the receiver.

I need to speak with Granddaddy! I have to tell him about the Sonic Boom I saw hanging over Harlem. I have to know what I gotta do to rescue Captain Fleet. I have to ask about the space missions and why they go from 51-D to 61-D without missions 52 to 60 and A to Z in between.

But instead I just go back to the television set and watch

Sue Simmons, who's still talking about no-good, terrible, and awful things. I hope that there'll be news coming out of the Marshall Space Flight Center in Huntsville, Alabama. Maybe then I'll be able to see Granddaddy, and if I press my forehead against the screen, we'll mind meld and he'll be able to read my thoughts.

After Al Roker's forecast of a heat wave headed to No Joke City (which, of course, is really the Sonic Boom!), I switch to channel 7 for *World News Tonight with Peter Jennings*. Now, it's about the no-good, terrible, and awful things happening in the galaxy.

By sunset, I leave the TV on while the theme song to *Diff'rent Strokes* begins, and climb the stairs to the third floor of Daddy's brownstone and the special bedroom that he's been saving for me all these years. It's not fancy like my bedroom back home in Huntsville with its canopy bed and white furniture.

Daddy keeps the tall windows wide-open. "Don't you lean too far out, you hear?" he says.

I nod even though he can't see me standing against the wall way on the other side of the room. "Why don't you close those windows, Daddy?"

"Aww, you afraid of heights, Broomstick? It'll be hot as hell if I don't let in some cool breeze."

But it's not just a cool breeze. What's coming through the windows is not the sound of whispering leaves on oak trees, singing cicadas, the *squeak-squeak* of Granddaddy's rocking chair on the porch, or Momma's soft humming. It's the sound of old roaring cars, wailing sirens, crashing glass bottles, and cursing—way too much cursing—that's easing up through the windows and crawling into my ears like the Ceti eels in *Wrath of Khan*.

Daddy takes one look at me and how I'm still pressed against the wall like a scaredy-cat, pulls down the windows, and says, "All right, Broomstick. I know you're not used to all this noise. And you probably don't mind all this heat, anyway."

I don't tell him that I'm not used to this heat. Granddaddy's house has a General Electric air conditioner in every room, especially mine. Maybe when I leave here, I'll have the Huntsville post office deliver to Daddy one of our air conditioners. And one of our JVC VCRs, too. That way, he could record his Saturday afternoon *Kung Fu* and Bruce Lee movies and watch them whenever he wants.

I think of all my videocassettes back in my room in Huntsville. I've got shows like *Battlestar Galactica* and *The Powers of Matthew Star* I taped off TV and then there's all the videocassettes Granddaddy ordered from the Columbia House catalog. It was hard to decide which ones to bring. But they won't do me any good now.

When I'm undressed and all cleaned up for the night, Daddy sits on the edge of my bed—a bed he's had ever since I last came to visit him. He had tried to convince Momma to let me stay and got the bed and dresser and small desk to prove to her that he could take care of me.

"Broomstick," he says, looking at the closed windows and not at me. "You tell me if everything's been all right at home down in Huntsville."

I don't say anything because I can't tell if it's a question or a comment.

"I don't want you to keep any secrets from your momma or your pops," he continues, rubbing his hands together. He had cleaned up and didn't smell like car grease anymore, thank goodness.

"Or Granddaddy," I say, yawning out the words. Sleep is pulling at my eyes.

"I don't want you keeping secrets *for* your grandfather, either."

These last words pull me out of that sleep-wake place. "Huh?"

"You heard me, baby girl. Don't you keep his secrets from me or your momma."

I shift to my side to get a better look at his face. "Daddy, you wanna come on the *Uhura* with us?" I ask. That must be the only secret he's talking about. And it's not a secret at all. Momma knows about the *Uhura* and our outer-space missions, but she chooses to close off her imagination location.

"The what?"

"The *Uhura*!" I sit up in the bed, rubbing the sleep from my eyes. "You know the nice brown lady on the Starship *Enterprise*? She's actually named *after* Granddaddy's spaceship since she's from the future and all, and we're in the present. *Uhura* means 'freedom.'"

Daddy takes a deep breath and hangs his head down really low. "So this is what your momma was talking about? All these crazy stories about spaceships and planets with Jerry?"

It's the first time I've heard Daddy call Granddaddy by his nickname. *Jerry* is short for "Jeremiah," and only his friends from the space center and the other grandpas in our town and church call him Jerry. Not even Momma calls him Jerry 'cause that's her own daddy.

"But, it's . . . ," I start to say. "Never mind." As soon as he said "crazy stories," I should have known that there was no hope. He sounds just like Momma, and just like my neighbors and the kids in my neighborhood in Huntsville who don't like to venture into their imagination locations. Daddy is my daddy, all right, but he's also king of No Joke City, sighing heavy and hanging his head down as if it were the end of Planet Earth. He is King Sirius Julius, for sure.

I turn over in my bed to let him know that I'm done talking about this.

"And you stay away from that Lester, you hear? If he come asking for a dollar or even a nickel, you get away from him as fast as you can."

"Okay, Daddy," I say, not caring about why I need to stay away from this Lester.

"And your Uncle Rich, too, 'cause he's a wheeling and dealing schemer, you hear, baby girl? He'll sell you the shoes on your own feet if you let him."

I don't answer him because Uncle Rich has never tried to sell me anything. He didn't even make me pay for all those high and low fives.

He gets up from my bed, but before he takes a step, I turn over and ask, "Daddy, why'd you pay Bianca to be my friend?"

He laughs without even smiling. "Oh, I just gave her five bucks so you two can go to the store and get yourselves some candy. You don't know your way around just yet, so I let Bianca hold the money, is all. Ain't nobody paying anybody to be your friend. You can make friends here all on your own, ain't that right, Broomstick? You got Harlem in your blood. This is my home. Your grandfather was born here. Your people got roots here. So why wouldn't you be able to make friends? Them 'little street urchins,' as your momma likes to put it, could be your cousins."

I furrow my brows at the thought of that, and shake my

head hard to let go of any ideas that I might be related to any of those nefarious minions.

He reaches down to pat my head, then walks out of my bedroom that's really not my bedroom, because I'm only here for a week, and not a minute or a second or a millisecond longer.

CHAPTER
9

The next morning Daddy's still in bed and the whole house seems to still be asleep. But I woke up on my own. Right away, I washed the stupid press 'n' curl out of my hair. My Afro was a soft, round moon around my head. I found four rubber bands that I used to make four pigtails that stand up like antennas. (Granddaddy tells me that when I use my imagination location, the very ends of my pigtails light up like fireflies. Momma just frowns and looks for her hot comb.) Then, I put on my Superman T-shirt and matching shorts set (it's for boys so Granddaddy bought it for me and Momma doesn't like it one bit). The stiff, ironed-on S feels like the burlap potato sacks Momma keeps in the kitchen, and the whole outfit will make me sweat like a hog because of all that polyester, as Momma says. But I don't care. I'm Superman. So, I fly down the stairs and make myself a bowl of cornflakes with milk. There's no one around to see the little smile on my face or the spring in my step. My soulglow, as Granddaddy calls it.

I let this soulglow take over my body from my kinky hair down to my funky toes because today is the day that I will save Captain Fleet from the clutches of the Sonic King, and save Bianca Pluto from the spell of the nefarious minionettes!

I'm standing in the doorway, staring out at the broken,

raggedy brownstone soldiers lined up along the street. I glance down the block. The nefarious minions are gone. The minionettes are not jumping rope. Only an old man strolls by pushing a cart full of plastic bags. He nods at me and tips his dusty black hat.

Then, I look up at the clear blue sky. Yesterday's Sonic Boom has dispersed and I wonder if it's Captain Fleet's doing from behind the Sonic King's prison walls.

"Why are you up so early, Broomstick?" Daddy asks from inside the house.

His voice makes me jump and I step back in and shut the door. "Where is everybody?" I ask.

"It's Sunday," he says, coming down the last few steps wearing a dingy T-shirt and cut-off blue jeans. I get my knobby knees from my daddy, but not his hairy legs, thank goodness. "Things slow down in the city on Sundays. It almost feels like Alabama." He comes over and puts his arm around my shoulders to pull me into the living room. "*Almost* like Alabama. Now, look here, Broomstick. I got some work to do so why don't you go watch some TV, have some more cereal, and take it easy for a while? Get acclimated to your new home."

He walks away on the word *home* and I want him to take it back. This is not my new home, and I will not get *acclimated*. He disappears into the kitchen and I race to the front door and into that cool Sunday morning No Joke City air.

I take a moment to make sure none of the nefarious minions are watching me. But the coast isn't completely clear. A lady and two boys walk by. The kids stare at me and I stare back. I take a few steps down the stairs. They look familiar. But they're both wearing disguises that make it hard for me to tell if they are indeed the nefarious minions: long pants, white shirts, and neckties. The older one sticks his tongue out at me and I immediately recognize him as the Pigeon-Chest boy! I stick my tongue out at him, too, extra long, putting my whole face into it. "I will crush you!" I call out.

He keeps looking back and making ugly faces at me, until he almost trips and his momma pulls his ear telling him to hurry.

I stand on the steps waiting for any other nefarious minions to come out of their hiding places wearing shirt-and-tie disguises. A lady walks by with a wide church hat and waves.

"You must be Julius's girl," she says, stopping right outside the rusty black iron gate. "I'll come by later to drop off a plate from church, if you like?"

I only nod.

She smiles and walks away, thank goodness.

Finally, the coast is clear. If I remember correctly, there's a secret portal beneath the stoop that leads to Bianca Pluto's lair. I head down to it and look around for a doorbell. There isn't one, but before I get to knocking really hard, the door opens and a woman wearing a hat just as fancy as that other lady's opens the door.

She gasps, smiles big and wide, and reaches for my face. I step back before she even lays a finger on me.

"E-bone-y!" she sings.

She pronounces my name with an accent, stretching the bone sound. It's Bianca's abuela, Señora Luz.

"So good to see you. Oh, you got so big!" She gets ahold of my shoulder and motions for me to turn around like all the other grandmothers do down in Huntsville. She giggles as if I'm one big joke. Poor Señora Luz. They got her, too.

Bianca comes out right behind her grandmother and the

sight of her makes my eyes pop out. She's in disguise, too!

"Hi, Ebony-Grace," she says really soft.

She's wearing a sky-blue fluffy dress that looks like a layer cake. Her hair is even curlier, but neater than yesterday.

"Bianca Pluto, are you okay?" I ask.

She rolls her eyes. A sure sign that some otherworldly entity has gotten ahold of her mind.

"What happened? Did something happen to you, Bianca?" Señora Luz asks her granddaughter.

Bianca rolls her eyes again, and I'm sure that she won't tell her grandmother the truth.

I inhale deep and brace myself to be an agent of truth, a messenger of good, a princess of peace. "I'm sorry to report, Señora Luz—" I start to say.

"The Sonic Boom!" Bianca cuts me off. "You should've seen it, Abuela, it was all over the sky!"

A warm, bright smile starts to rise from a deep place in my belly. It eases up to my throat and it's trying to make its way out of my mouth and through my face so that I shine like the sun—my soulshine! It's more than just a soulglow. But I stop it. I force it back down because Daddy is peering over the steps and looking down at us. I can't let him see me smile. I can't let him see me happy.

"Broomstick, why'd you leave the house without telling me?" he asks.

Señora Luz steps out of the doorway, wearing a purple dress with tiny flowers. "Julio, it's so good to see your daughter. Look at how big she got. Why don't you let her come to church with us?"

"Fine by me. Is that okay with you, Broomstick?"

Before I even answer, Señora Luz says, "But you have to put on a nice dress."

CHAPTER
10

I don't put on a nice dress because I hate church. Church is where Momma pinches my arm if she thinks I'm not paying attention to the pastor, and that's all the time. Church is where Momma's friends talk about her when she's not around and call her a *divorcée*. Church is where everybody from the deacon to the little kids in Sunday school try to convince me that Jesus is not an astronaut. "You do know there's a whole universe beyond the clouds, don't you?" is what I always whisper to the Sunday school kids. "Why would Jesus want to stay in boring heaven when he could visit other planets?"

But if Momma ever heard me say those words out loud, I would get a licking right in front of the whole congregation. And then she'd blame Granddaddy for putting these *demonic* thoughts into my head. Granddaddy stopped going to church after Nana died.

Upstairs in my room, I pretend to toss my clothes out of all my suitcases searching for a fancy church dress until I hear Daddy return to his room. I tiptoe back down the stairs still wearing my Superman short set to go to church with Bianca and her grandmother.

"I don't have a dress," I lie to Señora Luz. I hold my head down pretending to be ashamed.

"You don't have a dress? Ah, that's not true. I remember

your mother. . . . So fancy! Like Dominique Deveraux on *Dynasty*. She didn't put a nice dress in your suitcase?"

I pout and shake my head. Momma is not around to see me fib. Granddaddy once said that fibs are like deflector shields. It's okay to protect yourself or someone you love with a deflector shield.

Señora Luz just shakes her head and motions for me to join them as they walk down 126th Street. "We're almost late for church so Bianca can't give you a dress. Next time, you dress up, okay?" she says as she walks ahead of us.

I look down at Bianca's shiny shoes—the grown-up ones without the straps. But she still wears young lady socks, the ones with the lace trimmings that fold over. I had on those same socks yesterday. But Momma isn't here to make me dress *accordingly*.

Bianca starts taking long steps, landing on her tippy-toes each time. "Don't step on a crack so you don't break your mother's back," she says.

"Break my mother's back? What?" I ask.

She glances over at me. "You broke your mother's back," she says, walking as if trying to avoid craters on the moon.

"Why would I want to do that?" I ask.

"You just did it again. You broke your mother's back."

I freeze. I won't take another step. I would never want to break Momma's back, no matter how many fancy dresses she makes me wear. That would be no good, terrible, and awful!

Bianca grabs my hand. "If you step on a crack on the sidewalk, you break your mother's back."

"Who told you that nonsense? The nefarious minions?" I say.

We're at the corner of 126th Street and Lenox Avenue

waiting for the light. The streets here are wide as if every single block were supposed to be a freeway.

"What's a nefarious—" Bianca starts to ask.

"Those kids from yesterday. All of them are nefarious—evil, despicable little street urchins."

Momma's exact words ring in my ears: *And make sure you stay far away from those despicable little street urchins.*

"They're not evil. They're my friends. And why do they have to be onions?"

"Not *on*-ions. *Min*-ions! They're sent to carry out the unspoken rule: No visitors shall smile, or giggle, or laugh in No Joke City. King Sirius Julius commands it be so."

Bianca doesn't say anything as we cross the street. Other kids walk past us with their grown-ups, but they don't strike me as nefarious minions because they don't smile or laugh or wave hello. They're minding their own businesses. They're not trying to trick me into being happy. They couldn't care less.

When we reach the corner, Bianca starts again with her game of not stepping on a crack that will break her mother's back. I watch her grandmother walk ahead of us as she steps on crack after crack and wonder if there's such a thing as breaking your granddaughter's back.

So I try to skip all the cracks, too. But the sidewalk isn't the backs of everybody's momma. It's the big, fat, giant silver moon instead. "If you step on a moon crater, Earth will explode!" I say.

We get to 127th Street and we stand on a safe piece of the sidewalk, waiting for the light to change. In front of a corner building are a group of grandpas sitting around a small table playing card games. One of them waves to Señora Luz.

The buildings are taller and wider here, and they seem

to be all glued together side by side like the brownstones on Daddy's block. Some people lean out of their opened windows as if it's no big deal. They don't seem to understand the law of gravity. They don't have rocket engines in their shoes, so why do they think it's okay to lean out of windows?

Bianca pauses for a long minute before she asks, "Who cares if the Earth explodes if we're already on the moon?"

My soulshine starts to well up again. I push it down and make sure that Bianca Pluto stays in her imagination location. "Don't you care about your abuela?" I ask.

"She's on the moon with us," Bianca says.

"What about my daddy?"

"Well, that's your problem."

"That's not fair!" I say.

"That's because he's the king and he has to protect the nefarious onions," says Bianca.

I cover my smile and have to keep quiet for a little while because I want to laugh so badly. I just might burst out into *hysterics*, as Momma would say when Granddaddy and I are deep in our imagination locations—the kind of laughter that will make me float up to the air, through the clouds, and straight into outer space.

We reach a building with a big white cross in the front and a sign that says, HOUSE OF THE LORD. A few people stand outside with their fancy hats and church suits. I dust off my Superman shirt and get ready to be scolded by the church grandmas for not wearing a nice dress. But Señora Luz walks right past that church and doesn't even wave at the other church grandmas.

I shrug and step back into my imagination location. "But he's my daddy. I can't destroy Earth if he's still there. We have to go back and save him."

"If you save him, then you have to save the nefarious onions, too! They're my friends," says Bianca.

"Hmmm." I wonder, placing an index finger on my chin. "But we have to quickly get back onto the *Uhura*, leave the galaxy, and enter Planet Boom Box's orbit so we can save Captain Fleet."

We cross the street and at the other corner is another church—Mount Zion Baptist Church. People are walking into the small building, so we're right on time. That definitely has to be the church we're going to.

"What happened to Captain Fleet?" Bianca asks.

I can't help but to grin big and bright because, finally, this is a sign that I'm pulling Bianca Pluto out of the mind-controlling prison of No Joke City. I don't erase my smile. We're almost at church, and I'll be safe from the watchful eyes of the nefarious minions.

But we pass that church, too! Señora Luz keeps on walking without checking to make sure that she hasn't made a mistake.

"Hey, where are we going?" I finally ask.

"To church," Bianca says.

Señora Luz looks back, glances down at my clothes, and shakes her head.

"But we just passed two churches. And look! There's one across the street. And another down there!" I say, pointing at all the white or black or lit-up crosses on different buildings. How many churches can there be on one block, in one city?

"Yeah, but those aren't our church," says Bianca.

Finally, we turn on 138th Street. An even bigger church than the ones on Lenox Avenue stands in the middle of the block like a castle. Its bright red doors are like hearts pumping loud gospel songs, tambourines, and a preacher's shout to the rest of the block. Surely, that must be the one we're going to.

But we walk straight past it as grandmas in wide, colorful hats smile and nod at us.

We make a right up a street named Frederick Douglass Boulevard where we pass by open lots with even more old tires, torn mattresses, and garbage bags. There's a crumbled building at the very edge of one of the lots. It looks as if a giant Transformer had crashed through its brick walls, making it fall to pieces with a single blow. I even see a big round metal container with a large, blue-orange flame raging on top of it like it's a barbecue grill.

I've never been so far and deep into No Joke City. The last time we were here, Momma kept me cooped up in Daddy's house, away from the despicable little street urchins. Even as some kids rode their bicycles or played in the lots or leaned out of windows, there still wasn't anything funny about No Joke City.

If the churches in No Joke City are anything like the ones down in Huntsville, then I'll have to lock up my imagination location and act like the little lady Momma tells me to be. But Bianca is with me and she's already in too deep. She's been on the *Uhura* and has come face-to-face with Captain Fleet. There's no way we're going to be able to keep those doors closed!

CHAPTER

11

We make it all the way to 140th Street—fourteen whole blocks and more churches than I can count—before we arrive at the Holy Redeemer Church. There's another small crowd gathered outside—grandmas and grandpas, regular grown-ups and kids, lots of kids. And it's not even the church grandmas who shake their heads, scrunch up their faces, or wag their fingers when they see what I'm wearing. It's Pigeon-Chest Boy and some of his fellow nefarious minions.

"Why are *they* here?" I ask Bianca as we join the small crowd piling through the narrow double-doors of the church. The building looks more like one of the many stores along Lenox Avenue instead of a church.

"They come here for worship," Bianca says. "That's Calvin. We're gonna be in Sunday school together."

"Calvin," I repeat with disgust, as if I'm saying *cauliflower* or *cabbage* or *callous*. "Callous Calvin. Stone-Cold Calvin."

Stone-Cold Calvin is pointing at me. I furrow my brows and clench my fists, ready for an attack. He makes his way over to us with some of his nefarious minions.

"Oooh, you're gonna be in trouble! How come you don't have on church clothes?" he sings with a voice that sounds like broken concrete.

I scrunch up my face even tighter.

"You look like you wanna hit me," Stone-Cold Calvin says, stepping closer. "Go 'head. Right in front of church. See what happens."

I pull up my right arm in front of me with all my might and shoot out a strong "Pew!" in his direction. Before he even blinks, I do the same with my other arm. "Pew!"

Bianca touches my shoulder. "No, Ebony. Not here," she whispers.

But it's too late. Stone-Cold Calvin and the nefarious minions start to laugh.

"You think you're Wonder Woman?" he says. 'You ain't no Wonder Woman."

"And she has on boys' clothes!" one of them calls out.

They keep laughing and I'm ready to pull out my secret and most powerful weapon of all, but a grown-up pulls one of the boys by the ear and they all get really quiet as if the Sonic Boom has stolen their voices. My grown-up isn't here to pinch me or look at me sideways. Momma is all the way down in Huntsville and she won't see me act *insolent* or *unbecoming* or *discourteous*.

"Shawn, what'd I tell you about acting a fool right before church?" a woman says through clenched teeth.

She glances at me and scrunches up her nose. Even as she pulls the boy into the church, she keeps looking at me. Soon, the nefarious minions are making their way into the small building without paying me any mind.

Then, I catch another church lady staring at me, too. And then another. I slowly realize that a few of them have gathered around Señora Luz and they all have their eyes on me. These church ladies and grandmas are not nefarious minions, of course. They're grown-ups who've been locked out of their imagination locations. Bianca is no longer by my side, and it's like having Momma watching me through all these ladies' eyes.

If Momma were to secretly teleport from Huntsville to land right in front of me and see me on a Sunday, in front of a small and not-so-fancy church, wearing a Superman short set, I'd surely get a licking or two and be forbidden to have caramel cake or banana pudding for the whole summer.

I pretend to look away and kick around tiny pieces of litter from the sidewalk while activating my bionic ears. Their whispers become as loud as car horns.

"Julius ain't minding her. How's he just gonna dump her on you like that, Luz? You already got one of your own," a grandma says.

"I got a prayer cloth in my bag. Could wrap it around her skinny legs twice to cover up them boys' shorts," another church lady adds.

"Just this Sunday, okay? Next time, she'll be appropriate." Señora Luz says something else, but my bionic ears stop working.

I can't help myself, so I blurt out, "There won't be a next time!"

The ladies and grandmas all gasp. A few kids are left standing outside, and their eyes get really wide as if I'm about to get in the worst trouble. I'm sure this will make it back to King Sirius Julius. But I'm not smiling or laughing. So there's no reason for him to keep me as his prisoner.

"That is not the way to speak to your elders, young lady," a grandma says with a voice almost like a man's. She steps closer to me, and I step back. "This is a holy place, now you watch your tone."

I keep my eyes on her, staring her down, making sure she doesn't lay a finger on me. This isn't Huntsville where

Momma gives any and everybody permission to pop me one time if I get out of line.

"Ebony, sweetheart," Señora Luz says with her singsong voice like molasses. "Come inside for service. You can stay with Bianca for Sunday school."

Bianca is not looking in my direction. She's slipping from me. I have to save her! I can't lose this battle.

I walk over to Bianca, grab her hand, and walk right into the church with her—she in her fancy dress and me in my Superman short set.

CHAPTER
12

The Holy Redeemer Church is not really a church. It's a hallway. Chairs are lined up against the walls in rows of four on each side. A long, narrow walkway leads to the pulpit where there's an organ, a drum set, a box of tambourines, a pile of spare bibles, and six grown-ups in black graduation gowns—the choir.

Bianca pulls her hand from mine. She walks ahead of me and I follow her through the hallway church, past the pulpit, and through a secret door that opens up to a portal—a steep staircase leading down to a musty basement.

I knew the Holy Redeemer wasn't a real church. It's the command center for the No Joke City rebel alliance! Who knew that Bianca was plotting along with the nefarious minions to overthrow the king? Maybe she even obtained a complete tactical readout of his battle station!

"Wow!" I whisper as we reach the very bottom of the steps. The ceiling is so low that I can reach up and touch it with my fingertips. I have to duck to dodge the swinging lightbulbs.

We're in an even narrower hallway and a few doors line the walls. Laughter pours out of one of the rooms whose door is left open. I'm careful not to smile just yet. I have to know who exactly is leading this rebellion. I have to understand the terms of this impending war.

"It's so small. How can anyone breathe down here?" I whisper to Bianca.

She quickly turns around. "You've never been in a basement before?"

"Yeah, but not one so small," I say. Then, I lean in to whisper, "I will help you with your rebellion."

Bianca steps back. "*What?*"

"Your plot to overthrow King Sirius Julius and bring freedom to No Joke City!" I whisper-yell. "What else could be going on down here?"

She rolls her eyes. "¡Dios mio! Why are you so weird?" she whisper-yells back.

"But weren't you just talking about King Sirius Julius, and . . . ," I start to say, but she's already turned away from me and makes her way into the room with the laughing kids.

I take slow, careful steps toward the door. I peek in to see Stone-Cold Calvin's big ol' peanut head.

"You're welcome to join us," someone says from behind me, and I jump, putting both my Bracelets of Submission in front of my face.

A lady is smiling before me, wearing too-red lipstick and too-blue eyeshadow, almost like Momma. "I heard all about you upstairs. It's okay. You can go in."

The hallway is so narrow that I can't push past the lady to leave the secret headquarters. So before I know it, I'm in a small room filled with tables, chairs, nefarious minions and minionettes, and Bianca Pluto.

"There goes that weird girl!" someone calls out.

"Hush now!" Lipstick Lady says.

"Sister Linda, how come she gets to wear clothes like that to church?" a girl wearing a giant pink ribbon calls out. I don't recognize her, but still, she's definitely a minionette. I don't like her question and I don't trust her.

"Wendy, lower your voice," Sister Linda says.

"Is that a Superman shirt? Can I wear my Adidas track-suit next Sunday?" a boy's voice says.

"I thought you can't enter the house of the Lord worship-ping another idol," another girl's voice says. I can't spot the minionette who says all this, but my eyes land on Bianca, who doesn't even look my way.

The No Joke City gibberish escalates to new heights. There isn't much room here, so their voices bounce off the walls and ceilings like Ping-Pong balls in zero gravity.

Sister Linda takes my arm to walk me to a seat, but I pull away from her.

I was wrong! This isn't the secret headquarters for the No Joke City rebellion. Bianca Pluto is not overthrowing King Sirius Julius.

I slowly start to raise my arm to activate my Bracelets of Submission, and Bianca finally sees me. She shakes her head, her eyes pleading. I have no other choice. I will not be taken prisoner.

"Did everyone bring their bibles?" Sister Linda starts.

I take one step back. And then another. "Jesus is an astronaut!" I yell. I slowly extend my arms out on each side of me and just like Linda Carter turning into Wonder Woman, I spin right out of that small bible study room as Space Cadet E-Grace Starfleet, zoom through the narrow hallway, and rush up the steep staircase.

The preacher is at the pulpit leading his tiny congrega-tion in prayer. Everyone has their heads bowed down and eyes closed, thank goodness. So I sprint right out of that Holy Redeemer Church and onto 140th Street until I reach Lenox Avenue. I run down the whole fourteen blocks to 126th Street, passing dozens of grown-ups leading nefarious min-ions in church clothes.

Some call out, "Is it a bird, is it a plane? No, it's Superman!"

Another one yells, "It's Jesse Owens's love child!"

I zoom past a grandpa who says, "Look at Wilma Rudolph straight outta the Rome Olympics!"

"No way, it's Flo-Jo on her way to LA," says the teenager walking beside him.

But I am not running down the streets of Harlem. I am flying way up high over it, with the clouds.

CHAPTER
13

"Ebony-Grace, you can't just run around Harlem like you know the place. You're a spring chicken, baby girl—only twelve. You don't know these streets like the other kids yet. These kids—what your momma calls 'little street urchins'— have seen more hard life than any grown folk down in Alabama. I bet if a dope fiend asks for five dollars, you'll give it to him. If that same dope fiend asks you to use our bathroom, you'll let him in. You don't need to know about that kinda life, baby girl. But you don't need to be up in them clouds, either. There's a difference between knowin' and livin'."

"What's a dope fiend, Daddy?" I ask, when King Sirius Julius finally stops his lecture to take a breath.

"Proves my point, Broomstick," he continues. "Don't give Lester five dollars if he ever asks for it. And never, ever let him into the house."

I shrug because I don't have any problems with Lester, other than the fact that he smells funny.

I'm sitting on the creaky hardwood floors of my bedroom with my arms crossed and my legs stretched out in front of me. A stack of ten comic books sits next to my bare feet. I've already read them twice, even while a low-level Sonic Boom invades King Sirius Julius's lair and music pumps throughout every corner of the brownstone.

I can't really tell if King Sirius Julius is raising his voice so that I can hear him over the music, or if he's really mad at me. His words dip and dive around the rhythm, bass, and singing like a spaceship dodging meteors.

At least this is the music Granddaddy likes, too, and not the other sounds made up of hard beats and computer noise that gets down into your bones and makes you lose your God-loving mind!

Still, I knew King Sirius Julius was trying to control my mind when he put Al Green's "Love and Happiness" on the record player. He was trying to make me love Harlem, to make me happy, even as he stands yelling over me for running away from the Holy Redeemer Church and Señora Luz and Bianca.

King Sirius Julius takes in a long breath, places both his hands on his hips, and says, "Folks are already talking, saying that I should've left you with your momma, that I ain't got no business raising a girl out here with the shop and all. But I wasn't gonna stand by and watch all that stuff going on with Jerry and how it must be affecting you. I'm your father, and it's my job to protect you. But I'm not gonna fight you to do so, baby girl."

"What's the stuff going on with Jerry?" I ask without hesitating.

He sighs again, deeper this time, and King Sirius Julius melts off Daddy. His shoulders relax and his arms hang by his sides as if I'd defeated him with that single question.

"Come on," he says, motioning for me to get up from the floor and follow him down the stairs.

He still doesn't turn down Al Green and his mind-melding rhythms as he dials 1 . . . 2 . . . 5 . . . 6 . . . The number seems longer than before and I don't hear Daddy announce his whole name to the operator—Julius Freeman—to place the collect call.

In just a few seconds, he starts with "Gloria." Not hello or good afternoon or with a long string of names asking if so-and-so is well, and if a prayer for this-and-that has been answered by the Lord. This is how all conversations start on Sundays down home in Huntsville. But here in Harlem, Daddy gets straight to the point.

"You gotta let her talk to her grandfather," he says.

My heart skips a beat and I hold my breath. If there could ever be a time to smile in No Joke City, it's right now, even though this isn't a joke by far. I step closer to Daddy ready to take the phone and finally hear my granddaddy's voice after a whole month.

Granddaddy had not come to my elementary school graduation. Ever since last Christmas, he and I'd been preparing for that very day, which would be when I'd announce to the world my secret identity as Space Cadet E-Grace Starfleet. Granddaddy had said it was time to open the giant doors of my imagination location to the world. I didn't have to pretend to like church dresses or ballet class or etiquette lessons anymore. I wouldn't have to whisper anymore. I could be myself—inside and out.

He had a closet full of his blue NASA suits. Granddaddy called them flight suits and Momma called them coveralls, but I called them space suits. They're the same ones that Sally Ride wore when she boarded the Space Shuttle Orbital Flight STS-7 *Challenger* in June last year—the very first American lady on the crew of a spacecraft. When me and Granddaddy watched the launch on TV, he repeated in his very own way what all the reporters had been asking her: "How is she gonna get to her woman parts?"

Guion Bluford wore the same spacesuit when he boarded the Space Shuttle Orbital Flight STS-8 *Challenger* last August—the very first spaceflight to take place at night and the very first black man on a space mission. Granddaddy had joked, "Of course, they need a black man to guide them through the dark!"

I opened up the door to Granddaddy's closet in the back of his office. I counted five blue space suits, each with the patch of the American flag on the left arm. I grabbed one and tried to sniff out the smell of jet fuel, zero-gravity nothing-ness, and maybe even outer space. But it just smelled like Granddaddy and his cigarette smoke.

Granddaddy is not an astronaut; he's an engineer, and he doesn't think he'll ever make it to outer space. "That's your dream, baby girl, not mine," he'd said to me once. "Not any-more, that is." He's one of the nuts-and-bolts guys. There'd be no space shuttles without him and his work buddies Uncle Morgan, Uncle Charles, and Uncle James. There'd be no race part of the space race. There'd be no *Columbia* or *Challenger*, and not even the aeronautics part of the National Aeronau-tics and Space Administration because there'd be no one to screw in the nuts and bolts.

I pulled out one of the suits and ran my finger along the circular NASA logo. I traced each of the letters as I whis-pered the whole words that make up the acronym. National. Aeronautics. Space. Administration. Above the logo is a big, black rectangle with Granddaddy's name on it in white let-ters: Jeremiah.

On the right side of the suit, is the NASA 25th Anniver-sary commemorative logo where the red letters against the white patch look like they've been drawn by aliens, and the number twenty-five in red and blue separated by a small white star. Below the logo are the years 1958–1983. Aliens are older than NASA. The whole universe is older than NASA. Momma, Daddy, and Granddaddy are all older than NASA, too. Even the *Uhura*, Planet Boom Box, the Sonic King, and the Sonic Boom are older than NASA.

Then I trace the triangular gold trimming on the Space Shuttle patch right below that logo. So many patches. And if Granddaddy was planning on letting me wear one of his space suits to my sixth grade graduation, then everyone would know that I was already an astronaut; that I'd been to outer space, out of the galaxy, beyond Andromeda, and back.

No one would call me *weird*, *crazy*, or that I ain't got *no home training*.

One of the space suits didn't have Granddaddy's name patch on it, so I quickly pulled it off the hanger and put it on over my skirt and blouse. The skirt bunched up around my waist when I tried to zip up the space suit. It was loose, but it was perfect. There was enough room for me to fight off the evil Funkazoids if I had to.

I stepped away from the closet, aimed my right fist, and pretended to shoot my phaser gun at the walls, the ceiling, and the door. Pew! Pew! Pew!

There were footsteps headed straight for Granddaddy's office, and I was ready for those Funkazoids. The door slowly opened, and . . . Pew! Pew!

"Ebony-Grace Norfleet Freeman, you take that off right now!" Momma shouted. Her face was wound up into a knot.

I couldn't take Granddaddy's space suit off fast enough for her. So she rushed over and just about yanked it off me. She smoothed down my skirt and my hair and looked at me with her scrunched up face and said, "Don't you go meddling in your grandfather's things."

"Yes, Momma," I said. A stone was forming in my throat.

I swallowed it back down so Momma wouldn't see me cry about wearing one of my grandfather's flight suits.

"I've got a closet full of pretty dresses, and for the life of me, I can't understand why you don't go meddling in there!" she'd said.

I hung my head real low because Momma's closet is the last place on earth I'd want to be.

On the days leading up to my sixth grade graduation and dance, I had to listen to all the girls in my class talk about how they were going to coordinate their dresses. The only colors allowed were pink, yellow, sky blue, and lavender. And most of the girls were wearing their Easter dresses.

So the day before my graduation, Momma thought she was doing me a big favor by surprising me with a whole new dress since we weren't like the other families. We could afford a new dress, she'd said.

"Ebony-Grace, baby," Momma said with a big smile, holding up a brown paper shopping bag. "I managed to find something at the Heart of Huntsville Mall, but I can't wait for the new Madison Square Mall to open up this summer."

"The new space camp is opening up this summer, too, Momma," I had said without thinking.

Her smile disappeared for a quick second and she shot me a look that might as well have been a phaser blast. Her smile returned when she pulled out a frilly lavender dress that looked like a birthday cake.

The words, "No, Momma," spilled out of my mouth as easy as breath.

"What do you mean 'no,' little girl? It's your special day and you're becoming a young woman now. Junior high school is right around the corner. And before you know it, it'll be time for high school. All the girls in your class are going to look so pretty. Why should you be any different?"

There was no arguing with Momma about this.

But still, I was keeping hope alive thinking that Granddaddy would roll up one of those space suits into a bag and take it with him to my graduation. And since Momma would be sitting in the audience as all the sixth graders lined up backstage to walk down the aisle to Billy Foster's very bad alto sax rendition of *Pomp and Circumstance*, I'd have enough time to change out of that ugly lavender birthday-cake dress and slip into the E-Grace Starfleet space suit.

That morning I had done everything I was supposed to— sat still while Momma pressed and curled my hair near the kitchen stove as Granddaddy read his newspaper and ate his oatmeal. The phone was ringing off the hook with Momma's friends asking if she had an extra hot comb or a pair of stockings or some sponge rollers for their daughter's big day. Momma was friends with the mothers of the girls in my class. I wasn't friends with those girls.

I was polite and obedient to Momma as she laid out the lavender birthday-cake dress, white stockings, and white patent leather shoes on my bed because Granddaddy, with his short, gray Afro and clean-shaven face, had smiled and winked at me as he made his way into his office after breakfast.

That smile and wink was a secret, was a promise. I was sure.

I'd been announcing to my not-friends that I'll be revealing a very special surprise during graduation. I practically begged that everyone keep their eyes on me.

But the ceremony came and went, and there was no bag with a space suit. No NASA patches. No announcing to the world that I am Cadet E-Grace Starfleet. I didn't even get to show off my granddaddy, Jeremiah Norfleet, NASA Marshall Space Flight Center employee, who was supposed to be the first black man on the moon.

So I did what I always do during church or any one of Momma's fancy *formal affairs*: I folded up my imagination location into a tiny square and tucked it into one of my thick braids, or into my small pocketbook, or inside the fold of one of my frilly socks.

Even at the dance after the ceremony, as Michael Jackson's "Billy Jean" and "Beat It" played, and the boys tried to moonwalk across the gymnasium; and the girls pretended to be Donna Summer while working hard for the money; and the parents chitchatted, I sat in a corner, quiet and still, waiting for the whole thing to be over. The music was the stuff I'd hear on the radio, what Momma, with giant rollers in her hair, would dance to in the kitchen when she was tired of listening to Mahalia Jackson and Shirley Caesar sing from the bottom of their bellies about heaven and Jesus. Once I'd seen her shimmying her shoulders and whispering, "What a Feeling!"

The only time I got up was to get some snacks way on the other side of the gym. A big, round bowl of fruit punch sat in the middle of the snack table. I filled up a plastic cup and covered my paper plate with Cheese Doodles, Ritz crackers, vanilla wafers, and a thick slice of somebody's grandmomma's Lane cake. I went back to the line of empty folding chairs in the back of the gym and sat on the one closest to the corner. I placed my punch on the floor and my plate of snacks on my lap, not caring that I'll get crumbs all over that stupid lavender dress. Then one of Granddaddy's favorite songs came on—Lionel Richie singing "All Night Long." Even the teachers snapped their fingers. I started to tap my toes, too, but I placed my hand over my knee and forced my body to disobey that rhythm. Instead of dancing, I took a big bite out of the slice of Lane cake and chewed slowly, staring down at my plate and not at those spinning planets in that big, wide, lonely galaxy called school.

After graduation and the dance, Granddaddy was waiting for us back home. As he sat on his rocking chair on the porch sipping sweet tea, it looked as if he had dark, thick gray concrete clouds hanging over his head. He wore one of his many dark gray church suits, which made his light gray hair look white. Beads of sweat dotted his forehead and his dark brown skin seemed to shine in the late afternoon sun. He didn't even hug me and say congratulations. He didn't even tell me any stories about the *Uhura*—no Planet Boom Box threatening to take over the galaxy and no evil Funkazoids and their Sonic King. His imagination location was completely blank, like that stray rock we discovered just beyond Jupiter and thought it was a new planet. He was just a regular ol' grandpa.

But I'd been hearing the whispers and gossip with my bionic ears for weeks.

"His soul is lost," Momma's church lady friends had mumbled at Wednesday's bible study.

"Ain't no turning back from that kinda sin," Mrs. Headley had whispered to Mrs. Turner at last Friday's fish fry.

Surely all these whispers and mumbles and Granddaddy's sadness were signs of a much bigger problem that no one else could understand—not those chirping church ladies, not my nosy neighbors, and not my mysterious momma and her meddling questions about whether I'd seen Granddaddy's lady friends while Nana was alive.

No matter how loud I shouted above the hush-hush rumors and gossip, no one heard me or believed me when I told them the truth: Captain Fleet was being held as prisoner on Planet Boom Box by the Sonic King and the Funkazoids.

No one understood anything because they had all locked the doors to their imagination location and thrown away the key.

"Don't worry, baby girl. We'll hold off on the adventures of the *Uhura* for a few days. I'll activate the impenetrable force field so that she's protected out there in deep space," Granddaddy said to me as Momma brought out his suitcases for his long trip. He spoke in an unusually soft and quiet voice. He'd patted me on the shoulder and had not scooped me up into his long, wiry arms like he usually did at the end of a *Uhura* story.

"But, Granddaddy, I was supposed to reveal my secret identity today."

He placed his index finger over his lips and said, "You'll need to stay undercover for a little bit, Starfleet." He didn't make his voice sound commanding like all the other times he spoke as Captain Fleet.

Granddaddy had been wearing the church suit and tie as if he'd planned to attend my graduation. But instead, a shiny black car pulled up in front of our house. A man came out of the driver's side, walked around to the passenger side, and held the door open for my grandfather.

"What mission are you off to now, Granddaddy?"

"You're going to be just fine, Ebony-Grace. I'll try to be back before you leave for New York," was the very last thing he had said to me as he placed his empty glass on a small nearby table, stood from the rocking chair, picked up his suitcases, and headed for the shiny black car. The sadness around him seemed to have swallowed him up like a black hole.

CHAPTER
14

"Ebony" is the very first word Momma says when I'm on the phone with her. I want to wrap the springy telephone cord around my whole body and hope that it becomes a portal taking me back to Huntsville. "Ebony, baby? I heard you went to church today."

I don't answer her.

"Ebony-Grace, I am talking to you, young lady," she says. Her voice is hard candy again.

I pull the wide heavy metal doors to my imagination location closed—I become regular ol' Ebony-Grace again.

"Yes, Momma," I say.

Daddy looks at me funny.

"All right, now listen to me, and listen to me good," Momma continues. "I know I should've sat you down before you left, but we were rushing to get you onto that plane, and there was so much going on, Ebony."

Hard candy melts in your mouth after you let it sit there on your tongue, near the back of your throat. It's like the giant vacuum of outer space pushing and pulling everything apart until they're all just space dust particles. This is how Momma's voice sounds now—a tiny piece of sweetness that slowly disappears into nothing.

"Your grandfather's in a bit of trouble. I want you to

know that he's still a very good man who just made some bad choices, that's all. Do you hear me, Ebony-Grace?"

"Yes, Momma." Maybe my own hard-candy voice begins to melt, too, and it wants to seep out of my eyes and nose as salty tears and gooey snot. I feel it welling up inside of me like a rising flood, almost drowning me.

"Ebony, you're going to have to stay in New York for a few more weeks."

I don't say anything. I only think of the big, fat round moon and how it controls ocean tides. And maybe even tears, too.

"Answer me when I'm talking to you."

"Yes, Momma." My voice shakes.

"I have to help your grandfather out so I won't be around to look after you," she continues.

"Yes, Momma."

"Now, you have to promise me that you'll keep away from the auto shop and keep a good distance from those . . . children playing in the streets. I remember that lovely little girl, what was her name? Bianca. You're allowed to go to church with Bianca's grandmother and play in the front of the house, but inside the gate only. Do you hear me, Ebony? Don't go digging through any of the trash on the streets either, trying to find something to fix. And read your books. Your father will be taking you to the library. You're allowed two hours of television per day until your father signs you up for classes. I'll be sending money for your lessons. And don't stay out in the sun for too long. You already know that, Ebony. Do you understand me, young lady?"

"Yes, Momma."

"Good. Now, put your father on the phone" is how Momma says goodbye.

I hold on to the receiver waiting for more—more about the new space camp, more about this trouble with Granddaddy, more about when I'll be coming home. But more of anything is not going to come from Momma unless I ask for it. "What kind of trouble is Granddaddy in, Momma?"

"The kind of trouble grown-ups get into when they make wrong choices" is all she says. "Now put your father on the phone."

I don't activate my bionic ears. I don't wait to hear what Daddy has to say about all of Momma's plans for me. I run upstairs to the room that will be my room for a whole summer, and open up Momma's old makeup case. In it are VHS and Betamax tapes, including my favorite of them all: *Star Trek: The Motion Picture—Special Longer Version.* I take it out of the case and hold it to my chest. If there's anything I need most on this Planet No Joke City it's a VCR. Instead, I reach for another bag and grab the very first comic book I find— Volume One of *Star Trek, "The Wormhole Connection."*

Granddaddy had bought it when it first came out last February. That night, I sat next to him on the couch and we read it together. He'd fallen asleep when I read it a second and third time trying to understand what was happening in the story.

It's not until now, in New York City, in Harlem, in my daddy's house that was first owned by his father, sitting in this bedroom that my daddy has saved for me all these years, that I finally understand the wormhole connection.

There are pockets in time and space that fold over on themselves like pieces of paper.

I tear out a piece of paper from a blank notebook I had brought along with the comic books, and I fold it over and over again until it's just a tiny square as wide as my fingertip.

This is what happens to my imagination location when the doors are closed. There are a bunch of other doors that keep closing and closing, like folded paper. It becomes so tiny that there isn't room for any new ideas, even though the old ideas are still there, compact and dense like a tiny star. But there's always a sliver of space wide and tall enough for me to slip through—like that space in Daddy's kitchen between the fridge and the sink. And once I squeeze into that wormhole, I can go on a quest to save someone, anyone, or anything. No matter what kind of trouble he's in.

CHAPTER
15

After two whole days of playing in Daddy's house, watching TV, and eating cereal, I finally have a babysitter and her name is Diane. She's a teenager and she just graduated from high school. Momma says that anybody named Diane or Diana is a diva. Like Diahann Carroll, who plays Dominique Deveraux on Momma's favorite TV Show, *Dynasty*. Like Diana Ross and her diva hair and dresses. Like Diana Prince, who is a diva superhero in disguise. Even like Princess Diana, who is a real live princess!

Diva Diane meets me and Daddy in front of the shop, right before he opens up for the morning. A dog barks from behind the gates and I wonder if it's Albert, the old Lab.

I stare at Diva Diane from head to toe with my mouth open, catching flies as Momma would say. Her hair is straight and shiny and the very ends are flipped up like wings, as if her head were about to fly away. Bright gold earrings shaped like giant trapezoids hang from each ear, and her lips are as shiny as sunlight reflecting on glass. Her shorts are so short that they might as well be underwear, and her bright red jacket has a glow-in-the-dark white stripe along each sleeve. She keeps it open to show off a too-short T-shirt that hits right above her bellybutton. She has on see-through plastic sandals and her toenails match her jacket.

Diva Diane looks like a *Soul Train* dancer from outer space.

She bends down and rests her hands on her bare knees so that we're eye to eye. "Hi, Ebony-Grace! Remember me?" she asks, while chewing a huge wad of pink gum. She talks very fast.

I nod.

"I was fourteen last time I saw you. I watched you for one night while your parents went out dancing, remember?" she says, popping her gum.

I don't remember. In fact, I can't even wrap my mind around Momma and Daddy even agreeing to a song that they could both dance to.

"Well, we gonna hang out today, Ebony-Grace. We gonna go to the store, over to the basketball courts, and . . . " She stands up straight and examines my hair. It's still in the same four pigtails and I'm sure it's fuzzy by now, but I didn't check and I don't care.

"And we gonna have to do something with these braids. You want some cornrows and some beads? You want wooden ones or plastic ones? You want your hair going down or up? But first, we gotta wash out all this dirt. What you been doing? Rolling around in the junkyard? I'm gonna need some extra change to get some Dax hair grease for her, Mr. Freeman."

Diva Diane's words fly out of her mouth at warp speed. It's more than gibberish. It's shooting stars, flying asteroids, and a meteor shower mixed in with all that spittle, lip-smacking, and neck-rolling! And I can smell her strawberry-flavored ChapStick from where I'm standing.

I touch my hair and shake my head, afraid to say anything just in case she listens the same way she talks, and her hearing is way too fast for my slowpoke words.

The gates to Daddy's shop are open now and I quickly notice all the greasy men Momma warned me about gathering around on the sidewalk, including Lester, the itching man. Lester's clothes are even dirtier and more torn than before, but that's none of my business, so I keep my eyes and ears on Diane as she walks down 126th Street as if she were the princess of No Joke City. But I'm actually the princess 'cause the king is my daddy. Now, I'm convinced Diva Diane is set out to take my crown, even though I don't really want it.

I follow her around the neighborhood like a stray dog. This isn't babysitting; I'm the moon and Diva Diane is Planet Earth, spinning around and minding her business while I just orbit.

We walk over to 125th Street as she stops to say hello to other teenagers who are dressed just like her with their giant gold earrings, chains shaped like ropes, and sneakers with three black stripes along the sides. The laces are so thick that I wonder how they got them to fit the tiny holes in the first place.

"Hey! What's going down, D-Boogie?" one of the teenage boys says. He gives Diva Diane a big hug.

"D-Boogie?" I ask out loud.

"That's right. D-Boogie," the boy says. "Who's this? Your little cousin from Down South?"

"How you know she's from Down South?" Diane asks, looking me up and down probably to see if she'd missed the clues.

"Her knees, hair, face? Her whole situation!" the boy says, laughing, and gives another boy standing next to him a high five.

I want to say something really mean but the words don't form quick enough in my imagination location, and soon,

I'm distracted by two girls unraveling a telephone cord. One girl is wearing short-shorts like Diane, except hers look even more like underwear. Wooden beads are at the end of each of her braids and they smack her cheeks as she talks and stretches out the rope. The other girl is wearing blue jeans with a tiny horse sewn onto the back pocket—Jordache jeans like the ones I have.

"D, you wanna jump?" the girl with the beads asks.

Before Diva Diane says anything, the two girls are turning the ropes so fast, my eyes are crossing. Diane takes off her see-through sandals, tossing them to the side, and stands next to one of the girls turning the rope, doing a little dance, almost as if she were getting ready to run, but she can't make up her mind.

The ropes make music. A *bip*. A *bap*. A *bip-bap-bip-bap*.

Finally, Diane jumps in as the ropes circle around each other like dancing asteroids.

Bip-bap-bip-bap.

As soon as Diane jumps in, the ropes turn faster and she skips over each one as if her feet know exactly when each cord is going to hit the sidewalk. *Bipbapbipbap.*

"One up two, three, four, five, six, seven, eight, nine!" the girls start to sing. "Two up two, three, four, five, six, seven, eight, nine!"

I'm catching flies again, and Diane is doing a boogie-down dance with those ropes. She hops on one leg and turns the other way. Then she does a crisscross with her legs without skipping a beat. She puts both feet together and hops like a bunny rabbit.

Then the song changes. The girls only say, "Ten up . . . Eleven up . . . Twelve up!"

Even though they're counting up and not down, Diva

Diane looks as if she were going to launch into space as fast as she's jumping. So I yell out, "Blast off!"

Diane misses a beat, one of the ropes get caught beneath her feet, and she almost trips.

"Dang it, Ebony!" Diane yells. "You made me mess up!"

"Y'all don't jump double-Dutch Down South, do y'all?" the girl with the beaded braids asks.

"Yes, we do!" I lie. But I've never seen anything like that anywhere in Huntsville.

Diane sucks her teeth, grabs me by the arm, and says, "Come on, little girl!"

After hours of hanging out on other people's stoops, going to the laundromat, a hair supply store, and a stop at a corner grocery for some sandwiches that Diane says I'll have to pay her back 'cause it's being taken out of her salary, I play Bianca's game of avoiding the cracks in the sidewalk.

"Oh, you still play that game? Not trying to break your momma's back, huh?" Diane says, but she makes sure to step on every crack on purpose. "See, these are not my momma's back. These cracks are all my ex-boyfriends' heads. That's Jamal, that's Chris, that's Devin . . . "

"Well, I'm trying to avoid moon craters," I say.

Diva Diane looks over at me and smiles. "Moon craters? You're outta sight, Ebony-Grace."

Before I return the smile and even try to pull Diane into her own imagination location, we reach a wide, colorful, and loud playground. Outside its tall metal gate is a sign that says, MARCUS GARVEY PARK.

Suddenly, kids, lots of them, run past us and into the park screaming, yelling, laughing—letting out all kinds of sounds as if they were forced to keep quiet for a whole year.

"Last day of school," Diane says. "I remember those days."

I spot Stone-Cold Calvin's big ol' peanut head at the other end of the block. The same group of boys always follow him around like magnetic dust.

"Hey, Calvin!" Diane calls out to him, waving. "Y'all gonna practice in the park? Michael and them got the boom box. But the rain from last week done messed up your cardboard."

I look all around me for somewhere to hide. I force back the urge to blurt out, "Beam me up, Captain Fleet!"

I don't want to be anywhere around Stone-Cold Calvin. But he spots me and his eyes widen. He taps the closest boy next to him and points. I want to teleport out of this place. I try to. I close my eyes and wish really hard that I was somewhere else.

Science is real. It has to be. We are stardust. Why can't we just fold time and space around us and become our very own wormholes?

"Diane, why you gotta bring that girl over here?" Stone-Cold Calvin asks when he reaches us.

I'm standing behind Diane as if she were a sliding door to a transporter room.

"'Cause I'm babysitting her, that's why," Diane says.

I take another step behind Diane wishing that she was wide enough to hide my whole body behind. I am not a baby and we haven't sat all day.

"Ha-ha! You need a babysitter!" Stone-Cold Calvin says, stepping around Diane to get a better look at me.

"Be quiet, Calvin. I'm babysitting *you* next Friday night," Diane says.

The rest of the nefarious minions laugh at Stone-Cold Calvin, but it doesn't faze him. He keeps his eyes on me.

"But she's ugly," he starts, not skipping a beat. "She's

gonna mess up your reputation hanging around you like that, Diane. All that ugly is gonna rub off," he says. "Look at her glasses! She can see through walls with them glasses."

If a thunderstorm is the opposite of sunshine, then a soul-storm begins to brew inside of me. E-Grace Starfleet is like the Hulk with giant muscles ripping out of too-small clothes. I'm like Diana Prince spinning into her Wonder Woman costume. A superhero breaks out of my body, and I now have the courage to stand up to that stupid boy.

"That's right!" I say, stepping out from behind Diane and putting my hands on my hips. "I can read straight through that thick peanut head of yours and ain't nothing in there but a black void!"

The nefarious minions laugh, of course. But I can't tell if they're laughing at me or their leader, Stone-Cold Callous Calvin.

Diva Diane waves her hand at Calvin and his followers and sucks her teeth. "Don't pay him any mind, Ebony. He just likes you, that's all. Big-headed twelve-year-old boys mess with you 'cause they don't know how to behave like gentlemen."

If there ever was a time I wanted to be beamed up onto the *Uhura* and aim for the farthest galaxy, it was now. If I wasn't so brown, I'd be as red as Mars.

"You better leave her alone, Calvin!" I hear someone say. "Or I'ma mush you in your big fat head!"

Bianca Pluto to the rescue! She stands over Stone-Cold Callous Calvin with her hands on her hips. She's my friend after all, and I'm sure Daddy didn't give her another five bucks to come to my defense.

The nefarious minions retreat even as they continue to spout out their No Joke City gibberish. Bianca Pluto just rolls her neck and waves her little finger with every single "don't mess with my friend" and "you better leave her alone before I bust your head." I stand there next to her with my arms crossed as the nefarious minions finally retreat. I turn to her and nod.

"Bianca Pluto and E-Grace Starfleet: a united front!" I say.

"Oh, be quiet, Ebony-Grace!" is all Bianca says.

CHAPTER
16

"But that was a good diss, Ebony," Bianca says. "Calvin's spent so much time trying to learn head spins, there's nothing left in that big ol' peanut."

So I step closer to Bianca with my head down a little. I have to ease into this, tiptoe quietly so I don't scare her away. "The nefarious minions haven't fully surrendered," I whisper above all the noise. "They've only temporarily retreated."

She moves away from me. "I told you to stop calling them evil onions! And I only stood up for you because Calvin was being mean. Not because he's an evil onion and you're a Starfleet and I'm a Pluto or whatever."

Before I even get a chance to respond, a small crowd of familiar girls walk up behind her: the nefarious minionettes!

They all gather around Diva Diane to kiss her on the cheek and hug her and examine her hair, clothes, and sandals. Bianca does the same, ignoring that I'm standing right next to her.

"Is this from Dapper Dan's?" one of the girls asks while touching the stripe on Diane's jacket.

"You know Dapper Dan ain't gonna make something cheap like this," Diane says. "Do you see a Gucci or Louis V logo on here? No. And plus, I ain't got no money to buy Dapper Dan nothing. I'm saving up for college!"

Then, one of them finally notices me. "I heard you're gonna be staying with your daddy for a while. You're not going to our school next year, are you?" It's their leader, Rainbow Dull.

I look around at all their faces and notice that their hair is done up in the same exact style—side ponytails that either hang loose or stick out like doorknobs above their ears. They're all wearing the same exact clothes, short sets in different colors: blues, pinks, yellows, and greens, like the rainbow. A few even have on mini versions of Diane's golden trapezoid earrings. Worst of all, Bianca Pluto blends right in with them as if she's one of the nefarious minionettes with her curly side ponytail and bright yellow outfit.

"She's not going to school here," someone answers for me. "She's from Alabama. She's too slow to learn all the stuff we're learning."

"No. I'll just be here for the summer," I say with my hard-candy church voice. "I'm Ebony-Grace, by the way. I don't think we've officially met." I extend my hand out to Rainbow Dull.

She doesn't take it. "I'm Monique," she says, tossing her side ponytail braid over her shoulder. "Mint Chocolate Chip Monique, that is, and we are the Nine Flavas Crew!"

They all pose as if someone is about to pop out of nowhere to take their photo. Some hold one hand on a bent knee and the other on their hip. The others, including Bianca, fold their arms across their chests and fix their mouths as if trying to sniff their upper lips.

"Nine Flavors Crew?" I ask, trying to make sense of why anyone would want to be a flavor.

"Not Nine *Flavors*," Mint Chocolate Chip Monique says coming up from her pose but still with her hands on her hips. "It's *flava!* You gotta put your whole body into it with some rhythm and soul. You gotta have *flava*." She rolls her neck with every word.

Diane places her hand around my shoulder. "Oh, good, Ebony! You get to meet the rest of Bianca's friends," she sings. "Nine-F Crew, what it do? What's going down around town? Y'all look fly! Y'all been practicing?"

"Uh-huh. We're gonna show you some new moves in the park. But we can't let Calvin see 'cause he thinks he's better than us," Monique says—Mint Chocolate Chip Monique.

The questions are at the tip of my tongue, but I've been completely disarmed by this strange proclamation. This is all highly illogical! The nefarious minionettes have claimed to be a crew and they are *nine flavors*.

I count out each head, and there are definitely nine of them. But they shouldn't even be allowed to use the word crew. Real crews man spaceships. Real crews launch satellites into space. Real crews lead space missions like the ones on the *Columbia* and the *Challenger*. Crews are not supposed to be named after ice cream flavors!

I can't hold it in much longer, so I blurt out, "Why do you call yourselves *Nine Flavors Crew*?"

As the crowd of noisy kids leave and I stand here with Diva Diane and this group of girls, I start to feel like an alien on another planet. Even though Bianca just stood up for me with Calvin, she stands away from me with this crew of hers. I keep my arms crossed and head down a little because something in my belly lets me know that Bianca will be a little bit different now.

"'Cause even though we only got nine, we got more *flava* than Baskin-Robbins," Monique says, flipping her side ponytail around. All the other girls introduce themselves, saying their names with their matching ice cream flavor.

There's Rum Raisin Rhonda whose side ponytail is in cornrows and beads; Coconut Collette with her gray eyes; Vanilla Fudge Vanessa who's chubby and short and is all smiles; Mango Megan is tall with a reddish-brown side Afro puff; Cookies and Cream Christine's glasses are almost as thick as mine; Strawberry Stacey's cheeks are so red it looks as if she's wearing makeup; and Pistachio Paula is so tall, she looks like one of those Harlem Globetrotters.

Finally, my No Joke City best friend, my fellow space cadet on the *Uhura*, Bianca Pluto, is not an intergalactic astronaut after all. She's an ice cream flavor! She's Butter Pecan Bianca.

I love butter, but I hate pecans. I've never had butter pecan ice cream, and I never will. And I don't like this new Bianca.

"Nine flavors?" I whisper to myself again, shaking my head.

"No, it's *flava*. *Flava!* Put your neck into it. Now, say it!" Coconut Collette shouts in my face.

"*Flava* is not a word!" I shout back.

In an instant, the reality that I'll be here for a whole summer starts to sink in. And this isn't like Huntsville where everyone knows that I'm the granddaughter of Jeremiah Granville Norfleet, pioneering aerospace engineer. So of course, I want to be an astronaut when I grow up. Of course, I love *Star Trek* and *Star Wars* and comic books just like my granddaddy.

And even though both my daddy and granddaddy wanted Momma to have a baby boy, I'm Ebony-Grace Norfleet Freeman, girl wonder, Sally Ride believer, Nyota Uhura worshipper. Not an ice cream flavor!

"Uh-huh. Flava is too a word 'cause we said so!" Rum Raisin Rhonda says with a voice that sounds like gravel.

"Yep, *flava* can be a word, like *dope* and *fresh* and *fly*,"

Diva Diane says, touching some of the 9 Flavas' hair and making them turn around to examine their outfits. "Ebony, you should be one of them, too."

"That's not gonna work," Bianca says.

This is the first time I hear her talking about me—not defending me, or making up stories with me, but she's actually agreeing with what the other girls are saying.

"Since when did you become an ice cream flavor?" I say to her. "I thought you were Bianca Pluto and you like rocket ships and outer space just like I do. Remember how we launched a rocket to the moon in the junkyard. Huh, Bianca? Remember?"

"I keep telling you," she shouts. "I'm not a little kid anymore. I can do more than just build rocket ships out of junk."

"Yep. She sure can," Mint Chocolate Chip Monique says.

"Enough with this baby stuff, Ebony," Diane says. "Can you pop and lock? Can you dance? Rap? Jump double-Dutch? Y'all can be the Ten Flavas just for this summer. Maybe get into some contests or something?"

My eyes are locked in to Bianca's. I give her the ferocious E-Grace Starfleet stare—a snarl, tight jaws, and squinted eyes. She doesn't back down either. I want her to say something, anything, but Mint Chocolate Chip Monique pushes her aside and steps to my face.

"She can't be one of us. She don't have no *flava*. She's just a plain ol' ice cream sandwich! Chocolate on the outside, vanilla on the inside," she says.

"But chocolate and vanilla *are* flavors!" I say to her face. I put my fists on my hips and stick out my chest like I'm Superman ready to take flight. "And who wants to be a *flavor*, anyway! I'd rather be an astronaut, a space cadet, a hero saving the planet, stupid face!"

"Oh, so you like outer space?" asks Monique. "That's why they call you Ebony? *Ebony* means 'black.' And you're so black, you look like outer space. You can't be no astronaut in space, 'cause no one would find you. You would just *blend* with all that black. Yep. That's your new name. Outer Space Ebony-Grace, 'cause you're so doggone black!"

Everyone standing around lets out a blend of "oohs" and "oh snaps" and "she dissed you!"

Slowly, I retreat, even though I'm still standing there in Monique's face. This is like an enemy attack on the *Uhura*. Captain Fleet and I toss about on the spaceship, and all the lights blink and go out, and it's dark and we lose power. "Status report!" the captain shouts.

I'm okay, I tell myself. *I'm okay.*

Monique doesn't move from my face and I don't either, even as the other girls giggle and repeat every word she's said to me.

You're so black, you look like outer space, echoes in my mind. I look around at this crew, some with high-yella and redbone and Indian-in-my-family hair, as my mother would say. And I don't even need a mirror to let me know that I've stayed out in the sun for too long, as Momma and all the church ladies down in Huntsville would also say. I don't mind looking like outer space, at all. But I don't say that.

I'm the first to step back and look away. "I wanna go home, now," I whisper to Diane.

"Go home?" she says really loud. "Child, please. Your daddy said I have to watch you till five o'clock, and I already told you that you're not messing with my ten bucks. But don't worry, Ebony. I'm gonna help you get some flava."

Diane puts her arm around my shoulders as she walks me into this Marcus Garvey Park along with the 9 Flavas

Crew. Bianca has blended with the other girls and I can't tell them apart anymore. If having some flava makes me like everyone else here, then I'd rather be an ice cream sandwich any day. But an ice cream made up of all the things in the Milky Way: lots of stars and planets and moons and suns that make me black like outer space. I'd be a whole galaxy all to myself.

Inside the park are swings and monkey bars and other kids running about as if the Sonic Boom had already taken over their minds. To the left are basketball courts where a whole bunch of tall, skinny boys dribble and shoot. To the right are two tall concrete walls with colorful, bubbly words scribbled all over them. Another group of kids bounce a small blue ball against it as if they're playing tennis with the dancing letters that spell out jumbled and mumbled things I can't even read.

At the other end of the playground, I spot Stone-Cold Calvin's big peanut head with the other nefarious minions. A giant radio sits up on an overturned metal trash can, and a bunch of flattened cardboard boxes cover the ground.

I don't dare step deeper into the park because a low, iridescent wave forms right above the park, making everything sway back and forth as if it's all sitting in a giant bowl of Jell-O.

"The Sonic Boom!" I whisper.

I can hear it this time, loud and clear. It pulses and makes everything under its control dance.

"Are you coming, girl?" Diane asks. She doesn't wait for me to answer and grabs my hand trying to pull me.

I pull my hand away from hers.

"Oh, no you don't," Diane says. "This is why I don't babysit toddlers. I am not leaving you here by yourself. Come on now. You gotta see the Nine-F Crew beat the other girls in double-Dutch, and breakdance with Calvin and them. Maybe you can learn a thing or two."

"I said, I want to go home!" I shout.

I don't mean to sound like a baby, but this is where the doors to my imagination location slowly swing open on their own. It's as if there's a broken lock or a stuck doorknob that doesn't quite twist the right way to make sure that door stays shut. A little breeze, an offbeat sound, or a vision of something strange will make everything open up like slow-parting clouds. Nothing is real, everything is strange. Everything is deep space and far-flung planets and otherworldly beings.

If the Sonic Boom is as clear as day high above this playground in this city, then I have to believe it's there and danger is not too far behind.

This is where Granddaddy's stories are not just stories anymore.

CHAPTER
17

The very first time Granddaddy introduced me to Planet Boom Box, the Sonic King, and the Funkazoids was the day I got a special delivery all the way from Harlem. Daddy had sent me a cassette tape labeled, "Fresh from the Boom Box."

Earlier that day, Momma and I had visited Granddaddy at the Marshall Space Flight Center and brought him lunch and a thermos of sweet tea. As we walked from the parking lot to the center's outdoor seating area, most of Granddaddy's friends from work recognized me.

"If it isn't little Ebony-Grace, astronaut in the making," Uncle Lawrence said when he saw me and Momma. I gave him a sharp E-Grace Starfleet salute, even though he didn't know anything about me and Granddaddy's stories.

"You're quite the celebrity around here, Starfleet," Grand-daddy said when he came out to meet us for lunch. He bent down to give me a kiss on my forehead.

I saluted him instead. "Cadet E-Grace Starfleet reporting for service," I said.

"Shhh! Not here, Cadet Starfleet. This is the last place we want anybody to find out about our secret mission," Grand-daddy said with a laugh.

Other men walked in and out of the space center build-ing. Some said hi to Granddaddy, others nodded, and some didn't even say a word.

"You two and these secret missions," Momma said. "And you better not try to launch any of your rocket ships in your father's shop again when you get to New York in June."

"It wasn't the shop. It was the junkyard," I corrected her.

There were no rockets at MSFC. Only a lot of thinking and talking and computing and building rocket parts. That's Granddaddy's job as an engineer. He wants me to be an engineer, too. That's why he taught me math when I was just a toddler, read me engineering books before I started kindergarten, showed me how to launch a rocket with seltzer tablets and soda bottles, introduced me to *Star Trek* and *Star Wars*, and told me stories about space heroes from his old comic books.

But we didn't like those space heroes with their blue eyes and slick hair. That's why I had to become E-Grace Starfleet, space cadet hero! Besides, he had a huge crush on Lieutenant Uhura, so that's why our top secret spaceship is named after her, or she after it, since she's from the future.

Momma, Granddaddy, and I walked over to a set of picnic tables at a nearby lawn next to the space center.

"You're going up there on that Planet Boom Box?" Granddaddy joked. "All that boom and bip and crack going on up there. Seen it on TV, Starfleet. Boys are spinning on their heads like they're losing their minds! And some of them are!"

If Harlem was a boom box, then that Alabama quiet was like a pair of headphones blocking out the music booming all the way from Daddy's house on 126th Street. In Huntsville, everything was muffled—all those voices making up stories about Granddaddy—the chirping church ladies' whispers and mumbles and hush-hush gossip making a low-hanging concrete cloud over Granddaddy's head.

To block out those murmuring whispers, I'd spent the

day before in the attic reading Granddaddy's old comic books and magazines. Inside those pages was a world of high-flying rocket ships, giant aliens, and heroes saving the world from disaster. Just like Cadet E-Grace and Captain Fleet on the *Uhura*.

And when I wanted to board the *Uhura*, to boldly go where no girl has gone before, I'd be beamed up by Captain Fleet. In no time, I was at the control boards helping ease the giant spaceship toward the edge of the Milky Way, toward a whole other galaxy in search of intelligence to protect our planet from ultimate destruction. That was super top secret, of course!

"Ground control to Cadet E-Grace! Ground control to Cadet E-Grace!" Granddaddy's voice had snapped me right out of the stars and pulled me back down through Alabama's wide blue skies. The air was hot and thick, like having my head inside a space helmet.

"Well, did your rocket make it into orbit?" Granddaddy asked, as he pulled out the egg sandwich I'd made for him. He asked this every time he'd see me go off into my imagination location—I stared into space as if everything around me had morphed into a whole other world.

"Not this time," I said, because I wasn't in another world. I was still right down there in Alabama thinking of Granddaddy.

He tried to smile and sound like his usual self, but his soulglow was a little dim.

"Was everything all right with the *Uhura*? Those buttons and lights working out okay?"

"Pop, please stop," Momma said. "No more comic book stories. Ebony will need to start focusing on her schoolwork." She smoothed down one of my braids as I took a bite from my sandwich. "Junior high school is gonna be real hard and she'll have to start studying now and keep her head out of all that nonsense space stuff."

Granddaddy chuckled. I could see the chewed sandwich in his mouth. The little gray hairs on his mustache curled over his lips and his eyes squinted just like mine when I smiled.

"Well, outer space is what keeps me grounded, ain't that right, Starfleet?" Granddaddy said.

"Outer space is not stopping those newspapers from saying not-so-nice things, Pop," Momma said.

And with that, the low-hanging dark clouds spread from just being over Granddaddy's head, to being over mine and Momma's head, and maybe our little spot outside of MSFC, and maybe all over Huntsville, too.

"The newspapers can say whatever they want, Gloria," Granddaddy said. "Fact is, me and Huntsville newspapers got a long, long history. Ain't that right, Starfleet?"

I only nod and take tiny bites from my sandwich. Momma and the other grown-ups keep secrets or speak in code. But Granddaddy is as plain as day. Our stories about the *Uhura* are more real than any of the hush-hush gossip.

"Listen to me now, Ebony-Grace." Granddaddy sets down his sandwich, takes a sip of his sweet tea, and faces me. Granddaddy talks to me. He tells me the truth even when Momma and the others around me hide their secrets behind their whispers. "Those same newspapers didn't bother me none when I first moved down here from Harlem when your momma was a lil' baby. Moving back to the South from New York was unheard of. They called us uppity Negroes down here just 'cause we knew a little bit about that fast life up in Harlem and we were *engineers* working for NASA."

I just nodded. I never liked when Granddaddy talked about when he first moved down to Huntsville and how he was treated. Instead, I asked, "You think they'll ever let a kid go into space, Granddaddy?"

"I don't see why not. And I'll make sure you're the first one in line."

Momma was glaring at me. Her red lips were pursed tight. "That's it, young lady!" she whisper-shouted. "And, Pop, you got bigger things to worry about now, don't you?"

Granddaddy looked down as if the weight of the concrete clouds were pushing down on his head. At the end of our lunch, I gave him a super big hug.

"I'll see you later at the control boards, Cadet Starfleet," he whispered into my ear. Then he stood upright, pulled up his pants, puffed out his chest like he usually did when he's about to announce something he's really proud of, and said, "We're working on plans for the next Spacelab mission."

I gasped. This was my chance. "Maybe I'll get to go on that mission!" I said.

"No, ma'am! I've got galaxies for you to conquer on the *Uhura*, young lady! Spacelab missions are small potatoes."

I stepped back away from Granddaddy and gave him another cadet salute without even looking Momma's way. I could still feel her piercing eyes.

Later that evening when Granddaddy came home, we went off by ourselves to his study and listened to Daddy's cassette tape from Harlem with the volume turned down real low 'cause Momma didn't like me listening to strange music.

"Your momma's gospel music ain't sonic *nothing*," Granddaddy joked. "It's the slow, humdrum rotation of the planets around the sun. Can't even hear it move your soul."

But Momma's soul *would* move, all right. Even I could see that. In church, while cooking in the kitchen, or while sitting on the porch, she'd close her eyes, lean her head back and wave her hand from side to side to praise the Lord.

"But, Granddaddy, Momma lost her mind, too, with all that singing," I'd said.

"She didn't lose her mind, Starfleet. She put it aside for a bit and let Jesus take over," said Granddaddy.

There was no talk of Jesus or the Lord on Daddy's cassette tape, "Fresh from the Boom Box." Granddaddy carefully placed it into his stereo (not a boom box 'cause it was tall, had a turntable, *and* a radio dial, and you couldn't move it anywhere else). We listened closely as some guy talked over these beats that sounded like a big ol' party in outer space where the stars and planets would boogie on down.

A boom.
A bip.
A bop.

The words flew out of the speakers of Granddaddy's stereo and floated around the room like fireflies—glowing and sparkling just the same. There was a story and the story made music.

Hip and hop and stop.
Beat and feet.
Bang, boogie, and bang.
Stop, rock, and bop.
Pop the pop.
On and on,
To the break of dawn.

"Granddaddy, what are they saying?" I asked. I moved as close to the speakers as I possibly could to let the words and rhythm and beats reach that part of my imagination location where everything makes perfect sense.

"Huh. Gibberish," was all Granddaddy said. "Gibberish and noise. That's not music, Starfleet. I bet they're not even playing instruments. Nothing that sounds like that can come out of a guitar or a piano or even a drum set."

Granddaddy quickly stopped the cassette tape. A weird quiet filled the room as if there'd been a giant bubble of sound and everything popped leaving nothing but thick, hushed air. I didn't tell Granddaddy that I wanted more of Daddy's music from Harlem. I wanted to take apart the words like the buttons and wires on a radio. I wanted to put them back together with the music like a puzzle so it could all make sense—the "break" with the beat, the "clap" with the bap, the "move" with the groove.

But instead, I said, "That's right, Granddaddy. Gibberish and noise."

Granddaddy's bedtime stories have always been about spaceships and aliens and planets and galaxies, even though Momma kept saying, "Pop, there's only one thing out there and it's our Heavenly Father."

Granddaddy would lean in and whisper, "That's the name of a spaceship—*Heavenly Father*."

I didn't do a good job of hiding my laugh from Momma.

That night, it was time to check up on the *Uhura*. Granddaddy always started the mission with "*Uhura* to Cadet E-Grace Starfleet! *Uhura* to Cadet E-Grace Starfleet!"

And I always responded, "Beam me up, Captain Fleet!"

Then, Granddaddy started his story—a brand-new one filled with new words and new worlds.

"Starfleet, lemme tell you about Planet Boom Box, the evil Sonic King, and his Funkazoids . . . "

Just yesterday, in a galaxy far, far away . . .
A cadet and her captain zoomed through
the long, wide black sky
in the funkiest mothership on this side
of creation—Mother *Uhura!*
The mothership parted the black sky
like Moses's red sea.
You ever seen a thing so black in your life?
Make you feel like you belong to it,
that you come straight from it
like it's your own momma's belly.
That's the source of all things,
Starfleet—the long wide black sky.
It belongs to you, and you belong to it.
Those same stars are what make up your bones,
your pearly whites, and that twinkle
in your eye at night.
So music pumped all throughout the
mothership—good music, soul music, funk music.
Until Mother *Uhura* got swallowed up
by a big ol' wormhole,
and the cadet and her captain went spinning
like a vinyl record on a turntable—
round and round and round.
The wormhole turned that Mother out!
The cadet and her captain ended up way on
the other side of a whole new galaxy,
and they stumbled onto a new planet that bounced,
and dipped, and spinned, and flipped,
and landed in a James Brown split. Ha!

Have you ever seen a planet
that boogies on down?
A whole world that booms and
bips and baps and clicks and ratatatats?
And standing right there on top of it all
at the very tip of a radio tower—
like a long, lean antenna—was the
Sonic King with his stereo speaker ears
and radio tower crown.
If boom, bip, bap, click, and ratatatat were aliens,
they'd be amplified, magnified, sanctified,
and funktified. Ha!
Now, lemme hear you say, funky!
"FUNKY!"
So the Funkazoids gathered around the
Sonic King as his royal court.
And at the end of the Sonic King's giant
golden scepter was the
loudest, the baddest, the mind-controllest
Sonic Boom in the entire galaxy.
The Sonic Boom will seal your doom.
With only a flick of his wrist, the
giant waving bubble
full of booms and bips and baps
and ratatatats
will tear the roof off the Mother!
So cover your ears and seal your mind,
before the Sonic Boom
makes you shake your behind!

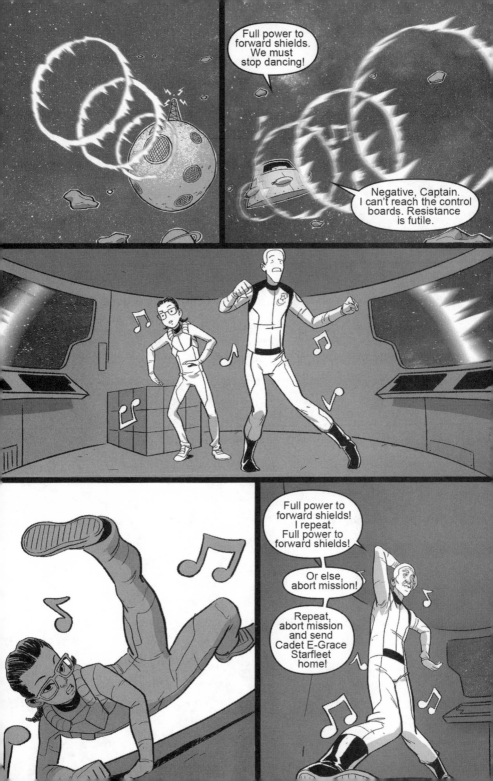

CHAPTER
18

Pluto is the ninth planet from the sun. It's the farthest and coldest—ice cold, just like the way Bianca is treating me. If there are nine planets in the solar system, then the 9 Flavas represent each one—Mercury, being the closest to the sun, is hot like fire and mean like Monique. I'd call her Monique Mercury 'cause she's so doggone mean.

But as I stood there in the middle of the park arguing with Diva Diane about whether I should just run home and have her lose ten bucks for not babysitting me until five o'clock, Monique comes over to take my hand and pulls me into the playground.

"Come on, Outer Space Ebony-Grace," she says. "You gotta turn the rope for us."

I thought she didn't like me. She's *Mercurial* Monique— mean one minute and nice the next.

Bianca comes over and hands me the two ends of the long telephone cord.

"Hey!" I protest. "This is for telephones!"

"Well, what y'all use down in 'Bama? Twine?" Monique says. She grabs my right hand and wraps the end of the cord around my index finger. Then she does the same with my other hand.

"Close both your hands, and you gotta keep the rope

around your fingers so it doesn't slip. Okay, Ebony?" Bianca says.

"It's E-Grace Starfleet to you, Bianca *Pluto*," I say, without thinking first.

"Escúchame. You wanna be one of the Nine Flavas, then you gotta show and prove," she says, rolling her neck and eyes. "Like this." She turns her arms around at the elbow like she's swatting flies.

"She's gonna be double-handed!" Rum Raisin Rhonda shouts.

"No she's not!" Bianca shouts back. Then she says to me, "I've seen you with a screwdriver, Ebony. How you twist and turn it . . . A double-Dutch rope is just like that. The screwdriver has to fit into the—"

"The groove," I say. "The screwdriver has to fit into the groove."

"Fit into the groove," she repeats.

"Yeah, Ice Cream Sandwich, fit into the groove," Mint Chocolate Chip Monique calls out. "Make your moves! Show and prove!"

Rum Raisin Rhonda is at the other end of the telephone-cord jump rope. She starts to turn. One hand over, one hand under. Over. Under. Over. Under. The rope kisses the concrete ground in a steady rhythm. *Bip, bip, bip, bip.* I follow the sound and keep my eye on the rope.

"You're doing good, Outer Space Ebony-Grace," Rum Raisin Rhonda shouts. "You're not so bad."

This is like all the times I watched Granddaddy's records spin beneath the needle on the turntable. The needle follows the record like the *Uhura* circling Saturn's rings—round and round and round. And music rises from those rings the way it rises from the telephone cord.

"If Butter Pecan is gonna jump in and do the Up Rock in the rope, then y'all gotta turn slower," Monique says. "We're doing something fresh and we gotta get it right."

Bianca is getting ready to jump, doing that same dance that Diva Diane did. And maybe, this turning and turning is a vortex that will swallow her whole and teleport her right up onto the *Uhura.*

So I turn faster and faster, and plan my exit strategy to join Bianca once she blinks out from between those telephone cords.

Bip-bip-bip-bip.

"That's too fast!" Rum Raisin Rhonda yells.

But I keep turning. I count down in my head: 10, 9, 8 . . .

BipBipBipBip.

"Slow down! You're messing up the rhythm!"

I don't listen to Rhonda. As soon as Bianca jumps in, I turn with all my might. I am an engine and both my arms are liquid nitrogen and oxygen pumping fire-hot fuel into a rocket.

Bipbipbipbip.

Bianca screams. The speeding cords get caught in both her legs, and she falls to the ground hitting her head really hard on the concrete.

Only the *bip* stops. Not the *boom-boom* from the radio in the distance. Not the nefarious minions' gibberish from across the playground. Not the dancing No Joke City air. And not the screams of the 9 Flavas Crew who all rush to Bianca and surround her like the universe contracting—the whole galaxy coming together as if a single planet were the magnet.

And then, in just a few seconds, they expand again into one big bang, and out comes their words in a torrent of shooting stars, asteroids, and meteor showers that will surely break the *Uhura*, or even Planet Earth, into a billion tiny pieces.

"What did you do, Ice Cream Sandwich?"

"What's wrong with you?"

"You can't even turn a rope right?"

"You didn't show and prove and you messed up all our moves!"

"You did that on purpose!"

"We thought Bianca was your friend!"

I let the jump rope slide out of my hands as they all sur-round me, and I surrender because this is the moment that they might just take me prisoner because no portal opens up, no captain beams me up.

CHAPTER
19

The Sonic Boom is here! It's in full effect, and at full force! My damage report for Captain Fleet would be bad. Shields are at less than ten percent. All systems in the critical range!

Bianca is okay. I am not.

When we leave the park, the sound wave in the sky is bigger and thicker like a storm cloud. I keep glancing over at Bianca to see if she looks up and notices it, too.

It used to be that way, the last time I was in Harlem back when we were nine. I would point to the sky or the distant horizon and see a quickly approaching meteor, an alien spaceship, or a strange light meant to lure us in and swallow us into another dimension. I didn't have to explain what I saw. I would see a color, and Bianca would add a shape. I would see eyes, and Bianca would add hair and arms and legs. But now there are no doors or windows or any openings to her imagination location. There isn't even a location. Or an imagination.

I walk behind Diane and the 9 Flavas Crew. Bianca holds a red freeze pop behind her head. The long plastic tube makes her look like an alien—as if the freeze pop is a long red tentacle meant to connect her thoughts to her mothership.

The other 9 Flavas eat their icees—holding the tubes to

their lips and sucking out all the sweet, syrupy juice that comes in all different colors. I don't have an icee.

"We needed two people on the rope, two people jumping, and six people to dance outside the rope," Monique explains to the rest of the girls. "That's why we made her turn. We were just trying it out."

"Well, we're gonna have to pick somebody different 'cause she's worse than double-handed. She's trying to kill us with that rope!" Rum Raisin Rhonda turns around to look at me and rolls her eyes.

I keep my head down.

We stop in front of a small store on 125th Street. The words on the window read DAPPER DAN'S LADIES & GENTLEMEN BOUTIQUE. Behind it are fancy fur coats and colorful leather jackets and bags with designs like the ones I see on Momma's favorite TV show, *Dynasty*. Momma doesn't know that I watch her watching that show. And she doesn't know that I listen when she talks about it to her church lady friends—all that lying, cheating, and sinning, she says. Momma would like this store.

All the 9 Flavas and Diva Diane rush to the store's window. Everybody points and squeals and jumps up and down, spilling out their No Joke City gibberish while they stare at all the fancy things.

"I want the one with the fly velvet stripe on the sleeve!"

"That's my fur coat! I'm gonna wear it in July!"

"Diane, you should wear that Gucci jogging suit on your first day of college!"

While they're all piled around the mannequins in the window, I spot a big colorful poster and step closer to read the words.

Again with these *crews*, I thought. *Rock? Steady?* Momma's Aretha Franklin album pops up in my head. She doesn't dance to it, but Granddaddy usually does a two-step, holds out his hand for me to slap, and repeats with the song, "What it is! What it is!"

So that's exactly what I say out loud while pointing to the flyer. "What it is, what it is?"

Diva Diane is the first to read the whole thing. "Get outta town!" she squeals. "Look, y'all. The Rock Steady Crew will be right here at the Apollo, and there's a contest!"

And don't they know Apollo was a space mission, not a theater?

The 9 Flavas Crew almost knocks me down to get a better look at the flyer. At the same time, a group of men walk into Dapper Dan's Boutique wearing the shiniest, biggest, heaviest jewelry I've ever seen. They wear matching jackets and pants that almost makes them look like a real crew getting ready to handle some serious business. One of their jackets is so shiny, they look like one of guys from that album cover— *Warp 9*. Maybe that's them. Maybe they're a real space crew come to save me from these nefarious minionettes! But they walk right past. Diane spots them and turns around putting her hand on her hip. She acts funny and smiles too bright.

But Monique pushes past her to get a better look at this crew.

"Ooh, y'all look fly!" she says, reaching out to touch one of the guys' pants. "Did Dapper Dan make them?"

One of the men nod and only half smiles.

"Does Dapper Dan make space-flight suits?" I ask no one in particular.

But Bianca rolls her eyes and shakes her head at me.

So I ease toward her, and say, "Hey. I'm sorry. I didn't mean to."

"Yes, you did!" she says. Her melted icee is now a tube of what looks like red Kool-Aid. "I never, ever fall when I jump into the rope. I'm real good. You were just jealous."

"But I never even seen you jump. How could I be jealous?"

"You're just mad 'cause I won't play those stupid games with you anymore."

"No, I'm not! I'm just—"

"Yes, you are!" she almost shouts. "Nobody cares about space, Ebony-Grace. And no, Dapper Dan doesn't make space-flight suits. He makes *fly* suits. Gucci suits. MCM suits. Louis Vuitton suits. Fendi suits. Church suits. This is Harlem, not another planet!"

"You can say that again," Monique says and comes over to pull Bianca away. "Let's get Dapper Dan to make our outfits for the contest!"

And they all cheer with their gibberish.

"I know that's right!"

"We gonna be fly and outta sight!"

"Dope and funky fresh!"

"Best dressed to impress!"

I step back away from the boutique. I close my eyes and cover my ears, but it's no use. The Sonic Boom pours out of every single crack and corner of No Joke City. It pounds out of radios sitting on tall boys' shoulders as they walk by. It beats out of cars with shiny wheels and all their windows rolled down. It even oozes out of Dapper Dan's Boutique with the fancy coats and bags and colorful jackets. It mixes with the *boom-bip-ratatatat* of the No Joke City gibberish. I drop my hands and open my eyes again.

"Y'all want Gucci suits or Louis Vuitton suits?" Monique asks.

"How we gonna pay for Gucci or Louis V? We ain't got that kinda money!"

"We'll pay for it with the prize money!"

"But we can't get the prize money until afterward."

"That's if we beat Calvin and them. They swear they're better than the Breakerz and Rock Steady put together. He said he wants to battle Crazy Legs."

Monique turns to Bianca and says, "Well, you're our only hope, Butter Pecan. You're better than Calvin even with that knot behind your head. And probably than PJ, too!"

"Oooh! Bianca and PJ!" Rum Raisin Rhonda sings.

The rest of the minionettes take their two index fingers and rub them against each other and sing, "Oooh! Bianca and PJ!"

I want to ask why the ice cream cones are acting funny about somebody named PJ. I want to ask what Bianca could possibly be better at than Calvin. Definitely not building rocket ships. But maybe jumping rope? The only thing I saw Calvin doing in the playground was try to spin on his head and twist and turn his legs all crazy as if trying to break them. Break dancing, they call it. I have so many questions, but I don't ask any of them.

The 9 Flavas Crew is mean to Lester when we reach Daddy's block. He's sitting in front of Daddy's shop on a plastic crate scratching his neck and forearms as if he's covered in mosquito bites or something.

"Y'all little ladies feeling all right?" is all he asks when we walk by.

"Shut up, Loco Lester!" Rum Raisin Rhonda yells. "Ain't nobody wanna hear a crazy junkie!"

"Yeah, shut up, Loco Lester!" Monique repeats.

"What did he do?" I ask Bianca, but she just kisses her teeth at me.

"Well, if it isn't the Nine Flavas," Daddy says as he steps out of the shop. "I guess y'all got ten now with Ebony and all. What's your flava, Broomstick?"

I shake my head, not wanting him to ask any questions or make any jokes about my being any part of this nonsense.

Two guys who look like they could be Lester's cousins, with their dirty clothes and messy hair, walk up to him holding big objects in their arms. One has an old radio with broken buttons and missing parts. The other one carries a car's steering wheel.

"Look at those junkies," Monique says. "I swear they will sell you to your own daddy if you're not careful, Ice Cream Sandwich."

Before I even get to ask her what in the world she's talking about, they all walk away. Only Diane stays behind, standing away from Lester's cousins. I watch as Daddy pulls dollar bills from his pocket to hand over to Lester's cousins. They set down the radio and steering wheel inside the shop, and just about run back to wherever they came from.

"I'm ready to collect my pay, Mr. Julius," Diane says, holding her hand out. "I watched her all day. Ebony-Grace had a good time!"

"No I didn't!" I yell. "I had a no-good, awful, terrible time!"

Diane shoots me a look that might as well be lasers.

Daddy chuckles, still without even smiling. "How about we try this again tomorrow, Diane? I'll owe you twenty by the end of the day, or fifty by the end of the week. Y'all can have a do-over so Broomstick here can really have a good time."

I freeze where I'm standing. I'd been a prisoner all along and Daddy planned to keep it that way for the whole week I was supposed to be here? And now, this is what he has planned for me for the whole summer? To follow Diane around as she forces me to be the tenth ice cream flavor?

"That way, you don't have to spend all your money in one shot," Daddy continues. "Save some up for college."

Diva Diane turns to me and smiles a mean, warning smile. "Deal," she says to my daddy.

CHAPTER
20

In Daddy's kitchen, I wrap the spiraling telephone cord around my body. This cord is not like the one the 9 Flavas were jumping double-Dutch with. This cord really is a portal. With only a round dial and a few numbers, my voice travels through that portal cord to reach Momma or Granddaddy on the other side.

"Operator, I'd like to make a collect call to the Marshall Space Flight Center in Huntsville, Alabama," I say through the receiver.

A man answers. I ask for my granddaddy—Mr. Jeremiah Granville Freeman, or Jerry if you know him pretty well.

The man puts me on hold. Another man comes on and says Granddaddy's whole name to make sure that I was asking for the right person. He asks who is calling. I tell him Cadet E-Grace Starfleet from the Mothership *Uhura*. He puts me on hold, too.

"Excuse me, who did you say is calling?" a woman's voice comes on now.

"Is this Sally Ride?" I ask.

"Is this a prank call?" she asks. "Because if it is, I'll have to hang up."

I close the doors to my imagination location so I can be taken seriously, as Momma would say. "I would like to speak to Mr. Jeremiah Granville Freeman, please."

"Are you a reporter?"

"A reporter? No."

"An attorney or a detective?"

"Huh?" I ask. Now, I want to slide through this portal to meet this lady. "What are you talking about, ma'am?"

It's quiet and I keep saying hello until someone comes back on the phone. Another man this time.

"Who did you say is calling, ma'am?"

I take in a deep breath. "I'm his granddaughter, Ebony-Grace. May I speak with him, please?" I make my voice sound like melted caramel.

"Ebony, sweetheart. Your grandfather is no longer working here at the space center" is all he says.

The morning before I left Huntsville for Harlem, I had visited Granddaddy's other office in our house.

In the wee hours of the morning when Momma was in deep sleep, and this side of the world was as quiet as outer space, I tiptoed into Momma's room, grabbed the stool from her vanity table, placed it under the attic door in the ceiling, pulled the ladder down, and quietly made my way up to the dusty attic.

I kept a flashlight behind an old trunk. I flicked on the button and the first thing I saw was a scrapbook sitting on top of an old wooden stool—the one I used to sit on when Nana would plait my hair; the one Momma would sit on when she was a little girl. The years "1964–1968" were written out in Nana's fancy script. I gently opened the scrapbook expecting to see pictures of Nana, but there was a black-and-white photo of Granddaddy standing in front of the Marshall Space Flight Center. The words "First Day" were written at the bottom.

I flipped through the pages to see photos of Momma as a little girl about my age with her fancy dresses and hairdo. She hasn't changed much. There were photos of New York City, and I recognized Harlem in the background. Then the rest of the newspaper clippings, postcards, and even parts of posters were all about Granddaddy. I paused on a photo of a man dressed like an Egyptian from outer space. Red beams spew out from his eyes like lasers. "Sun Ra, Space Is the Place" is spelled out across the top. "The Sonic King," I'd whispered, and flipped the page.

I let the flashlight sit on a nearby stool so I could read the newspaper clippings that covered the last bunch of pages in the scrapbook. The date on the first paper was March 14, 1964. I read the headline out loud, "Negro youth to boost first moongoer into space."

> **They say that there's a good chance that a Negro may be the first man on the moon. But if he isn't, there's a good likelihood Negro Collegian scientists will be performing their intricate duties at the launching pad as they wave the moongoer off.**

This article was about Granddaddy's friends. A year after a group of science students came from Louisiana, Granddaddy came down from City College in Harlem to work at the Marshall Space Flight Center. They were there to "integrate," the newspaper article said.

I untied the rest of the newspapers and there were more articles about how these Negro engineers were treated in Huntsville when blacks had to live in a separate section of the town from whites. I put the newspapers back into a pile and tied them up again. I didn't want to read about it. I'd heard enough stories about how Granddaddy had to live twenty-five miles out of town when all the other engineers could just walk to work.

This was also where Nana's things were. I crawled over to the far end of the attic, near the tiny window looking out onto Olde Stone Road. I could still smell my nana from here—a mix of mothballs and gardenias. Momma didn't want her things in plain old cardboard boxes. They were in wicker baskets and covered in the hand-embroidered tablecloths Nana used to make.

I sat up against the wood paneling where the ceiling meets the wall and let Nana's scent wrap around me. Then I scooted over to Granddaddy's telescope and peered into the peephole. The stars were dim now because the morning sun was about to come up. The edge of the Milky Way was too far away, and Planet Boom Box was all folded up into Granddaddy stories and the pictures in my mind—my imagination location.

I wasn't going to tuck away those stories just because I was leaving Huntsville for a little while. I was going to make them bigger, louder, brighter. Those stories would just fill up my head until they rolled out of my eyes and covered every inch of my thoughts. It would be everything I talked about and everything I saw. My imagination location would be as real to me as the air I breathed.

That morning, it was still dark enough for me to see the dulling stars. And the sky was big enough to hold Granddaddy's many stories of the *Uhura* and the not-so-final frontier. I pushed the telescope away and scooted over to the ladder. By the time I made it down, Momma was standing there with her arms crossed. Her hair was tied up in a scarf and her silky, flowery robe was on inside out. Momma didn't look like Momma when she didn't have on her makeup. Her eyes were smaller, almost like those dulling stars. Her lips were turned down at the corners, and her cheeks were sunken in—but that was because she was fixing her mouth to say something to me.

"What'd I tell you about messing with your grandfather's things?" she said with her hard-candy voice. "You're too nosy, Ebony, meddling in grown-folk's business. That's why you need to spend a few days with your father. Learn how to mind the business of becoming a decent young lady. Now, enough with this outer space nonsense. Leave that telescope alone. Ain't nothing out there for you to see but the Lord."

An alarm sounds, and it's like a farting elephant. There's been an attack on the *Uhura*!

I quickly get up out of bed, my head still fuzzy and my body wobbly, and turn about every which way trying to remember where I am. The cool wooden floors squeak under my bare feet, and the tall white walls feel as if they're spinning and inching closer to where I'm standing, almost squeezing me in. I'm not home in my own bedroom in Huntsville, for sure.

This is Daddy's house, and I'm in the bedroom he's set aside for me. *My* bedroom for now. I stand still when the alarm sounds again and realize that I'm now *acclimated*. This will be home for the whole summer.

The alarm buzzes a third time—it rolls and waves throughout the whole brownstone.

"Mr. Freeman, where's Ebony-Grace?" a girl's voice calls from outside. "I'm here to start my shift." *Buzz-roll-buzz. Buzz-roll-buzz.* "Mr. Freeman!"

I rub my eyes and shake my head hard to force myself into the present. It's morning. I'm in Harlem. No. It's No Joke City, and Queen Diva Diane is outside ready to take me as her prisoner again for the day.

I hear Daddy's bedroom door squeak open and it sounds like an old yawning dog. "Aw, come on, Diane. Ease up on that buzzer now!" Daddy's bare feet stomp down the stairs.

I can still hear Diane's big mouth at the front door three stories down. "I didn't get paid yesterday, Mr. Freeman. And you said if I watch her for the whole week, I'll get fifty bucks!"

"Broomstick!" Daddy's voice roars up the stairs. "Diane's here. Time to get up!"

I jump right back into bed and slip under the covers. Daddy calls my name again, and I squeeze my eyes shut when I hear him coming back up the steps.

He's standing right above me when I start fake-snoring really loudly.

"Broomstick? Aw, come on. I know you didn't sleep through all that noise. Your little country ears ain't used to all this racket. Wake up now."

Slowly, I open my eyes and moan. I roll over to my other side and moan even louder. I curl into myself like a baby and hold my belly and moan some more.

"What's wrong with you, Broomstick?"

"I don't feel so good, Daddy," I say, making my voice sound like sandpaper.

He steps out of my bedroom, stands at the top of the stairs, and yells, "Diane, what'd you feed my baby girl yesterday?"

"Oh no. Lemme guess. She's sick?" Diane yells back. "Don't you put that on me, Mr. Freeman. My job was to watch her, not spoon-feed her. Do I still get my twenty bucks for yesterday *and* today?"

I don't care if she gets her twenty bucks or not, I need her to go away so I can be free. "Daddy, my belly really, really hurts," I whine.

Daddy exhales and rushes down the stairs. I sit up in bed and press my ear toward the window.

"Look, these things happen, Diane. She can't come outside with you, but she'll be all right by tomorrow. I can't pay you for work you didn't even do," Daddy says.

"Well, Mr. Freeman. My auntie said her car still sounds like it got a bad cough after she *paid* you for that not-so-new muffler you put in," Diane says.

Then I don't hear anything.

"Thank you, Mr. Freeman," Diane squeals. "See you tomorrow."

I rush to the window to see if Daddy really did give her money when she didn't even work for it, and I catch Diane looking up. Our eyes meet. She smiles and waves.

"Feel better, Ebony-Grace. Too bad you'll be missing out on practicing with the Nine-F Crew."

I pull away from the window. Who said I wanted to practice with the ice cream flavors anyway, with their stupid moves and their stupid rope and their stupid outfits? And I refuse to call them a *crew*.

Daddy comes back upstairs. "I just paid Diane for babysitting you today, Ebony." His voice is different and he doesn't call me Broomstick. "Now, if your momma calls, tell her . . . No. Just don't pick up the phone. And don't go calling Huntsville, either. Just . . . lay low, okay. I gotta get to the shop. You know where the bathroom is, and there's some cereal, bread, and cheese downstairs. If you ain't feeling right, just ease up on the cheese, okay? I'll come back later with some Robitussin. I ain't got none in the house."

I remember to make a sick face and hold my stomach as he talks. He believes me! This whole playing-sick thing wouldn't fly with Momma at all. I never tried it with Granddaddy—never had to. When the door is closed, I stand upright, hands at my sides, ready to salute a captain, any captain. So I turn toward the window and salute the wide blue sky. "At your service, Captain Fleet!" I say loud and clear.

★ ★ ★ ★ ★

I quietly put on my Return of the Jedi T-shirt and a pair of acid-washed jeans that I begged Granddaddy to buy me because Momma said dungarees aren't ladylike. Then I wait to hear Daddy leave the house to walk over to the shop. When I'm sure that all is clear, I swing open the bedroom door because Daddy's brownstone is now a radio tower atop the highest peak on Planet Boom Box!

"All systems go!" I shout.

The stairs leading down to the first floor become a bunch of radioactive bars that will send shock waves up to my brain if I'm not careful. I gently step onto each wire to avoid being electrocuted.

"Cadet E-Grace Starfleet to Captain Fleet," I whisper into my communicator. "I'm here at the Sonic King's radio tower. Do you copy, Captain Fleet. Do you copy?"

"Copy, E.T.! I mean . . . E.G."

I jump and look all around because the voice comes from out of nowhere. Then, someone pokes his head out from the bottom of the stairs, giggling. It's Uncle Rich.

"You've got one heck of an imagination, little girl," he says.

A woman wearing a fancy silver dress tiptoes out of Uncle Rich's bedroom holding a pair of silver high heels in her hand. She smiles and winks at me before she comes down the steps. "Well, this here is Carol. And she was a figment of your imagination location. Okay?"

I nod and smile, then they both quietly leave out the front door. And finally, the house is all mine! "I'm coming for you, Captain Fleet!" I yell out to the walls, and ceiling, and dusty old furniture, and maybe even that stuffy No Joke City air.

I'm easing down the radio tower trying to get to Captain Fleet when a loud booming sound almost makes the whole planet shake. I don't have to move closer to the first floor window and look up at the sky to know that it's the Sonic Boom. The Sonic King will have it no other way. He's set on taking control of the whole universe with that booming sound of his. I don't even bother covering my ears.

Ever since I first walked into Daddy's house, I've imagined sliding down all these stairs as if it were a ventilation shaft in a space station. So I sit my butt on one of those steps. I've already been electrocuted by the radioactive bars, so I let my body slide down each step with a bump and another bump while I squeal, "Wheeee!" until I reach the very last step. I let my body fall back, and pretend to be unconscious. My body's been electrocuted and the Sonic Boom has taken over my soul. I've lost all control.

I don't even move when I hear the front door opening wide letting in more of that heavy pounding bass. It makes my heart jump and my inside dance. It's taken over everything!

"E.G.! You all right?" someone shouts.

I open my eyes to see Uncle Rich again bent over me with his gold chain swinging back and forth. Behind him is another lady friend, not the same one as before. She wears short-shorts like the ones Diane wears, and a tight striped shirt like the one Bianca wears. Her hair is slicked back to show off her gold trapezoid earrings. Again, with those earrings, as if they're magnetic receptors for the Sonic Boom.

I jump to my feet. My butt is sore, but I look back up those stairs wanting to go for another slide. "I was just trying to save Captain Fleet when the Sonic King trapped me with his Sonic Boom," I say.

"Is that right?" Uncle Rich asks, putting an arm around

his lady friend. "And what planet did you just come back from, E.G.? Lemme guess. Mars? Mercury? Uranus!" He laughs loudly, slapping his knee and pulling in his lady friend even closer. "I always liked that one. *Uranus.*"

"No, none of those planets," I say, walking over to Not-Carol to check out her outfit. "I was on Planet Boom Box trying to rescue Captain Fleet from the evil Sonic King and the Funkazoids."

Not-Carol giggles. "That's kinda cool, little girl. The Funkazoids? Sounds like a good name for a rap group or dance crew or something."

I roll my eyes. I wasn't talking to her in the first place. "No, *Carol.* The Funkazoids can never be a crew. Crews are heroes. Crews go on adventures. Crews work together for the good of all mankind."

Uncle Rich laughs, but Not-Carol cocks her head to the side. "Wait a minute, now. Who's Carol?"

"Go on up, baby. Gotta talk some sense into my niece," Uncle Rich says to his lady friend.

When she's at the top of the stairs, Uncle Rich walks closer to me, digs into his pocket, and pulls out a dollar. "Now, this is what we call hush money. I ain't got much of it, so if you spill the beans again, you gonna owe me double."

I don't take it and say, "A dollar's all you got, Uncle *Rich*? My granddaddy gives me a whole twenty."

"Your granddaddy gives you hush money, huh? Now I ain't got your granddaddy's kinda money. Nobody here does. So if you know what's good for you, little girl, you'll keep your little mouth shut, anyway. Why don't you go on outside to play with your little friends? That little Puerto Rican girl from downstairs is out there playing double-Dutch. Go on out there and be a little girl and play little girl games?"

"Be a little girl?" I mumble under my breath.

Not-Carol is making her way back down the stairs. "Don't make me wait too long, Daddy," she says in a syrupy sweet voice that hurts my ears.

"Daddy?" I say under my breath.

I watch as Uncle Rich goes upstairs with that woman. He pinches the lady's butt and she squeals, hitting him on the arm. So I yell, "Bye, *Carol*! Nice meeting you!"

"Who is Carol?" I hear her say.

"Go outside, little girl!" Uncle Rich yells back.

But I don't go outside because Bianca and the nefarious minionettes are busy playing with those stupid telephone cords. I stand in the doorway and watch as Bianca jumps in, the ropes gliding beneath her feet, her legs moving to the rhythm.

Bip-bip-bip-bip.

The minionettes start singing a song about a boy named Jack and how he's nimble and quick and jumps over a candlestick. Then they start counting down as if they're getting ready to launch Bianca into space.

"Ten, nine, eight . . . "

Bianca does a trick where she jumps over one leg as if it were a rope, too.

"Seven, six, five . . . "

Another girl is outside the rope getting ready to jump in. I can see a disaster coming, for sure. As a space cadet, I've learned to predict outcomes based on mathematical equations using space-time equilibriums. There isn't any space inside those spinning telephone cords, and there isn't any time for Bianca to jump out!

"Four, three, two . . . "

"No!" I yell as loud as I can. "Abort mission, now! I repeat. Abort mission, now!"

I open the door and run down the front stoop to stop the spinning telephone cord in enough time for Bianca to jump out. But instead of grabbing the cord by my hand, it slaps me in the face, gets tangled in my arms and legs, and I trip, landing right on my butt. The pain shoots up my back and goes straight to my head, forcing me to cover my ears because everything about that moment—the Sonic Boom, the spinning rope, the falling on the ground—comes crashing down right over my head. And it hurts.

CHAPTER
22

Bianca went all the way to the corner store—a "bodega" she calls it—to buy long tubes of red icees to soothe some of the soreness on my body. There's one on my head, one on my back, and one on my butt as I lie facedown on Daddy's beat-up, dusty couch. It smells just like him—car grease, cigarettes, beer, and Johnson & Johnson's baby powder.

"That's what you get for trying to make me fall again," Bianca says as she tries to stop the cold, wet icees from sliding off my head and back. "Boomerang! What goes around comes around."

"I wasn't trying to make you fall," I say. "I was just trying to save you."

"I don't need you to save me."

"Yes, you do. You just don't know it yet."

"Why are you so weird? And how come you didn't grow up already? You still act like you're nine."

She doesn't know what she's saying. Her mind is gone. The Sonic Boom has taken control. Then I say, "If *you're* so grown-up, then what were you doing jumping in that rope then? Is that your day job so you can pay your grown-up bills?"

"We're *playing*, but it's not like how you play. We're actually doing something, not pretending to be on spaceships and going to other planets or whatever."

"It's my imagination . . . ," I start to say, but I stop. It's no use. Explaining any of this to her will be like screaming on the other side of a giant blast door. She can't hear me. She can't see me. "Bianca, you can go home now."

"Okay. Adiós!" She gets up from the couch leaving me with my icy red alien receptors all along my back and on my head.

But when Bianca opens the front door, Daddy is on the other side holding out his keys. "Hey, Butter Pecan! I didn't know you were here hanging out with Broomstick."

"Hi, Mr. Julius. I was just leaving," she says.

"Oh, wait a minute, now," Daddy says, picking up a big, flat cardboard box from the ground and nudging Bianca to come back inside. "Got some pizza for lunch. You can help me and Broomstick finish it off."

I watch Bianca's eyes move from the box and then to me and back. "Did you get pepperoni, Mr. Freeman?" She closes the door and follows him into the living room.

"Sure did. And you can bring some to your grandmother if you like."

"Abuela doesn't eat pizza," Bianca says, and walks right past me and into the kitchen with Daddy.

Daddy doesn't even ask me what's wrong when he passes. So I slowly get up from the couch, still feeling a little hurt, let the red icees fall to the floor, and sit with my sometimes–best friend at the small kitchen table.

"Feeling better, Broomstick?" Daddy asks. "I knew a slice or two would get you out of your funk. But you gotta take some of this Robitussin first."

Momma makes me take Robitussin for everything from a skinned knee to a bellyache. I swallow a spoonful from Daddy even though I wasn't really sick in the first place. But it'll make my sore body feel better, for sure.

"I don't get to eat pizza down in Huntsville," I say, after letting the syrupy sweetness ease down my throat. I just want to have a regular ol' conversation. The doors to my imagination location are completely shut for now 'cause I'm glad Bianca stayed. I have to think of normal things to talk about.

"'Cause you don't have no pizzerias?" she asks, as Daddy puts out plates in front of us.

I shrug. "Maybe we do. I don't know. Momma likes me to eat food that she makes. Says she knows what's stirring in it."

Bianca giggles a little. "I'll get in trouble if Abuela finds out I'm eating pizza. She says her arroz con habichuelas is better. She doesn't like wasting money on other people's food."

I giggle, too. "Right. Other people's food might have some mind-controlling poisons that'll make you start eating your fingers and your hands and your arms, and before you know it, you'll be eating your friends and your mom and your dad, and whoever put that mind-controlling poison into the food will take over the world because everybody will start eating each other and it'll be an apocalypse, and Planet Earth will become the new home for the aliens and—"

"Ebony-Grace!"

I jump when Daddy yells my name. Bianca's eyes are wide, and her mouth hangs open as she stares at me.

I did it again. I didn't mean to. I shrink in my seat and put my head down on the table. My butt is still sore. It throbs against the chair, and I wish it was some sort of signal from Captain Fleet letting me know that I'll be beamed up onto the *Uhura* real soon.

But there is no *Uhura*. Everything is under the control of the Sonic Boom, including me.

"Now, would you stop talking crazy so you don't scare your little friend away?" Daddy says, as he places a warm, gooey slice of pizza on my plate. "Your mother warned me about this, told me not to entertain these outrageous stories of yours."

Daddy walks out of the kitchen to sit in front of the TV set in the living room. I sit up, and without looking over at her, I can tell Bianca is almost finished with her slice of pizza. Slowly, I pick at the pepperoni and cheese, and nibble on the crust. I'm still working on my first slice when Bianca picks up a second, and then a third.

"What's the matter? Your abuela doesn't feed you enough roots and parachutes?" I finally ask.

"Roots and parachutes? No. Arroz con habichuelas!"

"Whatever. My momma was right. You little street urchins ain't got no home training. Your grandmomma don't feed you right," I say, sighing before I bite into the pizza. I'm doing good. I'm making normal conversation again.

"What? *Excuse* you?" Bianca stands, puts her hands on her hips, and rolls her neck just like the minionettes.

I pop my eyes out at her. "You're practically eating the whole box of pizza by yourself."

"You are so stupid! My abuela does too feed me right. I just like pizza, that's all. And what about you? Your momma makes you wear boys' clothes? And you're just a five-year-old in a twelve-year-old's body with those stupid baby games."

"Baby games?" I watch her as she takes another bite of my daddy's pizza. Pizza that he paid good money for. And she's sitting on my daddy's chair, in my daddy's kitchen, and she even lives in my daddy's house. So I grab that pizza right from her mouth and right from her hands. "If you're gonna be rude, than you might as well not eat my daddy's pizza!"

"Give it back to me," she squeals. Her voice is like a whistle when she yells.

She grabs the slice, and I grab it back from her. "Like I

told you, you need to get out of my daddy's house if you're gonna be calling me a baby!"

"You called me a street onion!"

"No, I didn't!"

"Yes, you did!"

"Hey, hey, hey!" Daddy comes rushing into the kitchen. "Y'all gots to be kidding me!"

I'm squeezing half of the pizza slice in my hand and the cheese, sauce, and pepperoni are oozing through my fingers as if I'd just dug into Mars's red-hot soil. Bianca's hands are dirty, too, and she doesn't let go. We're both holding on to that pizza as if it were the last slice on Earth. I grind my teeth, scrunch my face, and try to use the Force like Darth Vader does to throw a nearby toaster at her.

"Both of you, put that pizza down!"

We don't move. We're staring so hard at each other that laser beams might as well be shooting out of our eyes.

"Let go of that food! Both of you!" Daddy yells even louder than before.

We let the slice drop down onto the table. Bianca just stares at her hands while I wipe mine on my shirt and jeans. Momma would give me a hard licking for doing that, but I don't care. She's not here. But I still want to go home.

I get up from the kitchen table, run out and up the stairs to my not-room. I plop down on my not-bed and bury my face in my not-pillow, and let out a loud and long not-cry.

CHAPTER
23

"Hey, now," Daddy says as he sits at the edge of my not-bed. "You are one spoiled little girl, you know that? You're acting out 'cause your mother ain't here. And she is mean, let me tell you that right now. Your momma would pop you one time if she saw how you were acting today."

My head is turned away from him, and I stare at the flaking white paint on the wall. Everything about Daddy's house is a little bit chipped and a whole lotta dusty.

"Ebony-Grace, I'm talking to you. If I gotta convince your mother for you to stay up here with me, then you're gonna have to start acting right."

I turn to my back and stare up at the high ceiling. There's even more chipping white paint up there, and if I'm not careful, it will all come falling down on me like a meteor shower. That would be outta sight!

"You were running your mouth downstairs with Bianca, talking about eating your mother and father. Now, where in the world did you get those crazy ideas, huh?" Daddy asks. "Say something, baby girl."

I search my brain for words—normal words. Sentences that have nothing to do with outer space or aliens or the *Uhura*—crazy ideas. "Uncle Rich had two different lady friends in the house. One after the other," I say, as plain as Wonder Bread.

"Uncle Rich had . . . Are you tattle-telling on your uncle, Ebony? That's grown-folk's business. You stay outta that. Now, how 'bout your granddaddy? How many lady friends did he have in the house, huh?"

"That's grown-folk's business, Daddy. I stay outta that," I say. I close my eyes, letting those normal words and normal thoughts bounce along the chipped-walls and swim around my not-imagination location.

Daddy chuckles and gets up from my bed. He pulls up his jeans even though they weren't slipping and walks around my bedroom as if trying to search the walls for the next thing to say to me. He finally stops in front of my bed with his hands on his hips and looks down at me with needle eyes.

So I sit up cross-legged and rest my chin in both my hands, waiting for him to yell at me.

"I'm gonna have to put you on punishment. Ground you or something," he says. "But I ain't about spanking kids." He's not yelling.

"'Or something' would be best, Daddy," I say, remembering how I got a spanking from Momma for trying to use her Conair hair dryer as a launching pad for my soda-bottle rocket ship.

Daddy chuckles again. He sits back down and looks at me. "You're gonna have to get some of that nonsense out of your head, Broomstick. You're gonna have to learn how to get along with the kids on the block and be normal. Now, you can wear what you want as long as you're all covered up, but I'm not gonna have you disrespecting me in my own house. Am I making myself clear, young lady?"

I take my hands away from my chin and rest them on my lap. "Daddy, I'm not being disrespectful . . . I'm just trying to be . . . " The rest of the words are stuck in my throat. They're begging to come out, but they form a ball right there. They want me to cry like a big baby. So I swallow them back.

"Trying to be what, baby girl?"

I can't hold it back. It comes tumbling out of my throat, slipping out of my mouth like a meteorite. "Regular and normal," I cry. I clench my fists and tighten my jaw trying to keep it in.

"Oh, Broomstick." Daddy sighs, pulling me in and holding me like I'm a big baby. "You don't wanna be regular. You wanna be dynamite. You wanna be outta sight. Just . . . not outta space."

"I wanna be extra-galactic," I say through tears.

"I know, I know, baby girl," he says, kissing my forehead. "You need to come back down to earth, that's all. The people ain't up there in the galaxy. They're down here on this planet, out on these streets. I don't care what your grandfather told you—and I blame him for all this—but you ain't no astronaut, Broomstick. You ever seen a black woman in space, huh? And that *Uhura* lady . . . she ain't real. She's an actress. And her name is Nichelle. I know plenty of Nichelles, but not no *Uhura*. And your name is Ebony-Grace Norfleet Freeman, not no cadet or captain of anything. And soon, you'll be a normal young lady. You can't be walking around Harlem pretending to be Wonder Woman or Superman, and running from church and everything."

I pull away from Daddy. "I wanna go home" is all I say.

Daddy's quiet for a long moment—biting his bottom lip, inhaling deep. And then he says: "You can't go home. Your mother's busy helping your grandfather out. It's too much of a mess down there. I know you miss your momma and all, but if she wants to see you, she got the money to pay for a plane ticket."

"So I'm here forever?" My voice cracks. I let the tears run down my face and drip onto my lap.

"You're home, Ebony," Daddy says. "It wasn't my idea to raise you in the South. I don't care what kinda job or how much money your grandfather has. The South will always be the South. Now, Harlem is where it's at. This is the heart of the city. Not Wall Street where all the money is, or Times Square where all the shining lights are. We got soul, over here. We got music. And way back in your granddaddy's day, we had books and words and jazz. We had revolution. And we still got all of that, despite what you see on the surface. We got talent, baby girl, talent mixed in with a lot of hopes and dreams. The world is at your fingertips up here in the Big Apple. You can take the train and go wherever you want. Now, don't get me wrong, you gotta be tough. And that's exactly how I want you to be—strong—like them girls out there. They don't take no kinda mess. Besides, there's more opportunities here, more jobs, more ways to start your own business. And more room to dream big. And what they say is true: You make it here, you can make it anywhere."

Daddy's words swim around the room as if it's zero-gravity in here. I don't pull them down and take them in. They're his words, not mine. I don't want them. So I nod, pretending that I understand.

"Why don't we start over fresh?" he says. "Fourth of July is around the corner. I got a little money saved up. I'll close the shop Friday, and take you and Bianca to the movies. How 'bout that?"

Daddy's words all fall to the floor, now, shattering like

glass. I don't remember anything he said before the word movies. Nothing else matters anymore because this is the summer of *Star Trek III: The Search for Spock*. I jump onto Daddy's lap, even with my long arms and legs, and hug him tight. "Thank you, Daddy," I say.

CHAPTER
24

It's finally Friday, and Daddy, Bianca, and I are walking down 125th Street. Daddy couldn't take everybody to the movies, thank goodness, but he asked Señora Luz's permission to take Bianca, and Señora Luz almost kissed him for giving her the afternoon off.

"You two are all y'all got on this block," Daddy says as he walks with us to the train. "Bianca, you look out for Ebony. And, Ebony, once you learn the lay of the land here, you'll look out for Bianca."

I try to stay normal and regular. I'm real quiet as Bianca walks beside me, and I keep my eyes on all the normal and regular things happening in Harlem. On almost every block, a fire hydrant spews out white foamy water, and perfectly *normal* kids jump in and out, screaming and laughing. In front of one of the boarded-up brownstones is a wide cardboard, and another small group of perfectly *normal* kids slide down the cardboard-covered steps as if it were part of a *regular* ol' jungle gym. A big *regular* radio sits on top of a broken car blasting *normal* heavy-bass music that seems to make the whole city vibrate. Some perfectly *normal* kids dance to it like robots. Others are spinning on their heads on another piece of cardboard and they look as if they're breaking their bones—break dancing. Perfectly *normal*.

I've never seen so much cardboard, broken glass bottles, old tires, torn mattresses, and messy colorful letters on crumbling walls in my life. This is normal. This is regular ol' Harlem. I just let my normal eyes rest on everything, watching, and not letting anything slip through the closed doors of my imagination location. And I don't say a word to Bianca, either. She's regular and used to all of this *normal*.

I do notice some things: Every other man in the neighborhood knows my daddy. They call him by different names.

"My main man, Julius!"

"What's going down around town, Jules?"

"DJ Jule Thief! When's the next block party?"

"Freeman! You think you could *free* this man by lending me a few bucks?"

Some of the men ignore Bianca and me, but one says, "These two yours? You get around town, Jules. Got you a Puerto Rican one and black one."

"No way, man! Just one of them's mine," Daddy responds. "Can't you tell?"

"Sure can. Put a mustache on her and you won't even know the difference!"

I don't let myself think that Daddy is the king here, but some men who look just like Lester—scratching their arms and necks and wearing dirty clothes—run toward Daddy offering to sell him all kinds of junk: a fancy doorknob, a pair of old leather shoes, a gold watch, and even a carton of milk.

"Word on the street is your kid's momma walked out on you and left you to raise a girl-child by yourself," the man says with missing teeth and only a narrow patch of hair left on his head. "Could use some milk, ain't that right?"

"Come by the shop tomorrow" is all Daddy says, without buying that junk.

We reach the long overhead train tracks that run along Park Avenue. I smile to myself thinking of the many ways a flying train can be a spaceship, a giant meteor racing through the galaxy, or a robotic weapon against the Sonic Boom. But I press my lips tight forcing myself not to say a word. I have to try with all my might not to blurt out something . . . crazy.

"I see you looking up, but we're not going on that train, Broomstick," Daddy says. "That takes you up north. We're going downtown."

He pats my head as he and Bianca start going down the steps that seem to lead to the very center of the earth. I stand at the top of the stairs, not moving one inch. Daddy's already at the bottom when he realizes that I'm not behind him. He sighs and shakes his head.

"I done forgot you've never took the subway before," he says. His voice echoes as if it were coming from a whole other galaxy. He walks back up and extends a hand out to me.

Bianca is covering her laugh, so I don't take Daddy's hand and walk down the stairs on my own. I stop midway because I can hear the loud boom rolling from that place at the bottom of the steps. I can feel the ground moving beneath my feet. *It's just a sound*, I tell myself. But *sonic* means "sound." And "boom" is exactly *how* it sounds.

"It's the Sonic Boom!" I blurt out.

"It's the train coming," Daddy says. "Don't start none of this nonsense now. It ain't a game down here, so you better act right. And we gotta catch the movie in time."

And that's the only thing to make me walk into the belly of the Sonic Boom. Down in the subway, there's a rolling, screeching sound, as if it were getting ready to make that *boom-bip-blap-ratatatat* music—like how the minionettes rock back and forth before jumping into the ropes. Bright lights shine on all those dirty tile-covered walls, but they're not bright enough to light the corners and faraway places that look like the end of all existence, as Momma would say—and that's called hell.

A big sign says that this is 125th Street. There's a little square house with wide windows in the middle of this underground place, and in it is a man in a blue uniform. Maybe he's the king of this place. No. There is no king. This is the subway. This is normal. We're going to see *Star Trek III* and that's when I can let the doors to my imagination location swing wide-open. For now, I lock them shut, stand against them, and hope that not even a little breeze—like the one blowing in from somewhere deeper in the subway—comes knocking them down.

"I got a token, Mr. Freeman," Bianca says, her first words since leaving our block.

"You keep it and crawl under that turnstile like every other kid," Daddy says.

Huge black gates separate the man in the small square house from the rest of the subway. We have railroads and train stations, too, down in Alabama, but they're outside and not underground. On the other side of the black gates and spinning metal bars called the turnstile is the train platform. Bianca runs onto the train platform as if riding an iron dragon deep under this already heavy city with its tall buildings and a million cars is the most normal thing in the universe.

Daddy motions for me to crawl under the spinning metal bars, too. This is not a portal. This is not a wormhole. *This is the subway*, I tell myself.

And it smells terrible. If Momma were here, she'd spray some perfume onto her kerchief and cover her nose with it.

"What an incredible smell you've discovered!" I say, just like Han Solo in *Star Wars*.

But Daddy just shakes his head at me, and I watch him put a bronze coin into a tiny slot next to the turnstile. He pushes through and it makes another strange sound like clinging chains. *Ching-ching-ching-ching*. Other than that, it's quiet now, and I turn to look down onto the train tracks. This is the ultimate void, the dark abyss, home of ugly aliens like the Klingons. Or maybe it's the meeting place for the nefarious minions. I was wrong about the church basement. This is where they all plot to take over the world. And here I am standing with their king, ready to plunge into this evil lair. I can't help it. Everything is as plain as the sun, the moon, and the stars.

This *is* another planet!

CHAPTER
25

"I've been taking the subway since I was a baby!" Bianca brags.

"So," I say, keeping my eyes on every scribble on the walls, every chewed-up piece of gum on the platform, and every drop of dirty water dripping from the tall ceiling.

"So, you've never been in the subway before," she says. Bianca has a smirk on her face. Here she is going to the movies with me and my daddy, and she's acting like she's the princess of this place. I should've thrown that slice of pizza on the dirty floor when I had the chance. I should've told Daddy not to take her with us.

"How do you get to the city in Alabama?" Bianca continues. "Monique says you walk on dirt roads. Barefoot."

"No we don't! My granddaddy has a brand-new Cadillac!" I yell, and my voice becomes a million other voices repeating every single word a million times. I'm sure there's a million tiny nefarious minions hidden behind every crack in this subway making fun of me.

"Hey!" Daddy yells, and both me and Bianca jump a little. "Y'all want me to turn right back around so I could send you off to bed, Ebony-Grace?" Daddy's voice is thunder, is a launching space shuttle, is the Big Bang down here in the subway. "Try me. Not gonna keep being nice."

So I shut my mouth for the whole time, even as a train comes slithering through the tunnel roaring like a dragon. Bright, colorful letters and words dance along its sides as it eases into the station louder than anything I've ever heard in my life. This is the mother of the Atomic Sonic Boom—the place where that *boom-bip-ratatatat* music is born and then learns how to walk, talk, and run loud and free in the world. And it sounds messy, like Daddy's junkyard, like the streets in Harlem.

I surrender. The doors to my imagination location are wide-open now because the writing's on the train: *Blast Off, No Limit, Pump Up the Volume.* And the best one of them all in big, bubbly, sparkling letters is the word *BOOM* stretched out in so many *O*s that it takes up the whole side of the train's car. Tiny dynamite bombs dance all around it, and if that isn't a sign as clear as the Alabama skies, then I don't know what is.

So I cover my ears, and Bianca does, too, as the train comes to a stop. It screams as sharp as a needle, and I press my hands against the sides of my head and purse my lips tight, trying to block out any way that the Sonic Boom might sneak in and take over my mind. Bianca and I look at each other again and she smiles. But this ain't funny. This is the dark, crusty belly button of No Joke City and I'm not gonna smile one teensy-weensy bit.

"Keep your eyes and ears open, Ebony," Daddy says as we take a seat on the train. My eyes are open, but not my ears.

He pulls my hand away, and Bianca has already put hers down on her lap.

There's also writing on the train's seats and walls—some too small and too strange for me to read. I spot the words

R.I.P. Michael Stewart written in big, red letters on the empty seat next to me. Other people take seats near us or stand against the sliding doors even though a sign above their head says not to lean against the doors. None of these people say a word to Daddy. No one seems to know him down here in the subway.

"If anybody stares at you, you stare right back," Daddy continues.

I can hardly hear him over the baby Atomic Sonic Boom. The train rattles through the tunnel as if it were the machine that puts together all the nuts and bolts of the loudest sounds in the universe.

Rattle-rattle. Rock-rock. Screech-screech. Rumble-rumble. Roll.

"Don't let nobody know that you're from Down South so they don't think you're country and rob the shoes from right off your feet," Daddy says.

I look down at my used-to-be-white sneakers. "Who'd want to take these shoes, Daddy?" I ask as loud as I could.

Rattle-rattle. Rock-rock. Screech-screech. Rumble-rumble. Roll.

"You don't have to talk so loud," Daddy says. "I can hear you just fine. And it don't matter about the sneakers, really. There's always somebody down here who don't have a pot to piss in, so a pair of sneakers can get them two bucks."

Rattle-rattle. Rock-rock. Screech-screech. Rumble-rumble. Roll.

The train pulls into another subway station called Fifty-Ninth Street, Columbus Circle. The doors slide open as more people come into the train. The doors close again.

Rattle-rattle. Rock-rock. Screech-screech. Rumble-rumble. Roll.

There's nothing but blackness outside those windows, and I remember what Granddaddy always tells me about all that black in outer space: *Astroblack, Ebony-Grace. Like Sun Ra says: You belong to it and it belongs to you.* But outer-space black is not like Alabama-without-electricity black. And this subway black is definitely not like outer-space black. But I can't help to want to reach out to it and touch it; see if it will yank my hand right out of this train car and pull me up into that blackness and let me swim in it. Maybe this blackness down here belongs to me, too.

But unlike quiet outer space, it's loud. The train screeches. I cover my ears. Bianca moves from the other side of Daddy to come sit next to me. She takes my hands away from my ears.

"You gotta get used to it," she says.

"No, I don't," I say, putting my hands back over my ears, but then Daddy moves them away and stares me down with those laser-beam eyes.

"Why are you so mean? You used to be nice," she says.

I shrug. "I'm still nice. You're the one who acts all different when those minionettes—I mean, *girls*—come around."

"They're my friends. And when you leave, they'll still be my friends."

"Good" is all I say.

As I stare out into the darkness through the window in front of us, another train comes speeding past it and I push back into my seat thinking that we're going to crash and everything will explode! I gasp. The train is a whirl of black and silver and bright, bubbly color. Then it slows down and I can read the words: *R.I.P. Michael Stewart.*

I quickly look down at the seat again to see those same words there.

Bianca gasps, too. "Do you see that?"

"Who's Michael Stewart?" I call out, and Daddy puts his finger over his lips and shushes me.

"That's the A train going back to Harlem," Bianca says. "Mike Stewart was tagging the L train when the police got him."

"Bianca!" Daddy whisper-yells, puts his finger over his lips again, and shakes his head.

"Police? Tag?" I ask and uncover my ears and look around for the kind of tags that comes with all the new clothes Momma likes to buy from JCPenney. And there weren't any police around on this train, either.

"The police killed Michael Stewart 'cause he was tagging trains," Bianca whispers.

"Why was he running after trains?" I figured it out. He was chasing a train, like a game of freeze tag.

Bianca looks at me funny, and I turn away. I said the wrong thing.

"No, not like the game," she says. "Like graffiti."

I glance at her and wait for more.

"Tagging is when you put your name or your crew's name on a train or on a wall for everybody to see. But mean ol' Mayor Koch wants the police to arrest anybody caught tagging. Michael Stewart was caught on the L train, and they beat him up, then he died."

Bianca's words sit heavy in my mind. I remember hearing this story on the news down in Huntsville and Momma had said, "I hope your daddy's not up there spray painting on cars. They could do it on trains, next thing you know, they'll be all over cars, too."

I ask Bianca, "Did . . . King Sirius, I mean, my daddy know him? Michael Stewart?"

"Maybe. Mr. Julius knows everybody. Maybe he'll take us to those art places downtown. If you could tag a train, what would you put on it?"

"What do you mean by 'tag'?" I ask, still thinking about the game. I imagine myself chasing a train through the subway. I'd get tired real quick. I can't even run a relay without my glasses flying off my face and my heart feeling like it's gonna leap out of my chest.

"*Graffiti.* Those bright words on the train. What would you put? I would tag my Nine-F Crew name, Butter Pecan. And draw a giant ice cream cone with little pecans all over and a bright yellow square on top. That'll be the butter." She motions her hand in the air as if she were drawing something with an invisible paintbrush, but she makes a shushing sound. "You should put Ice Cream Sandwich and draw one, too."

"No. I'd put . . . Cadet E-Grace Starfleet, and draw a spaceship called the *Uhura.*" I do as she does, pretending to paint my name into the train's cool air.

"That would be funky fresh," Bianca says with a wide smile. "And then you'd make it look like outer space with stars and planets. I don't think I ever seen that kinda tag. All I see is cartoons. But yours would be so fly! And then, you could do it in secret and all the guys wouldn't know that it's girls doing all those tags."

I stare at Bianca wide-eyed. "Can we really do that? *Tag* a train?"

"I don't wanna do graffiti. I wanna break-dance and I wanna rap. I wanna be the best B-girl MC in Harlem. No. In the entire city. That way, I can be in movies like the Rock Steady Crew and be famous. Watch, I'm gonna beat Calvin in that contest."

I can see Bianca's soulglow. She likes talking about stuff like this, break dancing and graffiti. Not outer space, not NASA, but breaking-bones dancing and colorful, bubbly words on walls and trains. So I say, "I wanna be the first kid to go to outer space. If those Russians can send a dog into space—his name was Laika—then NASA can send a kid. You know, to remember all the cool stuff for the future."

"That'll be dope," Bianca says.

"Yeah . . . *dope*," I say.

The train is now at Times Square 42nd Street. Daddy gets up and we follow him out of the train and onto another platform that's way more crowded and smelly. I look back at the train as it zooms out of the subway station. This time, I don't cover my ears. Maybe this is what it's like to have the Sonic Boom take over your whole mind and soul. The sounds are normal now. And I had a *normal* conversation with my best-friend-again, Bianca.

"Y'all hold hands and follow me," Daddy says as he pushes through the crowd. "And stay close. Don't wanna lose nobody."

Bianca doesn't even think twice about taking my hand as we walk up the long staircase together, and out of the subway, and into the brightest, loudest place I've ever seen. I don't even crack a smile at all the flashing lights because this is the capital of No Joke City.

CHAPTER
26

"If you two can't make up y'all minds on what y'all wanna see in the next two minutes, then we're outta here." Daddy stands aside as Bianca and I look up at the movie titles in shining white letters above the movie theater. I only look up because she's looking up. I made up my mind from way before I even knew we were going to the movies.

"Ghosts are way better than stupid spaceships," Bianca says.

"Hey! And no name-calling," says Daddy.

There's a long line near the ticket booth and I can't even tell who's going to see *Star Trek* or *Ghost Busters* or *Gremlins* or *Indiana Jones* or *The Karate Kid*. Unless they're wearing a *Star Trek* T-shirt like this one blond boy. I'll make sure to sit next to him in the movie theater.

"You could see ghosts anytime, but you don't always see spaceships," I say.

"That's stu—" she starts to say, then glances over at Daddy. "That doesn't make sense. It's the other way around. Didn't a spaceship go to the moon? It was on TV and every-thing. When's the last time you saw a ghost on TV?"

"*Poltergeist* on the television from my granddaddy's video-cassette recorder."

"Why you gotta brag all the time? Anyway, that wasn't a ghost, that was a demon."

"Ghost, demon. Same thing. But aliens? When's the last time you saw a Klingon up close, in your face? They're way better than ghosts!"

"Y'all got one minute," Daddy says, with his arms crossed and whistling.

And with that, I remember who I am and where I am. If he's King Sirius Julius, then I'm the princess. "I wanna go home," I say. "I miss my momma, anyway. Daddy, can we call her when we get home? Granddaddy, too."

"Oh, you talkin' crazy, Broomstick. Y'all got me down in Times Square and now you wanna go home? Oh, no."

So I win. Daddy makes the decision for us. We're on the line to see *Star Trek III: The Search for Spock* because Daddy is my daddy, after all, and he's the king of this place. He's taking me to the movies, and Bianca is just tagging along. He wasn't going to leave, anyway. But *I* was going to leave if I had to sit through a bunch of crazy people in fake astronaut suits fighting ghosts. That's just highly illogical. You can't even see ghosts.

Bianca and I share a bag of popcorn even though she's mad at me. Every time I look her way, she rolls her eyes. I don't care. We're about to see Uhura and find out how in the world Admiral Kirk is looking for Spock when Spock is already dead.

"Did you see the *Wrath of Khan*?" I ask Bianca before the movie.

"No. I didn't even see *E.T.*," she says.

"How come?"

"Abuela doesn't take me to the movies. The one time I get to go to the movies, I can't even see what I want."

"So you never been to the movies before?"

"Abuela doesn't like movies, okay? She likes TV shows instead. She says the seats are cleaner at home."

"I guess that's why you don't have an imagination location," I say, stuffing my whole mouth with warm popcorn.

"A nation *what*?"

"One nation under a groove," I say with my mouth stuffed and thinking of Granddaddy's funk-music albums.

"Groove? What groove?" she asks.

"Bless your heart."

"What are you talking about, Ebony?"

"Shush. The movie's starting."

I don't sit up in my seat until I see her name appear on the screen: Nichelle Nichols. "Daddy, that's her," I lean over and whisper. "That's Uhura's real name."

"I know who that is, Ebony," Daddy mumbles, sliding down into his seat and leaning his head back. I'll nudge him if he takes a nap. He has to stay awake so I can talk to him about the movie later.

Uhura's real name fades from the screen but not from my mind. Nichelle Neptune, I'd call her. Nichelle Nebula. Or Nichelle, the noble Nubian queen, as Granddaddy would say. But Nyota Uhura is way better. *Nyota* means "star." *Uhura* means "freedom." Free star. As free as a star in outer space.

"Admiral Morrow looks like you, Daddy. And he's commander of Starfleet." I lean over to whisper into his ear again. Daddy's not sleeping after all. He's watching the movie just like I am. "His mustache is thick like yours. You can't even see his lips move."

He shushes me just as Spock—after being dead, born again as a baby, a boy, then an old man—finally recognizes Admiral Kirk, and reminds him that they're still friends, even though he can't remember anything about all their missions together. Just like Bianca. I glance over at her as she sits with her face all screwed up, not even looking up at the screen. She's picking at the bottom of the popcorn bag and spitting out the kernels against the back of the seat in front of her.

It's as if I'm between Admiral Morrow, who didn't even want Captain Kirk to return to the Genesis Planet, and Spock, the half human–half Vulcan, who can't remember anything about the spaceship or the friendship.

Then I remember the Genesis Device was first created in *Star Trek II: The Wrath of Khan*. (I've watched it dozens of times on Granddaddy's Betamax machine.) The Genesis Device can make anything dead, anything broken, come back to life again. It can make everything old new again. Like Spock dying, coming back to life, and growing up to be himself again on the Genesis Planet.

"Can the Genesis Device help the starving children in Ethiopia?" I'd asked Granddaddy the last time we watched *Star Trek II*. Earlier that evening, Momma yelled at me for not finishing my meat loaf. She'd said there are starving children in Africa, and I believed her because the white lady with big blond hair was always talking about sponsoring poor children in Third World countries on her commercials.

Granddaddy only chuckled and patted my head.

Maybe everything here in No Joke City—and everything down in Huntsville, too—can be born again.

"I must have your thoughts. May I join your mind?" I ask Bianca as we walk out of the movie theater with Daddy.

"I know where you got that from, Ebony-Grace," Bianca says, yawning. "Spock's father wanted to find him through Captain Kirk's brain. I'm not Captain Kirk and you're not Spock. *And* you can't mind meld."

She says this while rolling her eyes and neck as if everything about No Joke City never left her and followed her into that movie theater, even as she watched all of outer space stretch out in front of her and she could just touch it with her index finger.

When I'm watching movies on the VCR with Granddaddy, everything about Huntsville, Alabama, and the sixth grade and my little house on Olde Stone Road, and even my being Momma's only child melts away like ice cubes in sweet tea in July. The screen pulls me in, and I forget about everything and everyone around me. Except for Granddaddy. But Granddaddy wasn't with me this time, and I was left with King Sirius Julius and Butter Pecan Bianca. More like *bitter* pecan with her face all screwed up like that.

"Hey, daddy!" a woman says with a syrupy sweet voice as we walk down 42nd Street. "Those your little girls?" She's super tall with even taller high heels, a short sparkling skirt, and enough makeup to make her look like Bozo the Clown.

Daddy takes both our hands and speeds up toward the train station.

"Why don't you come over and tuck me in after you take them home, daddy?" the woman says.

"No thanks, ma'am" is all Daddy says.

Bianca giggles. I only look back at the tall woman who

smiles, winks, and waves at me as we walk away. Then I say, "Lady, he's *my* daddy!"

The lady laughs. "Ain't nobody trying to take your daddy from you, little girl. I just know he gotta whole lot more love to spread around, that's all, sugar."

"No he don't!" I say, but the lady is too far away now to hear me.

Daddy is looking over at me when he says, "Rule number one for walking out here in these streets, Broomstick: You don't have to argue with crazy. And there's a whole lotta crazy out here, and before you know it, you'll be one of them. Ain't that right, Bianca?"

"That's right, Mr. Freeman," Bianca says. "Or all that crazy will snatch you up and put you in the back of a van."

"Is Uncle Rich crazy, Daddy?" I ask. "'Cause that lady looked like one of his lady friends he brought over to the house today."

"Is that right?" Daddy slows down. "But don't let me hear you tattle-telling one more time. You can't be putting your uncle's business out in the streets like that."

I didn't mean to, really. I'm just tired of Daddy and everybody else calling other people crazy 'cause that's exactly what they say about me—crazy. My stories about the *Uhura* and Planet Boom Box—crazy. How I want to be the very first kid in outer space—crazy. So, crazy Uncle Rich and that crazy winking lady are perfectly fine. Nobody told Gene Roddenberry that he was crazy when he wanted to make a TV show about people in outer space, on a spaceship, and visiting other planets and aliens. And nobody told Nichelle Nichols that it was crazy to play a black lady on a spaceship in the far future.

I look up and out at everything in this crazy city—all the

neon lights, the people sleeping on the sidewalk, the man wearing a dirty business suit and dancing by himself, the boy carrying a giant radio on his shoulder, and even all the fancy ladies who smile too much and talk to every single man who passes them. There isn't a single tree or shrub or blade of grass pushing its way out of slabs of concrete on the ground. The only thing alive here is all that electricity—blinking lights, zooming cars, and dancing ladies in sparkling dresses. And it's all crazy. Ain't nothing funny about No Joke City, all right. I'm starting to like it here.

I smile a little because there are no nefarious minions around to see me. Except for Bianca. But she's not smiling. She's not looking up. She looks down as if trying to not step on any sidewalk cracks. The cracks here are wide, as if they're fault lines in the earth. The concrete crumbles around them as if the Sonic Boom itself had made all of Times Square rumble and jumble. So we're astronauts again, avoiding giant moon craters.

I take her hand when we're about to cross the street.

"You think something like that would work here?" she asks quietly. "The Genesis Device?"

My heart lights up. My soul glows. I smile big and bright. "You were watching after all!" I squeal.

"Well, I couldn't help it," she says. "It was right there in my face."

When we reach the other corner and start to head down into the belly of the Atomic Sonic Boom again, I say, "I definitely think the Genesis Device can work here."

CHAPTER
27

"Genesis is life from lifelessness." That's what Dr. Carol Marcus said in *Star Trek II* when she explained what the Genesis Device was. She also said a lot about reorganizing matter on a subatomic level, but the main thing was the Genesis Device could make dead places live. But the Genesis Device can only work somewhere or on something that is already dead. Nothing can be alive or have the potential for life before it's activated. We're gonna need a Genesis Device in the future when humans destroy everything with their Sonic Boom. It won't be another big war or King Kong or Godzilla or the Soviets that will destroy Planet Earth and our whole galaxy. It'll be the loudest, baddest sound in the entire universe!

That's what I'm thinking a few days after the movie on the Fourth of July, when it's not even high noon and already the heavy bass creeps through my bedroom window and pounds on my head, screams in my ear, and just about picks me up out of bed with its iridescent sound-wave hands. I look out my window to see that all the cars are gone. Even the broken ones that used to sit in front of Daddy's shop. And people are walking in the middle of the street likes it's nothing at all.

I want to open the window and stick out my head the way I've seen so many other people here do. Instead, I press my forehead against the glass and try to see down toward the front of Daddy's brownstone. And there she is. Bianca. I spot the tip of her white sneakers and the top of her head. I can tell from up here that her hair is done up in a side ponytail.

"Hey, Ice Cream Sandwich!" someone yells out so loud I can still hear it over the bass of the music—the Sonic Boom—and through the closed window.

It's Mint Chocolate Chip Monique standing across the street holding on to those stupid telephone-cord ropes. She's wearing a side ponytail, too.

"We need you to do something," she yells, motioning for me to come down.

"Good, you're finally up," Daddy says, startling me. He's standing in the doorway, wearing a clean T-shirt and clean blue jeans with a crease as sharp as Granddaddy's slacks after Momma irons them. "Block party's today. Make no sense for you to be up in the house. Get on out there and help, play, do whatever you want, Broomstick."

"I don't feel well," I say real softly.

It's not quite a fib. I couldn't sleep with all that racket outside last night. The Sonic Boom must've descended from outer space, passed the sun and moon, and passed the clouds to land right here on 126th Street. It pounded out of radios, cars, from opened windows, and shouting voices.

If there was a Planet Sleep, it would be full of warrior sheep fighting against the Sonic King and his Sonic Boom for some peace and quiet in the galaxy. The Sonic King won last night, but still, I slept anyway, tossing and turning and covering my ears with my blanket and pillow even though it was as hot as Venus.

"Ice Cream Sandwich, you coming down?" Monique yells again. I look back out the window to see three more of the

9 Flavas gathered around her. I swear they're like Tribbles—multiplying in just seconds.

"Go on," Daddy says. "You'll feel better once you get outside." He starts to walk away.

"I'll feel better once I speak to Granddaddy," I say.

He freezes where he's standing. Then he turns to me. "Oh, I get it," he says. "You're homesick."

I take in a deep breath. "Finally," I say. "Yes, Daddy. Can I please speak to my grandfather? I wanna tell him about the movie. He probably ain't, I mean, hasn't seen it yet."

This time, I'm not even trying to make my voice sound like hard candy. It just comes out that way. Maybe this homesickness, as Daddy calls it, is really the Sonic Boom making me all gooey like caramel or molasses. Not hard anymore—melted and sticky. And I wonder about the *Uhura* up there near Planet Boom Box. Maybe it's melting, too, under all those radioactive sonic waves. And the Sonic King will absorb it all into Planet Boom Box's atmosphere. And the Sonic Boom, with all its power from the melted *Uhura*, will become more powerful than ever.

I have to warn Granddaddy!

"You're still young, Broomstick. You'll get over it. And besides, ain't nothing that a little fresh Harlem air and some exercise can't fix. Go play with Bianca and them, and before you know it, you'll forget all about Huntsville." And then he walks away.

When I finally get downstairs, Uncle Rich is on the telephone talking to one of his lady friends. I can tell by the way he leans into the receiver and whispers and smiles and strokes the spiraling cord as if it were long, curly hair.

"When you gonna be done with the phone, Uncle Rich?" I ask while standing in the kitchen's doorway.

He puts his lady friend on hold and looks at me with red and watery eyes. "Oh, you must be paying the phone bill around here now."

He turns back to his sweet whispers and chuckling. I stand there and wait. I need to call Granddaddy again. Surely he's back home now 'cause it's the Fourth of July. But Uncle Rich never lets up, not even when the buzzer rings. I ignore it.

"Uncle Rich, I have to call my granddaddy. I have to tell him something very important!"

He shoots me a look, but still, I don't move away. The buzzer goes off again. Bianca's face is peeking through the curtained window in the door.

"Best to run along now and open the door for your little friend," he says.

I don't move one inch. The bell buzzes and buzzes. Bianca can wait. Uncle Rich can wait. But my granddaddy can't.

Finally, Uncle Rich hangs up the telephone and stares down at me with needle eyes. So I put my hands on my hips and stare back at him.

"Are you waiting for your other lady friend to call? Or else I need to talk to my granddaddy right now," I say.

Uncle Rich shakes his head and steps aside. "Julius was right. That grandfather of yours done spoiled you down there."

The bell buzzes again, followed by hard pounding. "Open the door, Ebony-Grace!" Bianca shouts.

I start to dial 1-2-5-6, but a flood of voices suddenly pours into the brownstone. Uncle Rich let them in.

"Come on, Ice Cream Sandwich!"

"You can't ignore us, we ignore you!"

"Don't act like you can't hear us, Outer Space Ebony-Grace!"

Uncle Rich walks up behind the 9 Flavas standing in the kitchen's doorway. "You can hang up now, Ebony. Your friends are here to bring you outside. Go along."

But I keep dialing Granddaddy's. If Momma picks up, I'll just *insist* that she put Granddaddy on the phone, just like how Momma *insists* that I do or don't do this or that. I don't care about these not-friends. They wouldn't know what to do with the Genesis Device if it hit them in the head.

"Get your friend, Butter Pecan!" Monique says. "'Cause I'm about to smack her upside her head for being disrespectful!"

"Nuh-uh! You're the one being disrespectful while I'm trying to call my granddaddy!" I say.

"That's enough, now, Ebony! Hang up the phone!" Uncle Rich shouts back.

I keep dialing until someone touches my shoulder. It's Bianca.

"We need you," she says. "We need you to help us fight the Sonic Boom."

Everyone's quiet, including Uncle Rich, who's looking at me as if I had two heads.

"The Sonic Boom?" I ask just to make sure that I heard it right, and I slowly put the receiver down.

"Yep," Monique says nodding. "The Sonic Boom!"

"Uh-huh," adds Rhonda. "The Boom is gonna get us."

Someone snorts and I can't tell who it is, but I don't care. Bianca's eyes are looking at me as if she really does need my help.

"Please," she says with a quiet voice.

"Yeah," Monique says. "Pretty please."

"More like ugly please," someone else says.

But I don't care.

I inhale deep and smile big and bright. I don't care

anymore about the no-laughing rule in No Joke City because it's time to save the day! "I'm coming for you, Bianca Pluto!" I shout as loud as I can, even while Bianca is standing right there in my face. "The needs of the many outweigh the needs of the few!"

I say those last few words from Mr. Spock as I push past Monique and Bianca, make my way to the front door, step out onto the stoop, put my hands on my hips, and stare up at the big blue sky here in Planet No Joke City. "I'm ready for you, Sonic Boom!" I shout.

CHAPTER
28

"We didn't take a vote on her," Rum Raisin Rhonda says, looking me up and down.

We're standing at the edge of the open lot down the block. Four torn and dirty mattresses are stacked on top of one another in the middle of dry grass, empty plastic bags, and a bunch of old tires. A group of nefarious minions are lined up in the distance. One minion speeds toward the stack of mattresses and tries to jump over all of them. He misses and lands on the edge, almost falling to the ground. Another minion tries and he makes it to the other side of the mattresses. They all cheer.

"Well, who else we gonna use?" Monique says. "The girls from 1-2-7 got their own thing going. And they might even wanna battle."

Rum Raisin Rhonda rolls her eyes. "Who made up that stupid rule anyway?"

"It's math," Mango Megan says. "Ten for ten. That's how we battle. Even on both sides. They got ten, we got ten."

"But they got ten *good* ones!" Monique says. "We got nine fly ones and . . . a chicken wing." She glances over at me and rolls her eyes.

"Chicken wing?" Bianca says, coming to my defense.

I push out my chest and fold my arms. I'm here to help *her*, not those other ice cream cones.

"Yeah. Chicken wing. That's what she'll look like when she tries to break-dance." Monique flaps her arms like a chicken. The ice cream cones laugh, including Bianca.

I roll my eyes hard, just like I've seen them all do, putting my neck into it and everything.

"Oh! There go that flava!" Monique says. "I know you can't be that black and not have some flava in you."

The cones all cheer as if I'd done something brand-new.

"But she can't be chilling with us looking like that," Coconut Collette says with her deep, raspy voice and steps closer to me. She looks me up and down as if I were an alien. And I am!

Monique comes closer to me, too, and stares down at the top of my head. "Your hair looks like the inside of Central Park where the bums don't even go. Bushy!"

"Oooooooooh!" everybody says at the same time. The boys from the middle of the lot hear Monique's big mouth and run toward us because even I can recognize a signifying monkey when it's standing right in front of me.

So I say, "Oh yeah? Well, with that bumpy forehead, you look like Valkris and Commander Kluge's first baby!" I put my hands on my hips and roll my whole body with the words, just like they do.

"What are you talking about? That's not a diss. You don't make no kinda sense," Monique says.

Bianca pulls me away from her. "She basically said you look like you a Klingon. Now, can we please get on with it? Calvin and them are already practicing, and I bet they got their moves down already. We need this money. And when we get it, we can fix her clothes and her hair later. We'll have enough to fix all our hair and clothes."

A sound blasts from across the street, and we all turn

to see Stone-Cold Calvin holding a boom box on his shoulder. Behind him are the rest of the nefarious minions coming toward the lot. They don't walk. They flow like river water, like swaying trees in the breeze, like iridescent sound waves to the beat of the music.

"Where do they think they're going?" Mango Megan says. "This is our practice spot. They need to go to the junkyard."

Monique gasps. "Bianca! Look! It's him. In the green shirt." She points with her chin and we all stare at the boys.

I spot a boy in the green shirt with a head full of outer-space black curly hair. Then I look at Bianca. Her cheeks are Mars red. Her eyes and whole face look funny. I can't tell if she wants to smile big and bright, or run away. She looks excited and embarrassed at the same time.

"Who?" I ask.

"I can't believe he's with Calvin and them now," Monique says. "They're definitely gonna beat us in that contest."

"Who are you talking about?" I demand. "Who is he?"

"It's none other than Pablo Jones," Monique answers, with her eyes and smile as wide as the galaxy. Pablo Jones must be as famous as Michael Jackson.

Vanilla Fudge Vanessa, who'd been sucking her thumb all this time, steps closer to Bianca and starts singing, "Bianca and Pablo sitting in a tree, k-i-s-s-i-n-g."

"Shut up, Vanessa!" Monique shouts. "Leave her alone! Bianca, don't lose your cool. You gotta focus."

Bianca just nods slowly. I stare at her trying to figure her out. So I step closer. "Let me have your thoughts. May I join your mind?" I ask.

But Monique steps in between us. "Child, if you don't stop with all that craziness, I'll knock you right back to Alabama. We gotta get ourselves together because those boys will beat us and win that fifty bucks from the block party. Now, keep your mouth shut, Ice Cream Sandwich!"

"No, you . . . ," I start to say, but Calvin and the minions reach the spot where we're standing, and they all strike a pose as if someone were about to take their photo. Five of them crouch to the ground and the other five stand back with their arms crossed over their chests. Calvin, still with the boom box on his shoulder, tilts his head back, looks down at us, and rubs his chin as if he were a six-feet-tall Gargamel and we're all just little blue Smurfs.

Mint Chocolate Chip Monique pushes us aside to step right to Calvin's face. "This is our spot. We agreed that you'd get the junkyard and we'd get the lot. Now, make like a basketball and bounce!"

The five minions who were crouching down get up and pose with their arms folded, and the five who were standing crouch down in perfect unison. They must've practiced for a long time to get that right.

"Lucky Lionel, gimme a beat!" Calvin says, while putting down the boom box and turning off the music.

Another boy puts his hands to his mouth and starts making a sound. A beat. A rhythm. A *boom*. A *bip*. A *bap*. All with his mouth! It's a teeny-tiny Sonic Boom coming from inside a boy!

Calvin clears his throat and starts, "I'm Cold-Crush Calvin and I'm here to say . . . " He sways to the beat of the boy's Sonic Boom mouth. His words move around the rhythm like the sound of piano keys or guitar strings. No. It's the sound of a whole other drum set! Another *boom, bip, bap, ratatatat*.

> *"I rock it to the beat every single day.*
> *On 1-2-5 we're staying alive,*
> *Breakin' and rappin', talkin' all that jive.*

Harlem is the greatest,
Rockin' all the latest.
My man Dapper Dan
Got us all lookin' famous!"

Calvin stops with his Sonic Boom words and another boy—Pablo Jones, with the green shirt—is about to begin, but Coconut Collette shouts, "Y'all not no Run-DMC!"

"Uh-huh," Rum Raisin Rhonda says. "Y'all wanna be the Furious Five, but y'all more like the Tedious Ten!"

"And plus," Monique adds, "the contest is not for rapping. It's for the best crew—breaking . . . and double-Dutch!"

"Double-Dutch?" Calvin's voice cracks, and he laughs. "It ain't no double-Dutch contest, Nine *Flavas*. This game is for men, so y'all can get on with your little jump-rope games."

"Nuh-uh," Monique says. "You must've never heard of the original Roxanne Shanté. My homegirl Butter Pecan Bianca can rap better than both Roxannes and is a fresher B-girl than Baby Love, too. Ain't that right, Butter Pecan?"

"I'm not better than Baby Love," Bianca quickly adds. "She's my idol. I'm not even gonna try to be better than her."

"You *can't* be better than her," Calvin says. "And I don't even know why the Rock Steady Crew let a girl in, anyway. That's why Genesis Ten will never have any . . . what do they call 'em, PJ? *B-girls?*"

"Genesis?" I ask, but no one is paying attention to me now.

"Oh, is that y'all's name now? *Genesis Ten?*" Rhonda asks with her hand on her hip and her face all screwed up.

"That's right," Calvin says, cocking his head back again. "Genesis Ten. My main man PJ, tell 'em what time it is."

PJ in the green shirt steps up and stands just like Calvin with his head tilted back and his arms crossed over his chest, except he does it in a way that makes it look like he's hugging himself 'cause he's cold.

"Pablo Jones!" Collette calls out. "You ain't no rapper. Why you faking it and trying to stand like a B-boy. Your momma will smack you upside your head." But the minions ignore her.

"Lucky Lionel," Pablo says with a much softer voice than Calvin's. "Drop the bass."

Lionel doesn't make the beats with his mouth this time. Instead, he presses a button on the boom box, and out comes the bass, the rhythm, the *boom*, the *bip*, the *bap*, the *ratatatat*.

> "I'm Pablo Jupiter,
> And your rhymes get stupider.
> You mess with me,
> and I'll burn you like Lucifer.
> Ashes to stardust, we're the survivors,
> Genesis Ten will destroy all the rivals."

Calvin stops the music, and the minionettes are as still as the quiet moon. I'm frozen and speechless, too, because I recognize something in his words—Jupiter and Genesis and survivors and rivals. These are the things *Star Trek* is all about—other planets and new beginnings and war and enemies!

"Genesis Ten, as in . . . the Genesis Device?" I ask, louder this time.

"No, stupid," Collette says in my face. Spit comes out of her mouth and lands on my forehead. "Genesis as in the first book of the Holy Bible. Pablo Jones is a shepherd for the Lord. I bet that name was his idea."

Pablo Jones shakes his head. "Yeah, it was my idea. But no, it's not from the Bible. That weird girl is right. We're Genesis Ten 'cause we're like the Genesis Device when we rhyme and dance. With our flow and with our moves, we make everything around come back to life!"

"That's right, Pablo Jupiter!" Calvin says.

"Jupiter? Like the planet?"

"Shut up, Ice Cream Sandwich!" four of the 9 Flavas yell at the same time.

But I gotta hear what he has to say. Both the minions and minionettes talk over him with their gibberish words that fly as fast as shooting stars, but not with a beat or rhythm, just plain ol' gibberish.

"Then what's *your* name, Calvin?"

"I already told y'all. Cold-Crush Calvin. I will crush you with my rhymes and leave you out in the cold!"

"Y'all sound like Run-DMC *wannabes*."

"Y'all got all that mouth, then lemme see what y'all got!" Calvin says.

"Show 'em what time it is, Butter Pecan Bianca."

My eyes widen and I gasp because Bianca licks both her hands and smooths down her curls as if she were about to do something outta sight. Collette drags a big piece of cardboard and puts it down right in front of us. Bianca steps right to Cold-Crush Calvin and Pablo Jupiter, folds her arms across her chest, cocks her head back, and says, "I don't need no boom box or a beatbox!"

Monique grabs my arm so I can stand next to her and the other minionettes, and before I know it, they're doing a two-step, side-to-side dance while clapping and stomping the beat to Bianca's rap.

"I'm Bianca Pluto and I run the show.
Smooth like butter 'cause I got the flow.
We're the 9 Flavas kicking the beat,
Fellas step back as I move my feet.
I don't need no mic 'cause I'm dynamite,
I blow up in your face rocking to this bass.
Gucci. Louis V.
Lee jeans, fresh and clean—
Check my Alligators,
Turn my back, see ya later."

She kisses two of her fingers and points them in Calvin's face.

I'm supposed to be clapping to the beat, too, but instead, I watch as Bianca's words dance right out of her mouth, out of her body, out of her soulglow—her soulshine. And she called herself Bianca Pluto! Pluto like the planet. And that boy in the green shirt called himself Jupiter. And the minions call themselves Genesis Ten like the device. And they're survivors, with rivals, and space, and bass. This is the Sonic Boom fully activated—pulsing and pounding through words and radios and kids just like me. The 9 Flavas don't stop clapping even as Bianca gets down to the ground and moves her body like an asteroid. She kicks and spins and dips and dives as if she has no bones. So this can't be the breaking-bones dance. It's not even a dance, really. She's a spinning planet. She's Saturn's rings. She's a shooting star. She's the universe expanding and contracting.

And it all explodes in a big bang when Pablo Jupiter joins her and they battle on the cardboard with their kicks and spins and headstands and handstands and poses. The Sonic King was right. The Sonic Boom makes you lose all control. It takes over your whole soul.

"You ain't got no 'Gators!" Calvin shouts when it's all over. "And you wish you had Gucci and Louis V. You can't even get no Lees! And y'all not rapping, y'all *cheering*. Cheerleaders can't be MCs."

"Shut up, Calvin!" Monique shouts back in his face. He just waves her away.

I guess Pablo Jupiter won that dance battle because he stood on his head the longest. But nobody will tell me.

"Bianca, you need more practice," Monique says.

"No, I don't," Bianca says as the Genesis Ten walk away, cheering and carrying Pablo Jupiter on their shoulders. "I was just saving my best moves for later. Why would I show them my secret moves now, anyway?"

"Good idea," Monique says. "Now they could go back to the junkyard thinking that they got this in the bag. And we didn't even show them what we could do with the double-Dutch rope."

"But, still," Vanessa says. "Pablo Jupiter is good."

"Uh-huh. He's better than Whodini!" Monique adds.

Then, they all talk at the same time.

"Nah, he's better than Kool Moe Dee, Whodini, and Run-DMC put together!"

"Girl, you crazy. He is not better than no Run-DMC. There's three of them and PJ is only one person."

"Well, his flow is better than Roxanne Shanté's!"

"Everybody's better than Roxanne Shanté."

"You shouldn't say that. She's a girl MC and we should have her back."

"Well, Pablo Jupiter needs to hurry and be famous so he can blow Kurtis Blow out the competition 'cause he's getting played out."

"You think he's gonna be on the radio or on TV?"

"Sure is. Watch. He's gonna be rich."

"Uh-huh. PJ's gonna be walking 'round here with the fat gold chain *and* medallion."

"And a Dapper Dan Gucci suit."

"Yep. And a fur coat, too."

"He's that good."

"Uh-huh."

"Well, I'm gonna be better!" Bianca shouts over all the gibberish.

I believe her. I will help her, and she will help me.

So when Bianca steps away from the minionettes to tie her shoelaces, I say, "You called yourself Bianca Pluto. Does that mean you're ready to help me with the *Uhura* and save Captain Fleet?"

"No, Ice Cream Sandwich!" she yells in my face.

I step back. "Don't call me that. That's not my name."

"Well, E-Grace Starfleet is not your name, either. But that's what you call yourself, and Ice Cream Sandwich is what we call you. It's your tag, just like we're the Nine Flavas, and Daisy Castro calls herself Baby Love, and Roxanne Shanté got beef with U.T.F.O. 'cause of that song that really wasn't about her, and Grandmaster Flash and Afrika Bambaataa . . . they all made up those names, and you think Crazy Legs's momma call him that? It's just a name, Ebony. So Bianca Pluto rhymes with *show* and *flow* and you *know*. And it doesn't mean that I wanna go to Pluto!" She looks at me as if I'm stupid and says this loud enough for her friends—her real friends—to hear.

"You tell her, Bianca!" one of them shouts.

She rolls her eyes and walks away from me to be with her friends. I'm left standing there like a lonely planet. I roll my eyes back at her even though she's not looking at me. But, there's still a Pablo Jupiter. Jupiter like the planet. Genesis Ten like the Genesis Device. It has to be more than just a name for the boy in the green shirt.

"I'm coming for you, Pablo Jupiter!" I whisper into the warm No Joke City air and hope that the Sonic Boom's iridescent sound waves will carry my words to that boy in the green shirt.

"Where you going?" Monique calls out when I start to walk away. "We need you to be the tenth flava."

"I'm not a flavor!" I shout without looking back. "I'm Cadet E-Grace Starfleet of the Mothership *Uhura*. And I'm about to turn that mother out!"

"Don't worry," I hear someone say. "She'll come back once she sees that she ain't got no friends on the block."

CHAPTER
29

"Broomstick!" Daddy calls out nice and loud from the top of the front stoop of the house. "I've been calling you. Hurry up inside."

I don't hurry up. I take my time watching everything on the block because all the cars that used to be parked along the sidewalks are gone now. Instead, two raggedy old cars, including Daddy's brown Buick, block off each end of the block. A big table is set up in front of one of the broken and abandoned buildings. A red-and-white-checkered tablecloth covers the top as if this block party is gonna be like a church picnic. On top of the tablecloth are plastic plates and cups and paper napkins.

A shirtless man sits on the edge of the sidewalk with a white plastic bucket between his legs. He's breaking apart a huge block of ice with an icepick as sweat runs down his forehead. I hope none of it makes it into that bucket of ice.

The little kids run up and down the street as if they've never seen a wide, empty road before. Down in Huntsville, that's all we see. And we can run as far as the setting sun. Here, they're only running from one end of the block to the next like hamsters on a wheel.

There's a line of people in front of Daddy's auto shop— some look like Loco Lester's cousins with dirty clothes and missing teeth; the others look like Daddy's friends, with the same mustaches and everything. There's even a small group of ladies who stare at me as I walk up to the shop. I need to get into the junkyard. I need to find Pablo Jupiter and ask him what he knows about the Genesis Device, and maybe, just maybe, I can tell him about the *Uhura* and the Sonic King and Captain Fleet who's been held captive by the Sonic Boom.

"Ebony-Grace, I'm calling you. Now come on in here!" Daddy's voice makes me jump and I quickly start walking up to the house. But not before I hear all the whispered gibberish from the grown-ups on the line.

"I hear she's from Alabama. I thought they train 'em better than that down there."

"Mm-hmm. She's as sassy as they come. Her father needs to spank her one time to set her straight."

"You see, her hair ain't even combed. Got her wearing boys' clothes."

"He need a woman in that house."

"Hmph, Richard got enough women coming in and out that house for both of 'em."

I turn around to face the line of grown-ups with my hands on my hips and blurt out, "Y'all need to mind your own beeswax!"

I don't even wait to see their screwed-up faces as I turn back around and walk up the steps to Daddy.

"Ebony-Grace! Have you lost your mind? Go on back there and apologize," Daddy says with his laser-beam eyes glaring down at me.

"Daddy, they said you need to spank me one time. Where do you keep the switch?" I say, glaring back at him.

"Girl, if you don't get your scrawny little butt up in here!"

I rush past him and into the house with my belly growling. I didn't even have cereal for breakfast, and I'm hoping Daddy is calling me back home for some lunch. He only steps inside for a minute to say, "You got a phone call. Told 'em to call back in five. Stand by the phone."

I gasp long and deep, thinking for a minute that Granddaddy called. But I couldn't be that lucky. I shuffle to the kitchen thinking of what fib I was going to put together for Momma.

"Oh, and Ebony?" Daddy says before he closes the door. "Don't try to call your grandfather back. It'll cost an arm and a leg to call the space center collect."

My eyes are wide, and my smile stretches from here to Mars. I hold my breath and count down from twenty. The phone doesn't ring, so I start all over again. By the third set of twenty and right when I got down to eight, the phone finally rings.

"Granddaddy!"

"Starfleet!"

"Granddaddy, did you see how Spock came back to life? It was the Genesis Device! You think that could work up here in Harlem? You should see it, Granddaddy. Everything's so broken. Even the kids are broken. They do this breaking-bones dance. Remember when you were trying to show me, Granddaddy? Oh . . . I'm supposed to be Cadet E-Grace Starfleet. At your service, Captain Fleet!"

Granddaddy chuckles. "You ain't skipping a beat, huh? Thought you'd move on from all that *Uhura* stuff by being in those Harlem streets."

"Well, last I heard you were under the Sonic King's control."

He laughs hard this time. "Under the Sonic King's control?

183

I guess you could say that. And this is the one phone call I'm allowed to get. See? I didn't even call your momma. I called you to see how you're doing up there."

"So tell me what happens, Granddaddy? How does Captain Fleet get from under the control of the Sonic King?"

"I ain't up to it right now, Starfleet. Tell me, is your daddy feeding you right? Getting some good greens into those little narrow bones of yours? He can't just be feeding you Corn Flakes. Tell him you want some biscuits, grits, and bacon. Your momma should come up there."

"Granddaddy, I don't wanna hear about no food!" I almost yell. "These girls, right? I call 'em the nefarious minionettes because they're all working under the orders of King Sirius Julius over here in No Joke City."

"No Joke City?" he says and then chuckles.

"Uh-huh. 'Cause ain't nothin' funny about No Joke City! That's what you'd say, Granddaddy. Right? Anyway, these girls, they call me Ice Cream Sandwich. And they go by different ice cream flavors. My *sometimes*-friend, Bianca . . . "

"Ebony!" Granddaddy says. "Are you making friends? I hope you're not doing what you do down here, pushing all those kids away by talking about spaceships and aliens all day. That's between me and you, Starfleet. Not everybody's gonna understand our little space adventures."

"Little space adventures? We're saving the galaxy, Captain Fleet! Anyway, this boy, Pablo Jones . . . You think the Genesis Device will work here? You should see all these broken buildings, Granddaddy," I say, almost running out of breath. I gotta tell him everything before it's time to go. But the words are coming too fast, and my mouth is moving too slow. I wish I could borrow Diane's speedy mouth.

"Starfleet! All right, now. If you wanna go there with

all this Genesis Device stuff, just remember . . . the Prime Directive."

"The Prime Directive?"

"That's right. The Prime Directive. You can't be messin' with what people already got going. You got to leave it the way it is. Respect it. Get to know what it's all about. That's the Prime Directive."

"But, Granddaddy, the Prime Directive has nothing to do with the people, it's for aliens." I pause, and he's quiet. Then I say, "Ohhh. We can't interfere with alien cultures on other planets. No Joke City is a whole other planet, and as strange and broke as it is, I can't change it, right?"

Granddaddy laughs so hard, he starts coughing.

"You okay, Granddaddy?"

"Ebony, Harlem's been a little broken ever since I was a boy, back when there was no Genesis Device or Prime Directive or even a TV set for me to watch *Star Trek*. Nobody was going up on spaceships back then, Starfleet. But we all had an imagination location. That's what I want you to keep tapping into, Ebony. You might change locations, but don't ever lose your imagination. And that don't mean you go around talking about spaceships and aliens all day. Imagination locations are not all about outer space. Your own daddy's got an imagination location with all that *boom-boom-bip* music going on up there. Ain't nobody got time for outer space in Harlem, Starfleet. And I sure wasn't thinking about it when I was a little boy."

"But what about Sputnik One, Granddaddy? That was when you were a teenager."

"The Russians sent that satellite up in space. It had nothing to do with a Negro boy like me up in Harlem."

"But you wanted to be an astronaut."

"No, I didn't. I wanted to build cars, Ebony. I learned how to fix 'em first and became real good at it. Wasn't thinking about no outer space till I got to Marshall, baby. All this planning and math and engineering work that went into rockets . . . It wasn't something I saw on TV. And just because we were a few Negroes working down here at the space center, black folks thought we were gonna make it to the moon. No siree! We were just the nuts-and-bolts guys, not the ones they were sending into orbit. And they let us know that as soon as we walked in—no astronaut pipe dreams for us! And I didn't even think that a black man could make it to the moon until Nichelle Nichols showed up on *Star Trek* as Uhura." He chuckles again. "Fine as she was. Boy, I sure wish that was me and not that playa Captain Kirk!"

"Granddaddy!"

"Sorry, baby. Point is, my dreams of making it onto a spaceship were as real as Sun Ra's Arkestra with all those outer space costumes and sounds. Sun Ra wanted us to know how outer space sounds, feels, and even looks. But these are just stories, baby. Like *Star Trek* and comic books. Like the stuff my own nana used to tell me when I was a little boy—her Brer Rabbit and Brer Fox stories from 'Bama. We had some good times on the *Uhura*. But you're in Harlem now. Got plenty of stuff happening out there on those streets to keep your imagination location wide-open. Don't go trying to change anything, okay? Remember the Prime Directive, Starfleet."

I twirl my finger around the spiraling telephone cord over and over again. "What about the cadet and her captain? And the evil Sonic King with the loudest, baddest, mind-controllest sound in the entire galaxy? And the Mothership *Uhura*?"

"They're still there, Ebony. Right in your imagination

location. And that's where they should stay. You tuck 'em in for a little while so you can do what you gotta do in this real world. You think I go around talking about the *Uhura* and the Sonic King at the space center? No sir. Go on, now. Next time I see you, I want you to teach me that breaking-bones dance. Don't care if I lose my mind so long as I can shake my behind!" He laughs and coughs, laughs and coughs some more.

"Cadet E-Grace to Captain Fleet. Do you copy?" I say real quiet, remembering that the real Captain Fleet is unconscious under the Sonic King's radio tower. The real Captain Fleet wouldn't tell me to "go on now."

"Copy, Cadet. Now I wired some money to your father and he should get it today. I wanna see you before the summer's out. Your momma was against it. But it's my money, and you're my only grandbaby. Tell Julius to get you a round-trip ticket to Huntsville. Stay the weekend, then go back to your daddy soon after. Your mother won't admit that she wants to see you, too. Would rather keep you away from me." Granddaddy coughs again. "Anyway. I'll see you in a bit, Starfleet. Live long and prosper. Go on now."

"Granddaddy?"

There's a click and then the sound of the dial tone, like the sound of the great black void—empty and forever. I hold the receiver to my ear until that other sound comes on—the one like a robot duck. Then I hang up.

I jump when I turn to see Daddy sitting at the kitchen table eating from a paper plate. He licks his fingers before he says, "You should run out there and get a plate from Ms. Fuller across the street. She put her whole soul into this food. And get an extra heap of 'tato salad for your daddy."

"I'm going back home. Granddaddy wired you some

money. So you can wire me back to Huntsville, too," I say, as plain and cold as ice water.

"You're not getting wired to anywhere," he says in between bites of his chicken leg. "Your momma don't want you down there just yet. Says she needs you to stay till she's good and ready. Makes no sense for you to go down for just a weekend."

"Why not? My granddaddy say I could come, and it's his money," I whine. "And his house!"

"Well, he ain't the one gonna be lookin' out for you when you're down there. Your momma is. And if she says she ain't ready, then she ain't ready. I don't care how much money your grandfather sends." He says this like the mean king that he's supposed to be.

I am as quiet as 'Bama skies. Only for a little bit. "He's my granddaddy. If he say he wanna see me, then he has the right to," I say, just as quietly.

Daddy finishes chewing his food, wipes his mouth with a napkin, leans back in his chair, and glares at me with eyes I've never really seen before. "And I'm your *daddy*. If I say you ain't going nowhere, then I have the right to."

Something heavy sinks deep in my belly. Not food. Nothing good, really. Maybe lost spacecraft swallowed by a black hole. Maybe the sun being swallowed by the horizon. It makes my soul dull. Nothing shines right now. I try to say something but even my words are in my father's prison. But Daddy keeps on talking as if he didn't just put a padlock on a door and locked me in a cold, dark room.

"Go on out there and get you a plate. Ms. Fuller knows who you are. She's Diane's grandmother. There's some music, some kids, some food. You'll be fine." He finishes his meal, throws the paper plate and bones into the trash, washes his hands in the sink, and leaves the kitchen.

It's not until then that I realize how hot it is. The heat presses down on me, and I wipe the sweat off my forehead. This isn't like 'Bama heat. It's bigger, louder even. It's not like a warm, steady breath. It shouts, even in this small, dark, dusty kitchen. Maybe this Harlem heat is the Sonic Boom's hot breath, like exhaust fumes from rocket ships.

"Come on, Broomstick. Don't make me tell you again. Get on out."

Reluctantly, I follow Daddy out of the brownstone. There's a white envelope sticking out of his back pocket. As he walks to the front door, the envelope rides up until it finally slips out without him noticing. He leaves out the front door without looking back, so I rush over to pick it up. Inside is a slip that says "Western Union." I've seen the commercials on TV. It's the fastest way to send money.

I open the envelope wider and see cash. Six fifty-dollar bills! I know it's the money Granddaddy sent for my airplane tickets to Huntsville—the airplane tickets that Daddy said he wasn't going to buy. I fold the envelope and tuck it deep into my jeans pocket and make sure it doesn't crawl out the way it did from Daddy's pocket.

By the time we're outside, I realize that Granddaddy was talking all that gibberish because of the Sonic Boom. It's taken over his mind! If I forget about the *Uhura*, then I'll forget all about Captain Fleet, and he'll just be stuck there under Planet Boom Box's radio tower forever. And I won't even be Cadet E-Grace Starfleet anymore because there won't even be a *Uhura* or a Planet Boom Box or a Sonic King. That whole universe beyond Andromeda will just explode into nothing.

But then I remember how, in the movie, Spock became friends with Admiral Kirk again. Kirk went back to save his friend, and because of that, Spock started remembering. "I'm coming for you, Captain Fleet!" I yell out into the street with all the kids running around and multiplying like Tribbles.

"Ebony-Grace!" Daddy snaps. "You're gonna have to stop that nonsense. You see all these kids out here? Go play with them. Leave your imaginary friend alone."

I follow him. "I need to go with you into the shop," I say.

"What for?" he asks.

"I need to build a rocket ship and launch it into space."

"I need you to stay out here. Shop ain't no place for kids today. And you need to build yourself a crew instead. Go and make some friends."

I look ahead at the entrance to the shop where there's even a longer line now, and see one of the minions running in. "But what about Calvin and them? I know they're in the junkyard."

"All right then," he says, turning to me and looking down. "You wanna get smart? The junkyard is no place for young ladies. Now, where's Bianca and her little double-Dutch crew? Go play with them. I can't deal with this right now, Broomstick. Got every Tom, Dick, and Harry up in here trying to sell what little they could find. It's the Fourth of July, they got the day off, and everybody's trying to make rent this month. Gotta let them down easy. You don't wanna be around for that."

I glance at the line of people—some with bags packed with stuff, others holding in their arms old books, clothes, car parts, and there's even a pair of boys I've never seen before hauling a whole fireplace. "Daddy, I want that fireplace," I say as he starts to walk away, but he doesn't hear me. I wonder if it could actually hold a fire even if it's not attached to a wall. I could lay it on its back and use it as a launching pad.

When I try to catch up to Daddy to make another request

for a toolbox and some broken radios, I spot the boy in the green shirt—Pablo Jupiter. He's standing at the edge of the sidewalk outside the shop kicking a fire hydrant as if trying to make it spew out flying water.

I walk over to him and say with a big smile, "Doesn't it look like R2-D2?" But then I remember that this is No Joke City and that he's really a nefarious minion and that the doors to my imagination location are supposed to be closed. I wipe the smile from my face.

But he smiles with big white teeth and deep dimples. "It does look like R2-D2. Except, I'd call him . . . FT-125."

I let my whole face smile, but I push down my soulshine because the doors to my imagination location are still a little bit closed. "FT-125? That's outta sight."

"Yeah. FT for Fire Trooper and one-two-five for 125th Street. Even though I'm from the Bronx, I gotta rap rhymes about Harlem now. In the Bronx, the Fire Troopers were like Storm Troopers because of all the burning buildings."

I swallow hard and say, "I don't call this Harlem or New York City. It's No Joke City, because . . . "

"There's nothing funny about this city, right?"

I'm real quiet as I stare at Pablo Jupiter, trying really hard not to smile. The Afro on his head looks like the surface of the moon with its curls like craters. But it's his smile that makes his whole face shine. He's digging up a piece of broken concrete with the tip of his dirty sneaker. "Yeah," I say even quieter. "So you think the Genesis Device can work here?"

He looks up at me. "But we ain't all dead. I mean, things are still alive. Maybe the Bronx. But still . . . "

"The Prime Directive. We can't really mess with the stuff that's already here, right?"

He stops digging at the concrete and turns all the way to

me, sticking the tips of his fingers into his jeans. "Yeah, *we* can. It's our planet, right. We're not aliens."

"Yes, you are. I'm not."

"What planet are you from, then?"

"Planet . . . " I have to step into my imagination location now because I've never ever thought about this question. "Earth. Planet Earth."

"This *is* Planet Earth."

"No. I already told you. It's Planet No Joke City."

"Okay then. What are you doing on Planet No Joke City? *You're* the alien."

"Yeah, well, I've been taken prisoner by King Sirius Julius and his nefarious minions. And you're one of them."

"A nefarious *what*?"

"Minion. Nefarious minion."

He shakes his head. "I'm not a nefarious minion. I'm one of the good guys. I'm a rebel. The rebel lord."

"So you're the leader of the rebellion?" I step closer to him, eyes wide.

He nods. "I'm going to take down the king. King . . . what again?"

"King Sirius Julius, like the bright star in the sky. But he's also very serious, too."

He looks around and spots my daddy who's talking to the first person on the line—a man holding out a cardboard box of spoons, forks, and knives. I can't tell from here if they're like Nana's fancy silver or just the cheap stuff, as Momma would say.

"But he's a good king," Pablo Jupiter says. "Look at all those people. He helps them out sometimes. I know he's helping Bianca's grandmother out by letting her stay there."

I shrug and say, "I must go back to my home planet. But

I have to save my captain first—Captain Fleet of the Mothership *Uhura*. Will you help me?"

"Hey, Ice Cream Sandwich!" someone yells, and it echoes all throughout the block and maybe even Harlem, too. I look up and of course it's Mint Chocolate Chip Monique's gigantic mouth.

"Is that what you go by?" Pablo Jupiter asks.

"Ebony-Grace Norfleet Freeman. But really, I'm Cadet E-Grace Starfleet of the Mothership *Uhura*," I say, holding out my hand to shake his. "Pleased to make your acquaintance."

"Nuh-uh! You can't be making deals with the enemy, Outer Space Ebony-Grace!" Rum Raisin Rhonda calls out as they all cross the street headed toward me and Pablo.

But he shakes my hand anyway. "E-Grace Starfleet of the Mothership . . . It's a rocket to Mars but it ain't no trip," he says as cool as a midnight breeze. He steps away, glaring at the 9 Flavas as they start to surround us.

"You better get away from her, Pablo Jupiter. We know you were asking her about our moves!" Coconut Collette says.

"We already won, Nine Flavas!" he says while walking backward to Daddy's shop. "Genesis Ten ain't clucking with no hens. We're the roosters, storm troopers, brand-name boosters, b-ball hoopsters, slam dunk in your face. I'll see you in outta space, Ebony-Grace!"

The 9 Flavas break out into a bunch of "oooohs!"

"You like PJ?" Monique asks.

Then they all start yelling with their gibberish at the same time.

I hold up my fists and send out protective laser beams. "Pew! Pew!"

But Bianca grabs one of my arms and flings it down. She only stares at me while Monique blurts out, "You betta stay away from Pablo Jupiter. That's Bianca's man. And plus, he's the enemy. You're on our team, Ice Cream Sandwich."

Bianca and I just stare at each other for a long, whole minute before she says, "I thought you were gonna help me."

"I thought you were gonna help *me*," I say to her face.

"I've *been* helping you! You just can't see it!" she yells.

All her friends say "Mm-hmm" and "You-know-it!" and "Got that right" and "Tell her, Bianca!"

I stand back to take a good look at this 9 Flavas Crew. For a moment, I start to see them as a real crew. There's a captain, all right, and it's Mint Chocolate Chip Monique. Then I realize that Butter Pecan Bianca has been *her* First Officer all along. Mango Megan and Strawberry Stacey are untangling the telephone cord. Rum Raisin Rhonda and Coconut Collette are showing Pistachio Paula how to do something with her hands—a robot dance move or something. Cookies and Cream Christine is helping Vanilla Fudge Vanessa tie her sneaker laces.

Maybe they're working together like a real crew.

And then, in the distance, in front of the auto shop, something catches my eye. The line of people has disappeared, and now Daddy is crouched down behind a streetlamp with a screwdriver in hand. A group of other men stand and crouch down behind him as if they're about to somehow take down that tall streetlamp with just a screwdriver.

All the 9 Flavas turn around to see what I'm staring at.

"Aww, yeah!" Monique blurts out. "Your daddy is about to hook up the sound system."

"Sound system?" I whisper to myself.

Then, Rum Raisin Rhonda steps in front of her and yells, "Hey, Mr. DJ Jule Thief! Make sure you pump up the bass nice and loud!"

"Pump up the bass nice and loud?" I repeat real quietly.

Daddy looks over at us and gives us a thumbs-up.

"DJ Jule Thief?" I ask.

"Uh-huh," Monique says. "Don't you know your daddy's other name?"

I can only shake my head. I can't even close my mouth right to make any words come out.

Bianca adds, "He's not a famous DJ like Kool Herc or Grandmaster Flash or Afrika Bambaataa. But he got all the equipment plus lots of records, so he does our block parties. See? You don't know nothing, Ebony-Grace."

The 9 Flavas step away from me as I stand there, watching Daddy and his friends open the bottom of the streetlamp revealing a tangle of colorful wires. Other men are bringing in tables and boxes that look like the control boards on the *Uhura*. Daddy tells the men where to put things as he pulls out a bunch of wires—blue, red, yellow, and green wires. Someone hands him pliers. The men put more control board machines on the table, and another man unravels long black wires from those machines and hands them over to Daddy, who starts disconnecting and reconnecting wires like Han Solo when he tried to hotwire the door to the Endor shield generator bunker. Daddy connects a red wire to a black one and suddenly a few sparks fly and then the speakers behind me start to hum and pop.

Behind me, I hear the Flavas cheering, "Aw yeah! DJ Jule Thief on the wheels of steel!"

Then, something washes over me like storm winds, and my head starts to spin like Granddaddy's records on a turntable. I close my eyes and take a deep breath so I'm not knocked off my feet by what I'm seeing and hearing. Then, all I can manage to say out loud is "It's the Sonic King!"

CHAPTER
30

I got you now, Starfleet!
Have you crawling to my feet.
The Sonic Boom has sealed your doom.
Come on now, E-Grace! Hear that bass
all up in your ace. Gonna make you dance
up in this space. Let go of that soul, let
the music take control. Move to the beat, Starfleet.
Shake your junk and feel the funk. Ha!
Get down, get down. Dip, trip, shake your
hips. Hop, stop, pop, and lock.
Make your body rock!

Cadet E-Grace Starfleet to Captain Fleet: Do you copy?

Cadet E-Grace Starfleet to Captain Fleet . . .

I've been compromised, Captain Fleet. The *Uhura* is unmanned and I've been teleported by the force field Sonic Boom and I cannot escape!

Location: Planet Boom Box.

Captor: The Sonic King.

Do you copy, Captain Fleet?

King Sirius Julius and Planet No Joke City were carbon *copies* of the Sonic King and Planet Boom Box. There's been a malfunction with the transporter caused by an ionic storm.

This is a mirror universe, Captain. No Joke City *is* Planet Boom Box! King Sirius Julius is the Sonic King!

The Sonic Boom is all around me, Captain Fleet. It hovers over the planet like a gigantic bubble floating over Momma's Calgon bath. And yes, it *is* the Atomic Sonic Boom—louder and prouder than James Brown at a Black Panther rally. That's what you would say, Granddaddy. As loud as a Hendrix guitar solo, yessir! As proud as Aretha's big, bellowing voice singing R-E-S-P-E-C-T. Sure is! Bass so low you can't get under it. Lemme say it again. So low you can't get under it! And volume so high you can't get over it. Say what now? So high you can't get over it!

Tiny sound bubbles float out of the Sonic King's mega speakers and explode like fireworks all over the block. You should see it, Captain Fleet. The *boom*, the *bip*, the *bap*, the *ratatat* combined with the *crack-crack-pop-pop* and you don't stop, body-rock shock waves all over the ground making everybody get down. So I tap my feet and bop my head even though I don't want to, really.

I can't lose control. I can't lose my soul.

The Sonic King shouts into a mic and everybody calls him DJ Jule Thief. He says my name over the music for the whole block to hear. "Shout out to my baby girl, Ebony-Grace!"

Then, he scratches the record and the *boom-bip-bap-ratatat* sounds go backward, sideways, and inside out. And out comes the "Planet Rock" and Soul Sonic Force and "Jam On It" like shooting stars, meteors, and asteroids landing on the buildings and sidewalks and right on the people's heads. They all lose control—swinging their arms and kicking their legs and moving their hips—dippin' and trippin'.

They gather around the Sonic King like moths to the lantern that sits out on our porch at night down in Huntsville.

They cheer him on, pumping their fists in the air like Muhammad Ali fighting the Sonic Boom itself. They call out names like Fab 5 Freddy, Afrika Bambaataa, Grandmaster Flash, Whodini, the Sugar Hill Gang, Warp 9, and Run-DMC.

"DJ Jule Thief, can you play 'Planet Rock' one mo' time?" Diva Diane yells out from behind the food table across the street.

I don't leave Daddy's front gate. Even though it's not locked, I still feel like I'm stuck here, that if I try to step out, there'd be a greater, more powerful force to keep me even more trapped, more imprisoned, more frozen in this ice-cold place. Still, a little drop of the Sonic Boom gets to my foot and I tap it against the ground. *Tap, boom-boom, tap.* A little of it lands on my head and I bop. I snap my fingers once until I spot Pablo Jupiter. He's waving at me to come over. I don't dare move because directly across from him, in front of another building, is Bianca Pluto staring at him, then she turns to me. She starts to walk over. A few of the ice cream flavors follow her. But it's Mint Chocolate Chip Monique who opens up her big mouth first.

"Your daddy is deejaying, so you should come out here and dance. He just gave you a shout-out over the mic, so the least you could do is show him some of your moves, Outta Space Ebony-Grace." She says this with her arms crossed as if this invitation were a threat.

"I can't. I'm a prisoner," I say.

"You're a *what*?" Rum Raisin Rhonda asks.

"She said she's a *prisoner*," Monique answers for me. "You don't know nothing about prison. I gotta cousin in prison. Ain't nobody stopping you from coming out that gate except your own doggone self."

Bianca is about to say something but a louder and newer sound makes everybody freeze and turn toward the Sonic King—that scratching sound that makes everything go backward, sideways, and inside out again.

"Come on, party people, crowd around!" Daddy says into the microphone with a deeper voice I've never heard him use before. "Crowd around, party people, come on!"

Then everybody starts clapping to a beat and Daddy repeats his rap again. "Come on, party people, crowd around. Crowd around, party people, come on!"

Bianca and the rest of the ice cream flavors leave me behind as they follow the king's orders. Everyone is hypnotized by his Sonic Boom voice and that rap and that clap. Then he stops. It's suddenly quieter than it's ever been on this block.

"Are y'all havin' a good time?" the Sonic King asks, his voice echoes over the buildings.

Everyone cheers, breaking the silence.

"All right now. So we're gettin' ready for this contest. There's a new and improved grand prize: two hundred and fifty bucks and a chance to compete at the world-famous Apollo Theater along with the Rock Steady Crew, and a new kid on the scene, Harlem's own Doug E. Fresh, the human beatbox."

Everyone loses their minds. This isn't like with the Sonic Boom music. They cheer and jump up and down as if every single person on this block had just won the jackpot after playing the numbers.

"So One-Two-Six got two crews competing," Daddy continues.

I step outside of the gate because this is the battle the

9 Flavas were talking about. This is the moment they've been practicing for and I've been messing it up for them all this time.

"Y'all gotta come correct if y'all gonna represent my block. Born and raised in this hood so don't make us look bad now," the Sonic King adds. "Okay, who we got here today?"

Some people in the crowd surrounding Daddy start shouting, "Genesis Ten!"

I watch as Pablo Jupiter rushes to find the rest of the nefarious minions. He gathers about five of them, but Calvin is nowhere in sight.

"We got the Nine Flavas Crew over here, DJ Jule Thief!" Diane shouts as I watch Monique round up her team. "They're going up against Genesis Ten!"

But Daddy ignores Diane and starts calling over Pablo Jupiter and them as the crowd parts to make way for their cardboards. They all pose with their arms folded across their chests, and some crouch down on the ground as if they're ready to do karate with Bruce Lee.

"All right now," the Sonic King says. "It's Genesis Five over here. Ladies, lemme hear you scream!"

"Five?" some of the 9 Flavas say out loud, rolling their necks and looking over at Pablo Jupiter.

All the girls in the crowd scream just like the Sonic King ordered. Everybody looks around. They're Genesis Ten. There are ten of them, not five.

But the crowd parts in the other direction and in comes Calvin and four of the other nefarious minions. Everybody claps and cheers them on as they drag an even bigger cardboard in front of the Sonic King's control boards. Calvin walks over to the Sonic King and whispers something in his ear.

"All right now," Daddy says again. "We got Cold-Crush Calvin . . . "

The crowd claps and cheers some more.

"And the Fresh Four! That's Cold-Crush Calvin and the Fresh Four! A new team on the scene!"

Pablo Jupiter and his crew don't make a move. But Bianca, Monique, Rhonda, and Diane are trying to get Daddy's attention.

"Mr. Freeman, *they* were supposed to be the other team! All of them!" Diane yells out pointing toward Monique and Bianca. But people only glance at her until she walks up to Daddy and tries to grab the microphone from him. Bianca and Monique are right behind her.

The microphone screeches, and everyone covers their ears until it stops. I keep my hands over mine because if the loud music is the Atomic Sonic Boom, then this screaming sound is the *Mega* Atomic Sonic Boom. I'm sure it's done something to my brain at this point, as loud as it was.

Daddy puts the microphone behind him so no one could hear his conversation with Diane and them. And that's when I decide to step out of the gate and get closer to the very top of the radio tower on Planet Boom Box—the source of the Sonic Boom. I ease my way through the crowd until I get to the Sonic King, and I can't help but stare at his control boards with its spinning records and knobs and buttons and blinking lights.

"But, Mr. Freeman, they purposely split up just so they could compete against one another and whoever ends up winning, they'll still get the prize. That's not fair!" Diane says.

"Y'all just gonna have to wait for the double-Dutch

contest. We'll have it right after the boys finish," the Sonic King says.

"But we didn't sign up for no double-Dutch contest. We wanna break-dance like Calvin and 'em. And we wanna get on the mic, too!" Monique adds.

"Mr. Freeman, I could rhyme better than all of 'em," Bianca says.

Daddy puts his hand up while shaking his head. "The contest is for only two crews. They got their two crews. Now, wait for the double-Dutch teams. The girls from 127th are headed over here. There's even a bunch coming down from the Bronx and the East Side. No need to compete with the boys."

Just as he says this, the crowd behind us starts to get impatient and they call out, "Genesis Five," and "Cold-Crush Calvin."

Before Diane, Monique, and Bianca start arguing with Daddy again, he gets back on the mic to start the contest. "First up: Genesis Five. We got a request for a song off the *Breakin'* soundtrack. Let's go!"

The Sonic King ignores the 9 Flavas Crew even as more of them come up to his control boards arguing that they should be the ones battling Genesis Ten and how Calvin and them purposely broke up their crew just to keep the girls out of the contest. But the Sonic King isn't hearing any of it, neither are the people standing around waiting for the battle to get started.

The music comes on at full blast and I cover my ears again. We're all pushed out of the way so the boys can do their thing. I follow Bianca and the ice cream flavors as they stomp down the block and away from the crowd. Bianca is pouting. Monique is cursing so much that if my momma could hear her now, she would wash her mouth out with Octagon soap.

"That's not fair!" Bianca blurts out.

And at the same moment the crowd cheers even louder. I could see Calvin's legs spinning around like a helicopter's rotor blades.

"Why won't he let you dance like the nefarious—" I start to ask. "I mean, like the boys?"

"Don't you know? That's *your* father," Monique says. "He don't want us doing what the boys do. He just thinks we're only good at double-Dutch."

"We're good at double-Dutch *and* breakin' *and* rappin'!" Rhonda says. "That's way more than what Calvin and Pablo could do."

"What are they gonna do with that money, anyway?" Monique continues. "They don't need no Dapper Dan outfits. But we gotta look fly."

"And ain't nothing on that flyer that said an all-girl crew can't compete at the Apollo Theater. We don't have to mix in with boys just so they could take us seriously," Bianca says.

Her voice cracks, as if her whole soul were about to break apart into a thousand pieces. That's what happened to one of Granddaddy's records when I accidentally stepped on it. She sits on the dirty curb, even with its broken glass and garbage, and puts her head down on her knees. A dark cloud hovers over her. Her soulshine—the one that lit up bright when she was break dancing and rapping against Pablo Jupiter—is now dull, dark, and almost gone.

I sit next to her.

She scoots away from me.

"Leave her alone, Ice Cream Sandwich!" Rhonda calls out.

"That's my friend!" I call back.

"Then *do* something! That's your father and he's not being fair!" Monique says. Then, she starts counting off on her fingers and rolling her neck with each word. "You can't jump double-Dutch. You can't dance. You can't rap. The least you could do is get your daddy to let us battle those stupid-head boys!"

"You can't tell me what to do!" I yell at her. But after two seconds, I get up and stomp over to the Sonic King. I can hear the ice cream flavors walking behind me and talking over the music.

"What she think she gonna do?"

"Nothing. She's a daddy's girl."

"If she sticks up for us, you think we should make her the tenth flava?"

"She gotta learn how to dance first."

"At least learn to turn a rope."

"And jump, too."

"And rhyme."

"Yep."

"Don't you think that's asking too much?"

"She is country, you know."

"Well, she's in Harlem now."

"I know that's right."

"Uh-huh."

I stop suddenly and the 9 Flavas almost all bump into me. I turn around and look each one in the eye. "Okay," I say. "I have a plan. If you want me to help, then we have to strategize. We have to take down the king."

"Here we go again," Monique says, crossing her arms and rolling her eyes.

Bianca sighs. "What king, Ebony?"

"The Sonic King. He controls all the loud *boom-bip-*

bap-ratatat sounds in the entire galaxy! The meanest, loudest, mind-controllest sound in the whole universe. He sends out a Sonic Boom to the planets and takes over all the aliens' minds so he could control everything!"

"Ice Cream Sandwich!" Rhonda calls out. "Stay off them drugs."

"Now is not the time for those silly stories, Ebony," Bianca says, low enough for the others not to hear. I see sadness in her eyes, like blurry stars behind cloudy Huntsville skies.

So I step closer to her and ask, "Do you trust me, Bianca *Pluto?*"

"No. Not if you're calling me Bianca Pluto."

"I thought that was your rapping name," I say.

"It is. When I'm rapping. But when you call me that, I know you're gonna wanna take me to Mars or something."

"I'm gonna distract the king and all the nefarious minions. And when they're all not looking, the Nine Flavas can start doing their breaking-bones dance," I say. "It's like how Admiral Kirk tricked Kruge into going to the Genesis Planet in the movie. Remember?" Without waiting to hear what she thinks, I march up to the crowd, demand that they get out of our way, step over one of the Genesis Tens-now-Fives doing his dance moves on the cardboard, and walk straight up to the Sonic King even as the Sonic Boom pulses so hard, it reaches my bones.

I inhale, put my hands on my hips, and as regular ol' Ebony-Grace Norfleet Freeman, I yell, "Daddy, my friends wanna do that breaking-bones dance and win this contest! They need the money to get their outfits made by Dapper Dan for the contest at the Apollo Theater!"

He only waves me away, holding headphones to his ear and changing the record on his control board. I watch how he places his fingers on the black, shiny round disc, pulls it back, moves it forward a little bit, and pulls it back some more as the sound changes from a screech to a bass to a boom-boom, then back to a bass and a screech over and over again. I can feel the crowd, the block, and maybe even the whole city swaying and rocking to the beat.

The man in the song sings "Planet Rock" as everybody repeats each word with him. I am so small against this big, big sound. It pounds, swirls, and blows past me in a heavy wave as wide and deep as outer space.

I turn to see the boys moving their bodies to the beat. Every part of them pops and locks like a machine, like an engine, like a robot. I watch everybody's faces like a hundred suns gleaming bright. This isn't like church where my nana's friends let go of their bodies to make way for the Holy Spirit, as the pastor would say. This isn't like when Mrs. Headley and Mrs. Turner shimmy their shoulders and throw their heads back and put their hands up in the air saying, "Yes, Lord!" This isn't because of Momma's Jesus.

This breaking-bones dance, this pounding bass, these faces like a hundred suns as they clap and groove and make their bodies move is because of something bigger than this little planet. This sound, this music really did come from another world, and if what that man on the song is saying is right, then this Sonic Boom is really from a place called Planet Rock.

The Sonic Boom does make you lose all control. And the man talking over the song calls it the Soul Sonic Force.

One of the cardboard boxes on the ground is empty. Pablo Jupiter and his crew are doing a two-step dance like The Commodores or The Jackson 5, kicking out side to side and clapping their hands to the beat. No one is doing the breaking-bones dance on the cardboard. So I take my chance.

I look back over at the brown, rectangular cardboard—it's dirty and beat-up as if it'd been trampled over by every single person who lives in No Joke City. But it's for dancing, not for walking over. Then suddenly, the tears and footprints and stains start to morph into whirling black holes, like dark storms on the surface of a far-flung planet. The storms spin to the beat of the music, and in no time at all, the cardboard becomes a giant black void speckled with stars and tiny Milky Ways.

In the distance is a Planet Boom Box with its beaming radio tower bouncing and spinning to the music. It pulses like a heartbeat and before I even say Planet Boom Box, I spot the Sonic King holding out his scepter toward me as a giant iridescent bubble aims straight for me. It blows up in my face and out comes the loudest mind-controllest sound in the entire galaxy.

I lose all control and count down to the beat ready to launch: 5, 4, 3 . . .

The man on the song raps over the beat, "So twist and turn, then you let your body slide and glide / You got the body rock and pop, bounce and pounce . . . "

I hop right onto the cardboard, that becomes the galaxy, and I fall and fall and fall like Luke Skywalker falling through those giant shafts after fighting with his own daddy, Darth Vader, in Cloud City. Every time I think I land on something, I keep falling again. Atmospheric pressure pulls and pushes me in different directions as my arms and legs flail about and the Sonic Boom keeps pounding its mind-controlling beat into my ears and throughout my body. Still, I don't scream. I have to be strong so I can help the 9 Flavas. *I'm coming for you, Bianca Pluto!* Then, finally, I land on the surface of Planet Boom Box.

Gonna make you dance up in this space!

I am a meteor spinning toward Planet Earth.

I am R2-D2 and C-3PO moving about like hands on a clock—tick-tick-tick-tock.

I bend my arms and bop my head and pop and lock my bones like Michael's dancing machine and they don't even break. I let the groove take over my whole soul and ride on Planet Boom Box until it reaches the end of the galaxy. This Sonic Boom is what the spinning universe sounds like.

But it comes to a stop and everything is like it was in the very beginning—quiet, like floating in zero gravity.

"Come on, Broomstick," the Sonic King says over the microphone. "You can't just come in and bust up the contest like that!"

Everyone is booing me. The nefarious minions are shouting in my face, telling me to get out of the way. Their gibberish words are like laser beams attacking the *Uhura*. I can't even activate the deflector shields because I'm out of breath and my heart is racing.

"That's not what you were supposed to do, Ebony-Grace!" Monique shouts.

"You can't dance, Ice Cream Sandwich!" says Rhonda.

"You messed up the whole contest!" Vanessa yells.

"Why'd you do that for, Ebony?" Bianca asks, stepping closer. "*We* were supposed to dance. You didn't even practice. Why do you always want attention?"

"It was a distraction. You were supposed to jump in and do *your* moves!" I say.

Bianca clenches her fists and tightens her jaw as if she's ready to punch me.

"Hey now!" Daddy says. "Y'all take that somewhere else. Everybody's over here having a good time. Now don't mess that up, girls."

I watch as Bianca stomps away and the rest of her friends roll their eyes at me, stick out their tongues, or don't even look my way.

Everything continues to swirl around me as if I'm invisible, as if I'm an alien.

"All right, y'all. I think we gotta tie," Daddy says on the mic. "We gotta fifty-fifty split between the Genesis Five and Cold-Crush Calvin and the Fresh Four!"

Everyone claps and cheers. I look toward where the 9 Flavas are standing at the edge of the crowd near the red-and-white-checkered food table. I can't hear their words as they pout and point with anger spread across all their faces. Bianca sits on the curb again with her chin in her hands. She glances at me and shakes her head. I look down at my feet.

"Beam me up, Captain Fleet," I whisper against the blasting music again. This time, a robotic voice sings "Jam On it" and it sounds as if the Sonic King's Funkazoids are making fun of me from the control boards.

"That's not fair," someone says as they brush past me.

It's Pablo Jupiter, pouting and looking back at Calvin and them as if they'd just betrayed him. He walks toward Daddy's auto repair shop.

I look back at Bianca again, who isn't even looking my way. Then back at Pablo Jupiter who is walking away. So, like I'm being pulled by a tractor beam, I follow the boy who has the wide and tall doors to his imagination location flung open to let in all the dancing stars and bouncing planets and soaring rocket ships.

CHAPTER
31

"Hold up, now," I say, chasing after Pablo. "What happened over there? Didn't you all win?" His face is sweaty and he looks meaner than when I first met him. He doesn't say anything as we both head over to Daddy's shop where some men are sitting around a small table playing a card game.

"You ever been to the junkyard?" I ask as I try to keep up with his furious pace.

His face calms. "Yeah. That's where we practice."

"So you know there's enough junk to build new stuff. Maybe a . . . Genesis Device."

We reach the shop and he turns to look at me. "I really wanted to battle Bianca Pluto. She's good. It wasn't fair that Calvin took over the whole contest."

"So why didn't you stop him?"

"Who's that king you said he was working for?" he asks.

I smile. "King Sirius Julius. But it turns out that he's really the Sonic King." I turn to point to my daddy who has on his headphones now and is switching a record on his control boards. "He controls everything. He won't even let me save Captain Fleet."

"You think Bianca will let me join their crew?" he asks.

I turn back to look at the 9 Flavas. They've walked over to Calvin and them now, and they look like they're arguing. Diane is trying to break it up, but Monique and Rhonda are the angriest of them all. They point and roll their necks in

Calvin's face. "I don't think they're gonna want you in their crew, Pablo Jupiter. Why don't we form our own crew?"

"You can't dance, Ebony-Grace," he says, as plain as Granddaddy's Saltine crackers.

"No," I say. "Not *that* kinda crew. A real crew on a space mission. We need to get outta here, Pablo Jupiter. Either we build another spacecraft, or . . . plant a Genesis Device on Planet . . . Junkyard! Yeah, that's it. Planet Junkyard!" I smile because I've just created a whole new adventure in just a few seconds exactly like how Granddaddy would.

Pablo thinks for a second. Then he says, "Is there any room for break dancing on the spacecraft?"

"Only if it's to defeat the Sonic King," I say. "You'll make him think you're break-dancing, but it'll only be to trick him so you could take out his shield generator and destroy his warp drive."

I motion for him to follow me into the shop where it almost feels like an oven. The lights are turned off in the small space and it smells of engine oil, rusted metal, and sweat.

"Julius ain't got no cash in the shop, so y'all ain't gonna find nothing in there," a man shouts into the shop from outside.

As he says this, I tap my pocket to make sure Granddaddy's cash is still there. I won't need any of Daddy's money anyway.

We head straight for a narrow door at the back of the shop where Daddy throws all the broken, junky stuff he buys from people. I look for that fireplace those two boys were trying to sell him, but instead I spot the old refrigerator that's been there since I was nine. A pile of car doors are stacked against the rusty tin gate that separates the yard from the next building's yard, which has overgrown trees and shrubs making it look almost like Alabama.

"Everything here is dead. It could use a Genesis Device," I say.

"No way," Pablo says. "Everything here is still alive. People who don't know always say these neighborhoods are dead, but we're still here, still living. You know what I mean?"

"That's not really living, then, if everything around you is broken. Even the music is broken, and everybody does this breaking-bones dance."

"Nuh-uh. There's nothing broken about breakin'," he says, and starts to dance like a robot. "We just fix it up and it becomes something new and different. Nobody dances like this where you're from? I know they do the Electric Boogaloo in California."

"I'm from a different planet, remember?"

"But even the planet you're from gots to have music," he says, still moving about like a robot.

I think of Granddaddy's funk music: James Brown, George Clinton's Parliament-Funkadelic; his soul music: Al Green and Curtis Mayfield; his jazz: Sun Ra and Miles Davis; and even his disco: Donna Summers and the BeeGees. None of them sound like the Sonic Boom. None of them are from a place called Planet Rock with its electric bass and voices that sound like they're coming from another dimension.

I spot an old record player in the far corner of the junkyard. It's the kind with a wooden base and horn that looks like a brass flower. I'd have to climb over a motorcycle, a rusty bathtub, and a chipping wooden door to get to it. Before I could come up with a strategy, Pablo was already ahead of me trying to get to it. He lugs it over his head as he leaps over all the junk to bring the record player back to me.

We meet in the middle of the junkyard where he places the chipped and rusted record player on the ground with the broken glass and small car parts. We both crouch down to examine it.

Pablo is standing now, stepping away from the old record player as if he's about to leave the junkyard any second.

I stand, too, so I can say this to his face. "This is not what a planet is supposed to look like, and this is not what a yard is supposed to look like. All these people bringing their junk to the Sonic King with their torn clothes and missing teeth and all he gives them back is even more broken music."

"You don't know what you're talking about, Outta Space Ebony-Grace. The Genesis Device can go downtown where all the rich folks are and their fancy buildings! They need to come up here where it's about to be live in '85. Watch. When the Genesis Ten makes it big, we're gonna take over all of Harlem."

"And do what? Be like the Sonic King and blast loud music in the streets in the middle of the day?" I put my whole neck and body into those words.

"Yeah," he says, and puts his whole neck and body into it, too, but he's making fun of me. Then he waves his hand at me while saying, "I don't need this, Ebony-Grace! I don't need to fix what ain't broken, rescue what don't need saving. I just need to rhyme. I need to dance. And DJ Jule Thief ain't playing fair."

"Not DJ Jule Thief. The Sonic King. And of course, he's not playing fair. He's playing favorites with his minions. And he doesn't want me to save the captain, so he's punishing me and the Nine Flavas. But I can get him to change his mind."

Someone opens the door leading to the junkyard from the shop. Daddy pokes his head out. "Broomstick, get on outta there!"

Pablo rushes ahead of me, but Daddy stops me at the doorway and glares down at me. "Ebony, did you happen'a find a white envelope back at the house? It must've fell out of my pocket."

I shake my head. "A white envelope? No," I say as sure as the sun, and rush past him to catch up with Pablo. "Hey, Pablo Jupiter. I can ask the Nine Flavas Crew to let you join them." I follow him out of the junkyard with Daddy still glaring at me.

Pablo stops right in the doorway leading out into the block party. He crosses his arms and says, "As long as I could still be Pablo Jupiter. Then yeah. I don't mind being with an all-girls crew."

Before I chase after him again to tell him my plan, Daddy grabs my arm. "You sure, Broomstick. It had the grand prize money for the contest. Was gonna be just fifty bucks, but I raised it to two fifty. I thought I'd do something nice for the kids on the block."

I pause. I was too deep in the fib now to turn back. That money wasn't supposed to be for the contest and it sure shouldn't be going to Calvin and his crew. That money was for me to visit Granddaddy. "I don't know what you're talking about, Daddy" is all I say before I rush behind Pablo, and into the block party with the music turned down low.

There's a lot of talk and commotion. People are confused about the contest having no prize. I catch bits of conversation.

"Man, Julius was running game on us!"

"DJ Jule Thief got a lot of nerve doing folks that way."

"Who does he think he is?"

"He thinks he runs this block, but he's got another thing coming."

The minions of Planet No Joke City are plotting to overthrow the Sonic King. And it is all because of me.

CHAPTER
32

When I was little, Granddaddy told me the story of Apollo 13. That mission was supposed to go back to the moon. Since NASA had already landed on the moon, they thought they could go back over and over again—easy as a plane ride from Huntsville to Harlem. But accidents happen. Plans change. An oxygen tank exploded and, thank goodness, the astronauts survived. No one ever thought the moon would be easy again though.

Granddaddy said it was the same year Momma left Alabama to live with her new husband back in Harlem. My daddy. I wasn't born yet, and Nana was alive and well in that house on Olde Stone Road. That warm April day in 1970, Granddaddy came home sad and disappointed. But the world celebrated when those astronauts landed back down to Earth in three parachutes, all in one piece.

"It was one small step for mankind just a year before, Starfleet, when Apollo 11 made it to the moon safe and sound. Then, all of a sudden, we were ten steps behind. I tell ya, baby girl, you know what I was thinking. Maybe I was responsible for a bolt or screw, one itty-bitty piece in that whole big puzzle called the Space Race," Granddaddy had said.

That day, Nana had gone out and Granddaddy had the house all to himself. So, he was going to fill it up with music.

This was what he did when he was alone. Granddaddy liked his funk music because it was "the new frontier," he said. New music was like a space shuttle rushing to reach the farthest edge of the galaxy. "You ever hear a sound so outta this world, Starfleet, it could launch you to the moon?" Granddaddy would ask.

The day before the Apollo 13 disaster, the Beatles broke up. Granddaddy had said that there'd be no more John, George, Paul, and Ringo singing "Don't Let Me Down" and "Let It Be." It was the end of slow, dripping hopeful music like molasses swirling at the bottom of a glass of sweet tea. So he blasted Sly and the Family Stone instead, with their "Everyday People" and "Dance to the Music."

"You shoulda seen me, Starfleet. I was getting on down! Groovin' and movin'. Lettin' it all hang out without your momma and Nana there. That's how those astronauts must feel up in the great big sky, higher than high, so close to the moon they could kiss it!" Granddaddy had said.

But I couldn't shake the thought of how something went wrong. One itty-bitty piece in that whole big puzzle could've taken the lives of those astronauts. And that itty-bitty piece was like a bass guitar in a Sly and the Family Stone song or Ringo's drum set in the Beatles.

The night of the Fourth of July block party, it rained Sonic Booms. Fireworks lit up the skies and no one seemed to be asleep. I curled up in my not-room and covered my ears and dreamed of spaceships and moon landings and galaxies.

Bianca and the ice cream flavors were nowhere around and I had lost Pablo Jupiter in the crowd. I ate a plate of Ms. Fuller's fried chicken and mac 'n' cheese all by myself on the stoop while Daddy and his minions tried to figure out what happened to that white envelope. Still, I don't say anything.

As night came close, Daddy stopped playing that boom-boom-bip music with its Planet Boom Box sounds. Some of Grand-daddy's favorite funk and soul music danced all throughout Harlem, making everything sway slowly like leaves in a soft summer breeze. Those songs wrapped around me like Nana's knit blankets. The Five Stairsteps telling me that things are gonna be easier; Bill Withers singing it's gonna be a lovely day; and Earth, Wind, and Fire asking about September. And I sure couldn't wait one more minute to be back in Alabama, in Huntsville, in that house on Olde Stone Road where Grand-daddy filled up the empty quiet spaces with stories and that same music—and even Momma, too, with her church gossip over the telephone, Jimmy Swaggart's songs about Baby Jesus on the television, and the warm smells of biscuits and memories of Nana.

CHAPTER
33

Two weeks after the block party, the 9 Flavas avoid me like cod liver oil. Diva Diane came by a few times, but Daddy got the hint that I didn't want her to babysit me anymore. He figured it would save him a few bucks, just as long as I didn't tell Momma, if I stayed home and watched cartoons. So that's exactly what I did. My imagination location was closed for business. I shut all the doors and boarded up all the windows as if a hurricane were on the horizon. And I hoped there was one coming up to Harlem to sweep me away like Dorothy and plant me right in Huntsville 'cause there's no place like home.

Or, I could be my own hurricane and take my own dog-gone self home since I never told a soul about my little fib. I had tucked Granddaddy's money inside a comic book and at the bottom of one of my suitcases.

I search the whole house for a telephone book until I find one in Uncle Richard's bedroom. It's on his night-stand along with an ashtray and too many cigarette butts. His room is neat and almost empty, and he hasn't been home for days.

Daddy's in the shop again, so I rush down the stairs, go into the kitchen, sit at the table, and look up the telephone number to the hurricane that will finally set me free.

"Hello? American Airlines?" I say with my sweet regular ol' Ebony-Grace voice. "How do I buy a ticket to Huntsville, Alabama?"

I listen for instructions. I'll have to go to the airport to buy that ticket. I recount Granddaddy's money. Three hundred dollars. I'm gonna need extra to take a taxicab to Kennedy Airport.

Since I'll be gone from here in a few days, I call Grand-daddy anyway, even though every morning Daddy reminds me not to. It's gonna cost him a lot of money, but that's what he gets for not buying me the ticket in the first place.

The phone rings three times before Momma picks up. I choose my words carefully, as she would say. I make sure that my voice is even and steady, like when I answer a billion questions from the church ladies about bible study, piano lessons, and my marks in school. "Good morning, Momma. How are you?"

"Ebony? Oh, good morning, darling. It's good to hear from you. Don't you have your classes now?"

I was so close to asking her what classes, but I know it would get Daddy in trouble. "Oh, yes. I have ballet in the afternoon. I have Tuesdays off," I fib.

"Ballet? I thought they didn't have ballet at the Y on 135th Street?"

"Well, Daddy just signed me up at another place, and I love it, Momma."

"Is that right?" she says.

"Uh-huh, and I wanna tell Granddaddy all about it. Now, where is he?"

She pauses. "Ebony, honey? I know your grandfather wanted you to come down last weekend. But, it just didn't make any sense, sweetheart. Now, listen. You're grandfather's not doing too good. I know you want to see him. But now is not the right time. You'll be back by the summer's end. I promise. And then, you can see your grandfather. Okay?"

I don't answer her.

"Ebony-Grace, I'm talking to you!"

"Yes, Momma." I hang up.

Sadness doesn't get a chance to form a concrete cloud over my head because I have to make plans. I have to focus. I have money. I have a way to buy a plane ticket. And I know how to be on that airplane all by myself. I just need a way to get to the airport.

Daddy's auto repair shop is full of cars. Most of them are broken, but still, there are cars and they can get me to the airport in no time. Then, I'll just need a driver. I wonder if Loco Lester can drive. He always wants to help.

I go to the stoop and look around. There's no sign of Lester. The streets are quieter now, almost like Huntsville. Almost. Everybody has settled into summer, and instead of slow drives and visits to neighbors' porches, people hang their heads out of windows, sit on plastic crates and play cards, take over whole front stoops, or turn on the fire hydrants to let the Old Faithful flying water cool them down.

Everything is like it was yesterday, and the day before. Just like in Huntsville when Granddaddy isn't telling his stories. The trees and skies don't bend to become a whole other planet. Instead, I slowly get used to it all, and I'm as alien as the rap music that blasts out of the boom boxes on boys' shoulders, as strange as the people bringing junk into Daddy's shop for a few dollars, and as different as Diane's many outfits and jewelry.

I don't see Bianca from where I'm standing on the stoop, but I can hear her voice so I go looking. I finally spot Bianca and her friends behind a table propped up at the curb, the same one that held the food at the block party. There's an emptied-out milk jug that now holds a red liquid, a stack of plastic cups, and a sign that reads KOOL-AID 10 CENTS. ALL PROCEEDS 2 BENEFIT THE 9 FLAVAS CREW.

I dig into my pocket and find a quarter. "I'll take two," I say when I reach the table.

Every single one of the 9 Flavas Crew are here, and they talk and roll their necks and laugh out loud like they usually do. So I'm quiet and regular.

Bianca places two cups of Kool-Aid in front of me and I gulp them down in less than five seconds. I search my pockets for more change, but I left the rest of my money in that comic book in my suitcase. I don't want to leave. So I ask, "How come y'all not practicing or something?"

"Mind your own beeswax, Ice Cream Sandwich!" Monique yells before anyone else answers me.

But still, I don't go away because, in just a few days, I won't be seeing any of them. They'd all be a distant memory. "Where's Diane?" I finally ask.

Bianca points with her chin and I turn to see Diane walking over with a tall boy who has on almost the same outfit as her—white T-shirts tucked into blue jeans and long gold chains shaped like ropes. Diane has on even bigger gold trapezoid earrings that almost touch her shoulders. As she comes closer, I spot a ring on her left hand so big, it takes up four fingers. On it is her name written out in script. She could just hold up her hand with that giant ring if anybody asks for her name.

"How much did y'all make now?" Diane asks the 9 Flavas without even looking in my direction.

Bianca holds out the quarter that I just gave her.

"You mean to tell me that in this heat, nobody out here wants a cup of Kool-Aid?" Diane says.

Her boyfriend laughs and shakes his head. "Y'all didn't think everybody got their own Kool-Aid at home? And it's way cheaper."

Diane smacks her boyfriend's shoulder. "Shut up, Ray. They're just trying to make some money. You got a hundred bucks for them to get to the Apollo? Fifty bucks for their outfits. And fifty bucks to sign up," she says with her motor mouth.

I immediately look at Bianca. She stares at this Ray with hope in her eyes so bright, they might as well have been blinking fireflies.

Ray laughs and kisses Diane on the cheek. I look away, but none of the ice cream flavors do.

"Well, Ray?" Monique asks. "Do you have a hundred bucks for us? It would be an investment."

"An investment? For a double-Dutch team?"

"No!" they all shout.

"We're break-dancers and MCs," Bianca says.

"Yeah, right. Y'all have to come up against, lemme see . . ." He starts to count off on his fingers. "There's Roxanne Shanté out in Queensbridge; and if you want respect from the B-girls, y'all have to go up against Baby Love."

"We already know all that, stupid head!" Monique yells.

"Seriously, Ray," Diane says. "They're really good. They're better than that crew Calvin put together. And if they get to go, then the Nine Flavas deserve to go. It's only fair."

He shakes his head. "Good luck, ladies. I don't have that kinda dough."

"Yeah, right," Monique says. "You just wanna spend it all on your girlfriend."

Before Diane and Monique start bickering, I go around the table to Bianca and say, "I can help."

"*No.* No more help from you, Ebony. I told you. I don't wanna play those games." She steps away from me and joins in on the bickering about Ray having all that cash in his pockets and not wanting to help them.

I think for a moment and look back at Daddy's brownstone—the place I'm supposed to leave in just a few days; the place I'm supposed to break out of so that I don't stay there forever and never see Huntsville or Granddaddy and never hear the stories about the *Uhura* ever again.

I think of my not-friends back home, the ones who used to treat me just like the 9 Flavas do; the ones who call me strange and crazy and a tomboy. The ones who probably said "good riddance" when I left Huntsville for Harlem for the summer. If they even noticed I was gone.

But those kids in Huntsville only jump with a single rope, and they don't spin on their heads and make their bodies move like robots. They play boring ring games and dare one another to kiss a boy. They wear fancy dresses to church and know all the answers about the bible in Sunday school. When they look up at the sky, all they see is what Momma sees: The Heavenly Father and angels and storm clouds and stars and the sun. There's way more than that up there. I know this for sure. So in Huntsville, I always kept my *Uhura* stories to myself, never letting any of those not-friends know what I know. Besides, Granddaddy is my best friend. I didn't need anyone else.

Then, it settles in my belly like a parachute finally landing. Granddaddy is my granddaddy. Granddaddy is not well. Granddaddy is not always gonna be here to tell me stories about the *Uhura.* I remember one of the last things he told me on the phone: *The Prime Directive—you can't be messin' with what people already got going. You got to leave it the way it is. Respect it. Get to know what it's all about.*

At least, these kids here know what outer space sounds like. They know how robots move and some of them even know enough to name themselves out of whole planets, even though they don't want to visit.

Granddaddy told me that when those astronauts on Apollo 13 realized the plan to go to the moon wasn't going to work, they made a new plan. They thought fast and they improvised with whatever they had on hand. They knew they only had one shot to make the right choice and make it back to earth alive.

In an instant I knew: *I have to help the 9 Flavas Crew.* Getting an all-girl crew into the contest at the Apollo Theater would be like getting an all-girl crew to man an Apollo space mission.

I look around at the whole block—the buildings with the missing windows, the colorful words that dance along their crumbling walls, the random tire or mattress that sits out on the curb. This is a planet. This is another world. I remember the lights in Times Square, the sounds of the underground train, so loud it must be where the Sonic Boom is born.

I walk over to Bianca and say, "If I get you into the Apollo, will you let Pablo Jupiter join your crew? And . . . can you teach me some of your moves?"

CHAPTER
34

We never even get to meet this Dapper Dan, who weaves gold thread that makes golden outfits from the tips of his long, brown fingers. At least that's what the 9 Flavas Crew says. But it'll take a whole week for him to stitch something called a Gucci logo onto the cheap sweatpants they paid for with my money. Granddaddy's money.

"All the fly rappers come to him for their outfits," Monique tells me as we walk from the store back to the block. She's Mercurial Monique again. She talks to me, puts her arm around me, and doesn't call me Outer Space Ebony-Grace anymore.

But I'm still the ice cream sandwich in this 9 Flavas Crew. I still don't have no flava, they remind me.

Bianca is nice to me, too. I don't talk about planets and spaceships. Not even around Pablo Jupiter, who abandoned the nefarious minions—I mean, Genesis Ten—to join our crew. He took the Genesis name with him, too, since he was the one who came up with it. So they're just the Cold-Crush Calvin Crew, and according to Pablo, no one likes it 'cause it makes Calvin the leader, just like Monique is leader of the ice cream flavors.

"Since Diane is hanging out with her boyfriend all the time now, then you should be our manager, Ice Cream Sandwich," Monique says when we reach the block.

"Me? A manager of what?" I ask.

"Us," Rhonda says. "You can manage us. Organize battles, get us into contests, and probably get some of the news reporters to come up here and tape us like they did for the New York City Breakers."

"And maybe even get us into movies!" Bianca says. "It's not fair that only the boys get the spotlight and not us."

"Mm-hmm," Monique adds. "I heard some news reporters are coming to videotape Doug E. Fresh and the Get Fresh Crew over there on 122nd. Calvin and them are going to be right there! But nobody told them about us."

"But we didn't take a vote on her!" Mango Megan says.

"We don't need to take a vote," Monique says. "Me and Bianca already agreed. So, Ice Cream Sandwich, you're the manager of the Ice Cream Flavas. You're paying for the outfits, paying to get us into the Apollo, and we need breakfast, lunch, and dinner while we rehearse. You heard?"

I push down a smile. I won't be happy yet. I won't laugh. "Well, can I be called a . . . captain instead?"

"Captain? Okay. Captain Ice Cream Sandwich."

"No," I say. "Captain E-Grace Starfleet."

"Captain Starfleet," Bianca says.

Monique shrugs. "Okay, *Captain Starfleet*. Now, can we get some sandwiches from the store?"

This will be the third time I've bought everybody food. No one asks where I got the money from. And only once did Bianca say thank you. Only Bianca, no one else.

So Monique grabs my hand and the rest of the crew fall in line behind her, except for Bianca who stands on the other side of her.

"What y'all want? Put in your orders now! Captain Starfleet, take note!" Monique shouts.

I want to tell her that I'm supposed to be *giving* orders, not taking them. I pat my shorts pocket to make sure I feel the wad of cash that's supposed to be there, and in that same moment, a shiny black car comes speeding down the block, music blasting from the stereo.

The 9 Flavas Crew all stop to dance. I can't see the driver but a pretty lady with big, curly hair, bright red lipstick, and giant gold hoops sitting in the passenger seat. And they all talk at the same time.

"Ooh, she looks like Donna Summers!"

"No, more like Diana Ross with all that hair."

"I bet you she's a *Solid Gold* dancer."

"What if she's looking for dancers to be on her show?"

"Everybody, pose!"

In the blink of an eye, the 9 Flavas Crew are in different poses as if the pretty lady in that fancy car were ready to take their photograph. I've seen fancier ladies in Huntsville, and fancier cars, too, like Granddaddy's Cadillac.

Daddy steps out of his shop across the street. The fancy car pulls up to the curb and none other than Uncle Richard steps out, runs around to the other side, and opens the door for the pretty lady, who is neither Carol nor Not-Carol.

"Uncle Richard must be a pimp!" Rhonda says.

"Oooh, don't call Captain Starfleet's uncle a pimp. She might beat you up," Monique says. "With her Wonder Woman bracelets!"

They laugh at her joke and at me. I lower my head until I hear Daddy's voice boom across the street.

"You went ahead and got yourself a new girlfriend with my money?" he shouts.

Everyone who is either walking by, sitting on their stoops, or hanging their heads out of windows hears my daddy's voice and turns to look his way. He's walking toward Uncle Richard really fast and real angry. He gets in his face. He shouts.

"You stole my cash, Richard!"

"Whatchu talkin' 'bout I stole your cash?" Uncle Richard shouts back. "I bought this car with my own money. I told you I was getting it."

"I'm sick and tired of all your lyin', stealin', and cheatin'! You gots to get up out of my house!"

Uncle Richard steps closer to Daddy and spreads his arms out as if daring him to do something. Other men come out of the shop and surround them.

Daddy and Uncle Richard shout about the new girl, the new car, the new suit, and the three hundred dollars.

If there was a Sonic Boom right now, it would be a bunch of exploding curses oozing in molten lava dripping over this part of No Joke City. There is nothing funny about right now, at all, even though Monique and them are giggling with their "ooooh!" and telling my daddy to just sock it to Uncle Richard one time for cheating on all those girls he brings around.

"We don't want no pimps, junkies, and hos on our block, Mr. Freeman. You tell him!" Monique shouts.

Bianca steps closer to me. "Why is your daddy and your uncle fighting?"

I shrug and touch the bulge in my pocket. I don't say a word.

No one stops them from shouting. So I walk closer to the shouting men and, with my teeny-tiny voice against their Sonic Boom curse words, call for my daddy. But no one hears me.

The pretty lady comes out of the car with her long legs and short dress, but she doesn't stop them.

Señora Luz comes out of her apartment, waves for Bianca to come inside, but she doesn't stop them.

Everybody comes to watch and tell my daddy to punch his little brother in the face—the same little brother who calls me EG 'cause I'm extra-galactic. They don't stop them.

Daddy says he took his money.

Uncle Richard said he didn't. This was his new car and that woman ain't cost no money.

Daddy said he's freeloading.

Uncle Richard reminds him that he's his brother, and pushes him.

Daddy pushes back and accuses him of taking that money for dope.

Then the fists start flying.

"Daddy!" I yell, ready to dive in to save him.

But someone holds me back. "Wait a minute now, little girl. This is grown men's business. Don't want you to get hurt."

I'm ready to pull away from that man, but Bianca comes over and grabs my arm. "No, Ebony," she says quietly.

There's nothing else to do but to watch two planets colliding and exploding, and everyone standing around watching like stars, doing nothing except taking up space. I do the same thing, even as my eyes well up with tears, as Uncle Richard tries to punch but he's too weak and skinny, so Daddy becomes like Admiral Kirk wanting to destroy Commander Kruge and they both tumble down on the ground and Daddy throws punch after punch until Uncle Richard can't do anything but just lie there.

I'm yelling, "Daddy, no! No, Daddy!" over and over and over again until my voice just gives in and all I can do was whisper, "Daddy, no!"

A noise coming from far away sounds as if it's doing all the crying and screaming for me. An ambulance. Or a sheriff's car. Or both. It gets closer and everyone starts scurrying away back to their stoops and windows as if nothing had just happened.

"Five-oh!" somebody yells.

Daddy stands over Uncle Richard, breathing hard, wiping his sweaty forehead and bloody mouth with the back of his hand.

So I run to him.

He pushes me away without saying a word.

Before I run back again—because maybe he doesn't know it's me, maybe he's too angry to even notice—two sheriffs rush to him to grab both his arms and put them behind his back.

By this time, no words fall out of my mouth. And without thinking, I dig into my shorts pocket and grab whatever's left of the money. I hold it up so those sheriffs can see that it's okay, that Daddy shouldn't go to jail, that neither he nor Uncle Richard did anything wrong.

"I took the money, Daddy!" I yell out, and then the rest comes pouring out with it: "I just wanted to make things right. For Bianca and her friends—my friends. I didn't mean to lie. Take me prisoner instead. Please!"

CHAPTER
35

I see fights in movies and on TV all the time. Kirk is always kicking somebody's butt. Mr. Spock can do his Vulcan nerve pinch. And there's sometimes a phaser or a lightsaber. But someone's always the bad guy. Two good people could never get into a fight. Somebody's gotta win.

The only real live fight I've ever seen was between Mrs. Turner and some other church lady from another part of town. I didn't really know what they were fighting about, but it was at a church picnic and they knocked down a pan of cornbread. That fight was funny.

But Daddy and Uncle Richard's fight was not. Everybody on the block was talking about it for days afterward.

They talked about what a shame it was to see brothers fighting over money. About how Daddy wouldn't see that cash again after one of the police officers snatched it out of my hand to keep as evidence. About how they'd never seen a skinny little girl from Down South cause so much trouble.

I never thought that this was going to be the thing that forced Momma to get me back home to Granddaddy. This, and that other thing.

"Baby," Momma says so softly that I don't recognize her voice. "It's time for you to come home now."

Daddy is at the kitchen table eating a bowl of oatmeal. He's been eating oatmeal for two weeks, since after the fight and spending the night in jail. The left side of his face is still swollen. I had to stay in Bianca's room, where her abuela let us watch TV late into the night until the screen sizzled and fizzed like soda pop.

"I gotta stay and look after Daddy," I tell her. I'm like Momma now. While she looks after her own daddy, I look after mine.

"Your father's going to be all right, Ebony. He got his own self into that mess. You're too young to get all caught up in his stuff."

I watch as Daddy tries to chew with the bandage across his jaw. He broke it. He had a fat, busted lip, too, and a black eye from the fight with Uncle Richard, and from another fight while he was in jail.

"It's my fault, Momma," I say.

Daddy looks up at me and shakes his head. He didn't tell Momma about my fib, which was really a straight-up lie. All he ever said to me was, "Broomstick, it's my fault I didn't do the right thing with that money in the first place."

Momma says, "Nothing is your fault, Ebony. Now, I don't want you coming down here with those thoughts in your head. Especially when you see your grandfather."

I gasp. "Where *is* Granddaddy, Momma?"

"Ebony-Grace, your grandfather's in the hospital now."

CHAPTER
36

Bianca doesn't even look my way anymore. It's Sunday and she's off to church with her abuela. When I spent the night in her apartment, we both only stared at the TV. She fell asleep first, without saying a word. I left the moment I heard Daddy's footsteps upstairs. Before going in to see Daddy, I sit on the front stoop with my elbow resting on my knobby knee and my chin in my hand.

The 9 Flavas had no outfits or money and couldn't compete in the contest—the contest that the Cold-Crush Calvin Crew won with the help of Pablo Jupiter, the traitor, who turned around and begged Calvin to take him back so he could be in the contest.

None of that mattered anyway, because I was finally going home to see Granddaddy.

"I defeated the Sonic King and I'm now captain of the *Uhura*. If there still is an *Uhura*," I say to no one in particular as I sit alone on the stoop. I look up at the wide blue sky and the buildings in the distance that teased it. There wasn't an *Uhura* up there or a Planet Boom Box or a Sonic King. These stories were all starting to look and feel like those white, fluffy clouds—slowly moving away and pulling apart and dissolving like cotton candy at the county fair.

I spot Pablo Jupiter walking down the block and I try to

do something, anything, to avoid him. But he calls my name. My other name.

"Hey, Captain Starfleet!"

"You don't get to call me that!" I say, as he reaches the front gate of the stoop.

"Why not? Isn't that your name?" He's wearing a clean T-shirt and jeans with a long crease down the fronts of the legs.

"My name is Ebony-Grace Norfleet Freeman," I say.

"No, it's not. It's Captain E-Grace Starfleet of the Mothership *Uhura*. That's what you told me. Why you gonna change up the story?"

"Why are you a traitor?" I ask.

"I'm not a traitor. One of us had to get into that contest. Now, since we won, I got a little bit of money to help the Nine Flavas. There's gonna be a back-to-school contest and I want me and the Nine Flavas to compete as a team," he says, digging into his pocket and showing me five twenty-dollar bills.

"I don't care," is all I say, shrugging.

"Why? 'Cause you're going back to Alabama to save Captain Fleet?" he asks.

"Captain Fleet is no more!" I want to take back those last words, but I have to remember that Captain Fleet is just a story, is just a part of Granddaddy's imagination location. Not mine. It was his all along.

"Did he die?" Pablo asks.

"No! Don't say that!"

"But you said he's no more."

"He's not a real person!"

"So, you're not going to outer space anymore? And isn't Alabama where they have that space camp?" He sits on the stoop a few steps down from me without me even inviting him in. "If I had the choice, I'd go to space camp. Forget all this MCing and break dancing, because that's what everybody here wants to do. I mean some of us are better than others," he says, rubbing his chin. "But at some point, so many people will be doing it that no one is gonna get to shine. You know what I mean?"

"But, Pablo, there are lots of stars in outer space. Every one of them shines," I say.

He doesn't say anything. Then he asks, "You think I'm gonna be a star, Captain Starfleet?"

"I guess you ain't never heard how the Nine Flavas talk about you behind your back."

"No. Not that kinda star. I mean, one in outer space," he says, biting his fingernail. "An astronaut like Neil Armstrong and Guion Bluford."

"You know who Guion Bluford is!"

"Of course, I do! And he's probably from Harlem. Everybody who's black and famous is from Harlem."

"Well, I wanna be like Sally Ride! And she's definitely not from Harlem. And I'm not either."

"Take me to Alabama with you. I wanna go to that space camp, too," he says, looking out at the block.

"Why would you want to go to Alabama when you have all this . . . ," I say. I look out to my right as the Soul Train passes by on the aboveground tracks on Park Avenue. A car drives down the block real slow blasting that *boom-boom-bip* music out from its opened windows. Rap, they call it. Or hip-hop. A kid shouts some curse words from an open window across the street, and a group of girls, including some of the 9 Flavas, shouts back with their own curse words. A grandma down the block yells out, "I'll wash y'all's dirty mouths out with soap if y'all don't stop all that cussing!" Another car zooms down blasting old disco music that neither Granddaddy nor Momma likes. A boy walks down the block holding a boom box over his shoulders, blaring some more of that rap music, and this time it's a song I recognize from the block party: "Jam On It" by Newcleus—like the center of an atom, where all the energy is stored. Pablo starts to pop and lock his hands and arms and I start to bop my head. A group of young girls come out from a building next door holding a telephone cord for double-Dutch, and in that moment, it's as if someone had turned up the volume real loud. It's the Sonic Boom, all right. But I don't cover my ears.

I stand to walk down the steps, out of the front gate, and onto the sidewalk. I'm Bionic Woman opening up my ears to every sound, every beat, every rhythm in Harlem. I can even feel the trains passing underground. It's all music. So I snap my fingers.

A boom.
A bip.
A bop.

"What are you doing?" Pablo asks from behind me.

I don't say anything for a second. Then, "If space is the place, then Harlem is the biggest, baddest planet in the galaxy!"

"You got that right!" *he* says.

Then Harlem's volume turns up at full blast.

Hip and hop and stop.
Beat and feet.
Bang, boogie, and bang.
Stop, rock, and bop.
Pop the pop.

On and on
To the break of dawn.

"Harlem isn't going anywhere," Pablo says. "It's never gonna change. But I'm gonna be a man soon and I have to live out my dreams. I wanna go to that space camp to practice being an astronaut."

"Well, you don't need a space camp to be an astronaut," I tell him. "You just need an imagination location. And you already have that here, Pablo. You're already an astronaut. You're a space hero!"

"You're a hero, too, Captain E-Grace Starfleet," he says, walking over to me and putting his arm around my shoulders.

I stop breathing for a long second, and maybe my heart skips a beat, too. Bianca is out with her abuela, and some of the 9 Flavas across the street are not looking in our direction. I breathe in deep and relax under the weight of Pablo's arm.

"Yeah, okay," is all I say at first. Then I add, "Captain E-Grace Starfleet and Cadet Pablo Jupiter trekking the stars in space . . . "

"The final frontier," we both say together.

"To boldly go where no man . . . or woman has gone before," Pablo says, deepening his voice.

We both laugh secret laughs. And for a little moment, I have a new friend, and I almost don't want to go home.

CHAPTER
37

My airplane leaves in the evening and as I wait for Daddy back in the house, I watch the small TV that sits on top of the big one in the living room.

Uncle Richard moved all his stuff out the other day, when he was sure Daddy wasn't going to be home. Word on the block is that Daddy's looking for a new tenant, someone who could pay and look out for his baby girl.

But I'm going home.

Just as Daddy is coming down the stairs with his keys clinging and whistling because his face was starting to feel and look better, the telephone rings.

I don't rush to answer it like I usually do because it didn't matter if it is Granddaddy calling because I'm going to see him by tonight, at least.

Daddy takes his time getting to the phone. It's still hard for him to talk.

"Well, we're just getting ready to head out to the airport. What's wrong, Gloria?" Daddy says, his voice quieter, less king-like than normal. Then he's quiet for a long time. "I need you to breathe so I can understand what you're saying . . . I'm so sorry, Gloria . . . Honey, I'm gonna bring our baby girl down. I'll bring her home."

I sit up on the couch and pretend to be watching Raj and

Rerun on *What's Happening!!* with the volume turned down really low so I can hear what Daddy is saying to Momma on the phone. I don't answer him until he says my name for the third time even though he's standing right there and he's practically shouting.

"Yes, Daddy."

"Your momma's on the line for you."

That kitchen and that telephone and that spiraling cord that used to be a portal could've been as far away as Neptune as long as I took to get there. I walk slowly, feeling like something heavy and thick is waiting for me on that phone.

"Ebony, baby?" Momma says, as soon as she heard me breathing on the phone. I don't say anything. I just breathe. "There's no other way to go about this. Baby, your grand-daddy passed away this morning."

CHAPTER
38

Daddy's jaw is really sore from trying to comfort Momma on the phone, so when he calls American Airlines, I do all the talking for him, even though my words come out slow-dripping like molasses.

"One round-trip ticket to Huntsville, Alabama, please," I say, trying really hard to be polite and sweet, like Momma taught me. "And please change the date for Ebony-Grace Norfleet Freeman's ticket, too. I'll be going home later."

Momma told Daddy that I needed to wait a couple more days before coming down because things were in *disarray*. Newspaper reporters were calling, neighbors were stopping by with casseroles, and she had to get Granddaddy's affairs in order. Just 'cause Daddy's words were slurred from his sore jaw, Momma thought he was hard of hearing, too. So she shouted her words, and I could hear her while sitting at the kitchen table. If the doors to my imagination location weren't closed from all this sadness, I would've thought it was because of my bionic ears. No. Momma was just yelling.

I never knew how quiet it could be inside my thoughts when my imagination location is not there anymore. I can hear more things now. And they're not as loud as before— there's no *boom-bip-bap-ratatat* as it beats out of boom boxes and cars driving by. It becomes like crickets at night on Olde

243

Stone Road in Huntsville. Regular. Normal. As plain as all the broken things on every corner of Harlem.

I don't argue with Daddy. I don't argue with Momma. I wait for anyone or anything to move me into the next adventure, one that doesn't come out of Granddaddy's stories or even my own imagination. Adventure now is every day, everything; it's waking up, eating, talking about nothing, watching nothing, and going back to sleep.

On the day we're finally ready to fly back to Huntsville, I spend most of my time roaming around the brownstone. There's no radio tower, Planet Boom Box, or a Sonic King. I just flip through Daddy's records, staring at the ladies with shiny dresses and red lipstick or the men posing with their friends and their instruments. The TV is off, and even though the streets are as loud as they usually are, there's a dark cloud hanging over me that seems to block all of it out. My bags are packed and there's nothing left to do, nothing left to say, nothing left to imagine.

So I step out onto the stoop, then the sidewalk, and my legs take me over to Daddy's shop, where one of his friends is gonna take care of business while he's away.

"Sorry about your granddaddy, little girl," the man says, as I walk straight through the auto repair shop and out into the junkyard. I inhale deep as I stare out at all the mess. There are a few more tires than there were before. The whole fireplace sits atop a refrigerator lying on its side. I blink a few times to see if my mind will play some trick on me and turn that fireplace into a launching pad, but after a few seconds, it's still a broken fireplace ripped from somebody's living room.

"Broomstick?" I hear Daddy say.

I turn around to him standing in the doorway leading

into the junkyard. I get ready to leave, but he nods and walks away leaving me to continue with whatever I was doing.

But after a short second, Bianca comes in. Her eyes are fixed on me as if she's expecting me to be broken somehow. She doesn't come too close at first, so we just stare at each other.

Then Monique comes out, and Rhonda, Collette, Vanessa, Stacey, Christine, Paula, and Megan. The whole 9-F Crew steps into the junkyard and they look so strange with all their bright colors against the dull browns and grays of the junkyard.

"What do y'all want? I'm sorry about the money. About everything" is the first thing I say, as I kick the tip of my shoe against a lonely brick on the ground.

"We heard about your granddaddy," Monique says.

"Yeah, my nana died last summer and I cried for a week," Rhonda says.

"Sorry about your grandpa, Ebony-Grace," Bianca says. "And I brought everybody here to say sorry."

I look up at Bianca, whose curly hair is out of its usual side ponytail. "Why?" I ask her.

She's quiet for a moment then she smiles a little. "Because the needs of my amiga outweigh the needs of my crew sometimes."

"Yeah, sometimes!" Monique adds. "You two are Ebony and Ivory all right. Always have to be in perfect harmony!"

Then Rhonda starts singing the song at the top of her lungs, "Ebony and Ivory—"

"Shut up, Rhonda!" two of the 9 Flavas shout.

And everybody laughs, except for me and Bianca. She's still looking at me as if she wanted me to say something.

"Sorry, too," I mumble and look up at her. Maybe I see

her soulglow a little bit, as if this little moment had made her happier than anything. Or maybe, it's my soulglow reflecting off her.

Daddy calls me in from the auto repair shop and scolds the girls for being there. "That's enough now. You all don't belong here. I don't want your mothers coming over here to see their daughters hanging out in a junkyard. You all are young ladies now."

"But you let the boys play in here, Mr. Freeman," Bianca says.

I smile big and bright on the inside. "Yeah, Daddy," I say. "If the boys can play in the junkyard, then we can play in here, too."

Bianca looks back at me with a smile that I think says "Thank you."

Daddy brings me a peanut butter sandwich on a plastic plate and a cup of milk as I sit on the couch watching Sue Simmons on the news. It's raining outside, and some of the kids on the block dance in it as if it were a waterfall on *Fantasy Island*.

Sue Simmons still looks like Momma. And the news about all the no-good, awful, terrible things that happen in New York City is the same as it was yesterday and the day before. Once, I made sure not to even blink so I wouldn't miss if Daddy and Uncle Richard's fight made it onto the news. But that was just a small fight compared to the no-good, awful, even more terrible things that happen in Harlem.

Daddy keeps me safe. He doesn't let any of it get to me. That's what he said to Momma.

I never got to say goodbye to Granddaddy. I push down everything that would make me cry, make me mad, and just stare at Sue Simmons as she announces a special message from the president of the United States, Mr. Ronald Reagan.

Daddy comes with his tuna sandwich plate to sit down beside me.

The movie star who used to play a cowboy hero in movies, Granddaddy told me, is the president, and he comes on the TV screen all serious. For a minute, I don't care, but then I see an image of one of the space shuttles. I set my plate down on the floor and sit up on the couch to hear every word.

Today I'm directing NASA to begin a search in all of our elementary and secondary schools, and to choose as the first citizen passenger in the history of our space program, one of America's finest: a teacher.

The screen shows an astronaut in outer space floating near a space shuttle. A teacher in space. I don't know what to make of that idea. What would a teacher do as part of a space shuttle crew?

CHAPTER
39

I'm not alone on the plane this time. Daddy is sitting next to me snoring like a junkyard dog. I press my face against the plane's window and look out at the concrete clouds. The sun is setting behind them and the whirling mix of colors look as if all the planets in the galaxy were dancing together at a block party.

The airplane doesn't push past the gray, blue, and orange colors to reach the giant, endless black sky called outer space. So I take control. I close my eyes, press my back against the seat, and pretend the plane is at an angle, its nose aiming high for the stars and planets and the very edge of our galaxy. I extend my arms out and press button after button, manning the control boards as the plane crashes through the concrete sky and becomes the Mothership *Uhura*. Once we've made the jump to hyperspace (no throwing up this time), I engage the autopilot. Then I sit up straight in my chair and summon my best captain's voice.

"Captain's log, stardate 08.31.1984. The *Uhura*'s mission to rescue Captain Fleet has come to an end. Unfortunately, we have neither rescued the captain nor defeated the Sonic King. The battle damage to this spacecraft will be repaired soon enough, but I cannot say when her crew will be recovered—"

Suddenly, the plane hits some turbulence and I open

my eyes. Out the window is nothing but endless blackness. Blackness beyond night that goes on forever. I can't take my eyes away from it, can't help wonder what it's all about. So I keep my eyes open.

"And yet I wonder if the mission wasn't a success after all."

Out of the corner of my eye, I see Daddy is awake and listening to me, and some of the other passengers glance in my direction, but I don't care. There's no reason to sneak around, no reason for secrets. *Uhura* means "freedom" and this captain does what she wants!

"Maybe this was never really a rescue mission. Maybe the purpose of this mission was for Space Cadet E-Grace Starfleet to become Captain Starfleet.

"I've changed, and maybe that was the point. Granddaddy is gone now, so that makes me feel different. But that ol' Captain Fleet is alive and well in my imagination location, same as ever. I can visit him anytime. And he's not in any kind of trouble out there in the big, wide universe.

"Maybe the Genesis Device can change how a captain sees a new planet, not the other way around. Maybe the captain thinks the planet is all broken and dirty, but she'll have to follow the Prime Directive: Don't go trying to change things up. Maybe the aliens like it just the way it is. A captain has to change her mind to see a place with new eyes. She has to wonder what it's all about. That's the only change that needs to happen, whatever's going on in her imagination location."

Next to me, I can see Daddy smiling. He's shaking his head, too, but there's definitely a smile on his face.

"That's what the teacher in space is gonna have to do. No sense in trying to teach aliens new ways. They've got their own way of doing things. So, I'll definitely have to be the first student in space to let that shuttle crew know about the Prime Directive and the Genesis Device. Besides, ain't that many kids out there who can call themselves captains. And they'll have to meet the Sonic King in Planet Boom Box. The whole Planet Earth has to know about the loudest, baddest, mind-controllest sound in the entire galaxy: the Sonic Boom!"

I look over at Daddy and wink at him. If his block in Harlem knows him as DJ Jule Thief, then I know him as the Sonic King disguised as King Sirius Julius. And right there in Harlem is the Planet Boom Box where the Sonic Boom lives. I didn't go messing with any of it. I followed General Order Number One: The Prime Directive. I didn't take down the king and I didn't destroy the planet. If that doesn't make me a darn good captain, then I don't know what does.

ACKNOWLEDGMENTS

This book took a long time to write, and there wasn't a moment when I was recreating the world of 1984 Harlem through Ebony-Grace's imagination location that I didn't have a smile on my face. This story brought me so much joy, and many people shared my enthusiasm and appreciation for science-fiction, early hip-hop, being twelve, and old New York.

I am grateful to photographer extraordinaire, Jamel Shabazz, for documenting little known parts of American history: the imaginative Black children of 1980s New York. What we dreamed up ultimately changed the world. Thank you for allowing us to see ourselves in the books *A Time Before Crack* and *Back in the Days*.

A captain's salute to the incomparable Nichelle Nichols and her role as Lieutenant Nyota Uhura on *Star Trek*. Your presence in the future, among the stars, meant the universe to us.

I am grateful to Rita Williams-Garcia's *One Crazy Summer* and the Gainther Sisters series for reminding me of the beauty, humor, innocence, and playfulness of Black girlhood. These books allowed me to reach back and step into child-sized shoes. I remembered myself.

Of course, my own children do the daily work of forcing me to reckon with all things teen and preteen. Bahati, thank you for your beautiful, pitch-perfect voice while reading Ebony-Grace's words. She was that much more real because of you. Abadai, it's my hope that you become an editor one day, given all the editorial work I put you through. Thank you for your keen insight into plot and characterization and for always keeping it one hundred. Zuberi, thank you for reading all the way to the end and having lots of questions. That is all.

To my dear husband, Joseph, an unwavering cheer-leader: if books could have a sound engineer, I'd give you this very important job. Thank you for sharing your love of music and early hip-hop, and lending your voice to daddy, grand-daddy, uncle, and even the Sonic King himself. They are that much more real because of you. And a huge thank you for that very first sketch of Ebony-Grace. You are indeed the co-creator of this very special girl.

Thank you to Frank Morrison and Anthony Piper for rendering Ebony-Grace and her worlds.

Ammi-Joan Paquette, thank you so much for seeing the potential of this story when it was just a seed of an idea. You get me and that means a lot to me.

Andrew Karre, I could not have asked for a more wise, thorough, enthusiastic, and patient editor. The process of bringing this story to life was definitely a mind meld. Thank you for being so deeply invested in, not just this story, but in Harlem, its people, its history, its music, the characters, and even all those old Star Trek and Star Wars movies. It was clear that you cared so much about this book, and as a result, it made the writing that much easier.

Thanks to my Penguin team: Julie Strauss-Gabel, Melissa Faulner, Natalie Vielkind, Lindsay Boggs, Kristin Boyle, Carmela Iaria, Felicia Frazier, and many others. I am so grateful for all the behind-the-scenes work and love that went into this book.

Lastly, to my dear friends Helen, Talana, and Ahmed, who shared all those old New York stories with me. Yes, all those questions were for this book. Your memories are so special and sacred—the carrying double-Dutch ropes in your bags, the partying with hip-hop legends before they were stars, the music, the clothes, the style . . . The world has no idea, and they need to know. I love you for supporting me in countless ways.

It wasn't a village that made this book. It was a block—from the corner store to the rooftops, and even the hidden stars. We made this sonic boom of a book. You too, reader. Thank you, all!